Bonjour Girl

ISABELLE LAFLÈCHE

DUNDURN
TORONTO

Cover image: ©istock.com/alvaher
Printer: Webcom

Library and Archives Canada Cataloguing in Publication

Laflèche, Isabelle, 1970-, author
    Bonjour girl / Isabelle Laflèche.

Issued in print and electronic formats.

ISBN 978-1-4597-4200-0 (softcover).--ISBN 978-1-4597-4201-7 (PDF).--
ISBN 978-1-4597-4202-4 (EPUB)

    I. Title.

PS8623.A35825B65 2018   jC813'.6   C2017-907758-9
                                                 C2017-907759-7

1 2 3 4 5   22 21 20 19 18

We acknowledge the support of the **Canada Council for the Arts**, which last year invested $153 million to bring the arts to Canadians throughout the country, and the **Ontario Arts Council** for our publishing program. We also acknowledge the financial support of the **Government of Ontario**, through the **Ontario Book Publishing Tax Credit** and the **Ontario Media Development Corporation**, and the **Government of Canada**.

Nous remercions le **Conseil des arts du Canada** de son soutien. L'an dernier, le Conseil a investi 153 millions de dollars pour mettre de l'art dans la vie des Canadiennes et des Canadiens de tout le pays.

Care has been taken to trace the ownership of copyright material used in this book. The author and the publisher welcome any information enabling them to rectify any references or credits in subsequent editions.

— *J. Kirk Howard, President*

The publisher is not responsible for websites or their content unless they are owned by the publisher.

Printed and bound in Canada.

VISIT US AT

 dundurn.com | 🐦 @dundurnpress | 👍 dundurnpress | 📷 dundurnpress

Dundurn
3 Church Street, Suite 500
Toronto, Ontario, Canada
M5E 1M2

For Frankie

Life shrinks or expands in proportion to one's courage.
— Anaïs Nin

Be who you are and say what you feel, because those who
mind don't matter, and those who matter don't mind.
— Anonymous

Prologue

@ClementineL's blog, Bonjour Girl, is a total fake-ass disaster. Don't bother reading it. It's a waste of your precious time.

THE NASTY TWEET hits me like a wall of vintage boots, handbags, and boho dresses. Or like a hurricane that goes on a rampage in my soul and leaves a gaping wound in my heart. I fight back tears while absentmindedly chewing on my nails. I cringe, knowing how many Twitter followers she has. Her malicious post has *lots* of retweets, too. Like, far too many. Somebody please shoot me now. This is dredging up old, unwanted emotions, all the pain and worry that nearly destroyed me last year. That's why I came here, why I escaped to New York.

I want to crawl into the nearest hole and lie there until the school concierge finds my decaying remains.

Okay, I'm being gross and melodramatic. I take it back. I just want to hop on the next flight to Paris and never set foot in America again.

I feel nauseous and dizzy at the thought that the entire Parsons student body has probably seen this awful tweet and is now laughing at me. To make matters worse, I think of a Latin proverb I learned at my private school in France: *verba volant, scripta manent*. It literally means "spoken words fly away, but written words remain." This totally sucks.

My mind goes into overdrive:

My chances of making any more friends are nil.

My existing friends will think I'm a complete loser and will desert me.

My chances of ever making it as a fashion journalist are ruined.

My transfer to Parsons will get revoked.

My parents will then kill me and ship me back to France on the next flight. (Not so bad an option considering the circumstances. Actually, that might be a good thing.)

Again, my eyes well up, but I'm too angry to cry. My classmate's biting words sting to the bone. Especially after all I've already endured in my personal life.

What did I do to deserve all this?

Chapter One

MY FATHER SAYS I'm his good luck charm. The thing is, I don't believe in luck.

Maybe that's because I haven't been all that lucky, but I have a feeling things are about to change. Big time.

I'm half Chinese, and luck plays a big part in our culture: lucky numbers, lucky symbols, and lucky colours. I also believe in the old saying, *luck is what happens when preparation meets opportunity.*

I did everything I could to prepare for my first day at Parsons' School of Fashion — convinced my overprotective parents, took on an extra summer job, let go of a toxic relationship, put together a portfolio, and made a kick-*derrière* video that knocked the socks off the admissions committee. It was a ton of work but was definitely worth it. I mean, Marc Jacobs, Donna Karan, Anna Sui, Tom Ford … they ALL attended this amazing school.

Camille, my neighbour in Paris who's an up-and-coming videographer, helped shoot a short film of me climbing the stairs of Rue Foyatier (one of the most famous streets in Paris, which leads to the Sacré-Cœur) in a flowing vintage dress, holding smoke bombs that billowed bright pink and blue clouds, all to 90s hip hop. My mother said the effect was a masterful mix of class and sophistication. I like to think it was just plain awesome.

I'm transferring to Parsons as a sophomore. I studied at the Parisian campus for a year but, for personal reasons, I decided I needed to get out of town and come to New York. So here I am, nervous as hell, standing in front of what they call The New School: Parsons School of Design. Being away from home makes me anxious, and everyone knows how competitive the school is. There are YouTube videos by Parsons alumni on the subject. I watched every single one of them, trying not to bite my nails. I need to protect them; my nails, along with my quirky sense of style, are my trademarks.

I stand in the middle of the Manhattan sidewalk with stars in my eyes as students rush past me. I'm looking up at the skyscrapers while taking in the city's electric energy and the billboard ads for the world's top fashion labels. My heart thumps with excitement.

My name is Clementine. Yes, like the fruit. I like to think that I'm tangy and just the right amount of sweet. My parents named me after one of their favourite colours. I know, it sounds cheesy but they're both kind of artsy-fartsy so I guess they just couldn't help it.

My father's a businessman from Beijing. He moved to Paris to open a shop that sells men's clothing and rare books. He wasn't thrilled about allowing his only daughter to leave Europe. New York *is* different. I get it; it's *the* big city. Thankfully, my mother's cousin Madeleine, a.k.a.

Maddie, who's ten years younger than my mom and teaches at Parsons, helped me find ways to convince him.

Maddie promised to take good care of me and even offered the spare bedroom in her cool Williamsburg apartment. I really lucked out — she lives in a huge loft with a connecting studio, where she keeps all of her stunning fashion collections. I just hope she lets me wear some of her precious things.

I'm not going to lie, I have big dreams. I'm hoping to find a job in the fashion industry after I graduate, one that allows me to write, draw, and share my fashion finds. Like many of the women I admire in the industry — Garance Doré, Susie Bubble, and Tavi Gevinson — I want to be a fashion influencer.

Lady Gaga said, "I'm just trying to change the world, one sequin at a time." That's my motto. I hope to help change the current fashion landscape and shake things up. There are so many issues to be addressed, like body shaming and the negative way clothing is advertised to my generation, using only the tallest, slimmest, most perfect models instead of real people. I think that clothing should be empowering, not objectifying, and that there isn't only one acceptable body type, skin colour, or hairstyle. I'd like to participate in the conversation in order to make a lasting impact. Call me a fashion-renaissance activist.

Speaking of style, for my first day of class I'm wearing a burgundy-flowered silk dress, a vintage Yves Saint Laurent wool cape, an old leather handbag that belonged to my great-grandmother, black tights, and a large floppy felt hat. I've also added some colourful vintage necklaces I picked up at a flea market, and I'm wearing Repetto ballet slippers because it's much easier to navigate the subway in flats. Thankfully, they also look great with my outfit. Fashion is my religion, fashion is my salvation, and fashion is the way I roll. I don't do conventional fashion; I'm quirky and different, I have a funny-looking button nose and lots of freckles, and I go my own way.

Am I worried about feeling lonely in New York? Of course. I'm nineteen, under the legal drinking age, and even if I weren't, New York City is expensive; I can't afford to go out as much as I did in Paris. And I no longer have a boyfriend to cuddle with on Friday nights or to take me to brunch on weekends in the Jardin du Luxembourg. But that's okay. The one I left behind wasn't that nice. As a matter of fact, he was a total jerk. Just like the Dior perfume, he was poison. But I don't want to dwell on that, or him, anymore. He's one of the main reasons I left Paris. I needed a clean break, a fresh *début*.

My dad told me that an elderly friend once asked him, "What are you willing to give up in order to pursue your dreams?" I've asked myself that question a lot. His wise friend answered it for me: "It should be no less than everything." Standing in front of Parsons' entrance on Fifth Avenue with the future a blank canvas, I have a feeling that wise man was onto something.

I look up at the expansive blue sky to thank my great-grandmother Cécile. I know she's somehow responsible for my being here. I lift my arm in the air and give her a thumbs-up.

One fashionable gal looking out for another.

Chapter Two

"THE ONLY EXCLUSIVE relationship I have is with my Nespresso machine," I recall a Parsons student saying in an interview for *Teen Vogue*. She was going on about the school's heavy workload and curriculum. I wonder if it's humanly possible to maintain a romantic relationship while studying here. I've heard so many stories about students suffering from exhaustion and burning out. Apparently, a lot of students drop out, and those who do stick around spend the majority of their time working on school projects.

Those are the thoughts going through my mind as I walk past the bustling school cafeteria on my way to class. I don't know why I bother thinking about romance — I was told by some students that most men on campus are either gay, party promoters, or the building maintenance crew.

I try to brush that off; dating should be the last thing on my mind. I'm here to learn, grow, and *expand*. I'm really looking forward to attending some of the design classes, even though I have no interest in launching my own label. I just love to be close to the creative process and all those luxurious fabrics.

After picking up a cup of tea in the basement cafeteria, I finally make it to the classroom and take a seat. I pick a spot near the window. I unload the contents of my bag onto my desk: my polka-dot agenda and a light-pink pencil case filled with pens in every colour. My accessories are met with a few side stares.

I'm not surprised. Compared to most students here, I look like a unicorn. Or Miley Cyrus, depending on your point of view. Especially with each of my nails painted a different colour, my rainbow-coloured backpack, and my ton of vintage necklaces. It's a look that's more feminine, more flamboyant than what others here wear. But it's a look that feels totally me.

I dropped by school yesterday to pick up some books and noticed that most of the kids wear all black — you know, that gothic look: oversize and baggy, with lots of skull jewellery. It's a style made famous by designer Rick Owens and it reminds me of Marilyn Manson videos. It's such a far cry from my own style. Maddie said the teachers joke that the school's palette is limited to black, grey, and white. I think it's a big yawn.

I knew I was going to stand out here and I'm okay with that. Personally, I'm a big fan of fashion bloggers who boldly dye their hair pink and purple and wear sparkly rainbow dresses. Don't get me wrong; I do appreciate the *bon chic, bon genre* Parisian elegance, but the fashion style? Not so much.

In addition to wearing all black, some of my classmates look like they have a major attitude. I don't let that get under my skin. I assume Coco Chanel was met with some nasty looks when she wore her avant-garde pieces, and I bet she ignored them. She was a total badass and one of my greatest inspirations.

I look around the room hoping to find a like-minded tribe and notice a few young women huddled together at the back, staring at an iPad. I recognize the host from *Project Catwalk* on the screen. It's no surprise; parts of the show are occasionally filmed here on campus. The women are laughing and cheering. I decide to walk over.

"Hey," a woman says without looking up from the screen. "What's up?"

"Hi there, I'm Clementine. Just wanted to introduce myself."

"Hi," one of them responds, not bothering to look up from the screen.

"Clementine. Now that's interesting," another says. I'm not sure whether she's being nice or sarcastic so I keep a cool distance. But I'm hopeful.

"Where are *you* from?" one of the girls asks, having torn her eyes from the screen and now staring me up and down.

"Paris."

"Oh, fancy ... *excusez-moi*," the tallest of the trio, a brunette, responds with a mock French accent. I respond with a tight smile.

"We love Paris, don't we ladies?" the girl says, and they all coo.

I still can't tell if they're being sincere so I try to look on the bright side: I might be making some friends. One of them is wearing a bright-lemon satin bomber jacket, a vintage striped cardigan, and rolled-up boyfriend jeans with royal-blue pumps. She has wild, curly black hair and piercing, feline green eyes.

"Hey, I'm Stella," she says, holding out her hand. She then introduces me to her friends.

"It's nice to meet you," I say. "Love the jacket. It's a great colour. Very refreshing."

"No kidding, right?" Stella says. "Not many people around here appreciate colour. I like to think we're the bold ones." She points around the room.

"Where are you from?" I ask. Stella looks not only older than my other classmates, but more mature and far more confident.

"Chicago," Stella says. "I'm a second-year transfer. I dropped out of law school to join the Parsons fashion program. I guess I wasn't cut out to be a legal eagle."

Stella's not only stylish, but classy and smart. She's the type of friend I'm looking for. I hope she feels the same way.

"Are those Repetto flats?" she gushes.

"Yes. You have a good eye."

"I can spot them from miles away. I wish I had a pair in every colour," Stella says. "I saw them in *Vogue Paris*. Major drool."

"Thanks. Very comfy, too," I say. I'm thrilled we've found a connection. Parisian fashion is always a good start.

"Hey, why don't you get a room?" a female voice calls out in the most condescending tone.

I turn around and come face to face with a woman in heavy makeup, arms covered in ink, staring at us menacingly. The left side of her head is shaved. She's wearing a ripped grey T-shirt underneath a black vest and looks as though she might eat us for lunch. I try not to judge her based on her looks (after all, I'm here to advocate for diversity), but my open-mindedness disappears when she throws her discarded gum wrapper at me, and it lands in my hair. This leaves both Stella and me speechless.

"What the —" I stammer.

The young woman gives me an exaggerated wink that makes my anxiety level shoot way up. I feel queasy. And it's only my first class.

I never thought I'd get insulted and attacked on my first day. It's worse than I thought. I picture myself giving her a piece of my mind. My mother always taught me to stand up for myself. But I decide to take the high road and ignore her instead. I just hope this woman will stay away from me and, more importantly, that I won't regret my decision to enrol at The New School.

Time will tell.

Chapter Three

"BEAUTY FADES BUT DUMB is forever," a male voice whispers.

"Excuse me?" I retort, spinning around. Okay, now I'm really offended. My father was right; I should have stayed in France.

"No, sweetheart, I'm not talking about *you*," the guy says with a wry smile. "I'm referring to that lame douchebag who just insulted you. I'm Jake. And you are?"

I relax and extend my hand. I like this guy already. "Clementine."

"Clementine? Wow, love the name. Don't worry about Debbie Downer, she probably forgot to take her tranks," he says, shaking his head and placing a pencil behind his ear.

"Thanks," I say, turning to face him fully and get a closer look. He's got a round figure and the sweetest smile. He's wearing large black hipster glasses, black and white checkered pants, and a grey sweatshirt that reads *MORE ISSUES THAN VOGUE* in bold white print. He's also sporting the coolest sneakers with silver shoelaces and shiny moons and stars. Jake looks older than most of the other students in class, including Stella. My guess is that he's in his midtwenties.

"Where are you from, sunshine?" he asks, putting a smile on my face.

"Paris," I say, throwing the gum wrapper into my empty paper cup.

"I should have guessed from the chic look." He points at my ensemble with his pencil.

Pfft. If only he knew I found the dress at the Salvation Army, my favourite place to hunt when I come to New York. I decide to keep that to myself. I don't need any nasty comments from the fashion police.

"Are you staying in the student dorms?" he asks.

"No, I'm staying in Brooklyn. With a roommate."

"Cool. You're missing out on some serious partying though. I hear the ladies can get pretty wild in there sometimes."

I shrug. That's not why I'm here. I don't tell him that my parents let me drink at home if I want to. To me, it's no big deal.

"What about you? Where are you from?" I ask.

"Queens. It's not as glamorous as the City of Light. We don't have the Louvre but we have the Louis Armstrong House — you know, the trumpet player?"

"That sounds interesting."

"Yep, it is. It's a shrine to his amazing talent and his wife's passion for vintage wallpaper. She was a woman after my own heart." He places his hand on his chest. "I just love *Toile de Jouy*." He says this with an exaggerated French accent that melts away my frustration.

"It's nice to meet you, Jake. And thanks for looking out for me," I say, giving the nasty girl a stare. She ignores me and pretends to look away. I brush it off; I have more important things to think about, like making a good impression on my first day at school.

I take a seat, wave at Stella, and wink at Jake. I like them both. I can already see them becoming part of my A-Team, my new "glamily," so to speak. I open my notebook while Jake stares at my nails. I can tell he's impressed by the tiny white daisies and gold hearts glued on them. I well up with pride. This could be the start of a great friendship.

Our teacher walks into class. She looks to be in her midthirties and is dressed in head-to-toe black, with a pearl necklace and Prada platform oxfords. She has vintage eyeglasses and her hair is tied in a neat ribbon. She's not as stylish as Maddie, but she looks elegant and smart. She goes over the class outline and asks us to partner up with a classmate to discuss our personal fashion history.

I freeze in my seat at the thought of being coupled with the class bully, but relax when Jake leans over.

"Okay, sweet pea," he says, adjusting his glasses, "we need to get intimate. Since I'm such a Chatty Cathy, why don't I start?"

"Please do," I say, happy to let him take the lead.

"All right, here goes nothin'. I come from a long line of shopkeepers from Queens. My father owns a fabric store that belonged to his father and my mother is a seamstress. Together, they've probably fixed all of the hemlines in Astoria. And they run a successful dry cleaning business, too. I work there nights and weekends in addition to doing freelance gigs. I'm the heir apparent to the family empire."

"Cool. That sounds pretty awesome." Jake is so authentic, I'm already under his spell. I can tell he and his family are all heart, elbow grease, and generous spirit. I could listen to him talk all day.

"But I'm looking to branch out — into fashion design," he says, his eyes gleaming. "The truth is, I'm no fashion spring chicken. I studied fashion history in college, I interned at the Met's Costume Institute, and I've been sewing since I was nine. I decided to study at Parsons to get some hands-on cred from the rigorous design program, if you catch my drift. And that's it, *ma chérie*. My entire fashion history."

"You want to be a fashion designer? With your own label? That takes a lot of hard work and discipline. But I guess you know that already, right?"

"Yup. Duly noted. The plus-size Zac Posen, *c'est moi*," he says jokingly. "My father's business doesn't appeal to me, but the craft of making clothes does."

"Do you have a muse?"

"My mom," Jake responds without hesitation. "She wears samples from Loehmann's and alters them perfectly; she transforms them into couture. It's like magic, really." His eyes are wide with excitement. I can tell he's found his calling. There's no doubt about it. He's full of passion and determination. "And I admire her guts. She's been in a wheelchair for the last ten years, but she never complains and always looks like a million bucks. She'll always be my number one source of inspiration."

My heart melts. I'd love to meet his mom. She sounds far more approachable, down-to-earth, and frankly inspiring than mine. My mom just gives me a headache most of the time with all of her drama.

"She sounds amazing. So what kind of designs do you have in mind?" I ask. I imagine him becoming the next Isaac Mizrahi, the New York designer who made it big in the 90s. He has the same witty repartee, the same belly laugh, and the same physique. My mother would say *il est adorable*. I think he's just adorbs.

"Well" — he looks around the room to make sure no one's listening — "I have this idea: I want to focus on clothing for people with disabilities. I want to make a difference in this industry and I know I can make an impact. That's my game plan, Clementine." He lowers his voice and waves his index finger. "I'm trusting you with my life on this; it's my secret strategy." He lowers his eyeglasses to the tip of his nose to make the point.

Wow. I'm really impressed with his concept. It reminds me of a Parsons student I read about who created a fashion line inspired by Syrian refugees. One of the key pieces of her collection is a wearable tent that easily converts into a jacket.

Not only is it impressive, it's a huge coincidence. What are the chances of me coming to Parsons dreaming of influencing the fashion world toward more diversity and eco-friendly choices, and the first guy I meet wants to design clothing with a conscience?

We must be soul twins. And I'm flattered Jake would trust me so quickly.

"Don't worry, Jake, you can totally trust me. I bet your designs will be a big hit."

"Thanks, doll. I appreciate that. So, what's your story?" he asks, his eyes brimming with curiosity.

"Well," I say, clearing my throat, "unlike you, I haven't studied fashion before, but I've been passionate about it since grade school. My French great-grandmother, Cécile, was a supremely fashionable woman in her day. She's *my* muse."

"Cool. Tell me more."

"Um, for starters, she was a model for the Parisian designer Madame Grès in the 40s."

"OMG! SHUT THE FRONT DOOR!" Jake hollers, making every head turn our way. My face turns Valentino red. I want to crawl under my desk but don't want any more attention. "Dude, are you kidding me?" Nasty girl glares at us again and I quickly stare down at my nails. Maybe I should've gone to beauty school instead.

"Shhhh. Stop it! I don't want any more attention from the haters," I whisper.

"Who cares about them? I want to hear about your great-grandma. She sounds fantabulous. My god, I fell in love with those fancy Madame Grès dresses when I was working in the archives at the Met." He puts his elbows on his knees like a sports fan watching a soccer match. It's thrilling to think my life is that captivating to him.

"Well, Cécile loved to go out on the town. She had an eclectic style and got noticed by Parisian trendsetters. She wasn't that wealthy but she had great taste." I have fond memories of spending afternoons window-shopping in Paris with her. "I remember visiting my first haute-couture salon with her. I was about ten years old, and although I was very young, I still remember some of the details about the day. Cécile passed away only months after that. I'm so grateful we shared that special time."

"I bet," Jake says. "Okay ... what else?" He's on the edge of his seat, drinking in my every word. He's so close to the edge, I worry he'll slide off his chair. That wouldn't be a pretty sight. "What about the designer?"

"Madame Grès was impressed with Cécile — she loved her style, her striking features, and her appreciation of fine clothes. She asked Cécile to be a house model and show her dresses to the local press." I point to my pearl necklace. "This belonged to Cécile."

"Oooh, that's gorgeous," he coos. "Do you have any pictures of her?" He pokes his nose almost literally into my bag.

"Who's Cécile?" nasty girl asks, appearing from nowhere and planting herself in front of me with her arms crossed. I'm tempted to tell her to screw off but instead I begin to laugh as Jake makes hilarious mocking faces behind her back. He wants me to say nothing but I decide to try a different tack. My gut tells me it's a far more effective way to handle her.

"She was my great-grandmother. She modelled for Madame Grès in Paris in the 1940s. That is all," I say, nonchalantly mimicking Meryl Streep in the movie *The Devil Wears Prada*. I turn to face Jake as if to dismiss her.

"La dee da," she says. Her cold expression changes, but to what, I can't tell. She's hard to read. "I studied Grès's work in college." Her voice trails off. She seems to want to say more but I have no interest in engaging with her.

"You need to watch your 'tude, girl — stay in your lane or swerve," Jake chimes in, wagging his finger. "What's your name?"

"It's Ellie." She crosses her arms, all attitude again, and stalks off, saying over her shoulder, "Guess I'm just not into the vintage boho vibe. That's my mother's style, and I haven't spoken to her in years."

I hear that. I have my own issues with my mother. I guess everyone has a story. If only we talked more instead of throwing gum wrappers. I decide to just ignore her.

Voilà. There it is. Cécile strikes again. Thankfully, keeping your cool runs in my blood. I'm grateful for having had one female relative who had it together. I just hope I can do the same and be as strong as she was.

Chapter Four

"OKAY, HON, I told you about my dreams. It's time for you to share yours," Jake says with a twinkle in his eye. He raises his eyebrows mischievously and it feels like we're exchanging dating stories, not future plans.

"Writing, fashion blogging, and creating an international platform."

He rolls his eyes and holds up his hand like a traffic cop. "Oh, puh-*lease*, not another fashion blog. Trust me little sister, that's not what the world needs. The market is pretty saturated already."

Ouch. I was hoping for more enthusiasm from him. It's true that there are tons of fashion bloggers out there. I should know; I follow a lot of them. I'm a big fan of the popular ones: *Bryanboy*, Nicole Warne of *Gary Pepper Girl*, *Mr. Bags*, and Aimee Song of *Song of Style*. But my concept is completely different. I wish he'd let me get to that before raining on my parade.

"It's not what you think. I'm not looking to promote fashion brands or labels. I want to write about diversity and eco fashion and become the voice of my generation."

"Right." He rolls his eyes again. I guess he's not grasping the concept.

"My blog will involve interviewing fashion trailblazers from all over the world who want to make a difference in this industry. People from diverse backgrounds, religions, and sexual orientations. A cast with strong political messaging, not just famous people. I want to portray a new kind of icon who can make a difference in the industry and make us think. In my view, that's worth paying attention to."

"Now you're talking my language," says Jake, coming around. "You have your great-grandmother's chutzpah in your genes. In that case, you go, girl. Be careful, though, diversity is becoming a hollow word in the industry. Just make sure it isn't a token marketing strategy."

"I get what you're saying. But I'm going to go beyond the surface. I plan to go deep. Inspired by my own life experiences." Just saying it brings back a flood of painful memories.

"Oh? How so?" he asks. I see I've piqued his curiosity.

"Just high-school memories of not fitting in with the popular girls at the private school I went to in Paris. I always felt judged and left out for how I looked. It was agonizing. I was unhappy and not confident."

"I'm sorry to hear that, hon. I can totally relate. I was a total outcast in high school and the butt of so many jokes and lewd comments you have no idea. But look where I am now. I'm about to take over Seventh Avenue. And the entire fashion world, too. Just like Cécile."

"You have some of her chutzpah, too. You also remind me a bit of my mother. She speaks her mind freely just like you do."

"Oh? What does *she* do?" Jake asks. He peers over at our teacher to make sure there's still time to continue our conversation. I hope so; it feels like we're just getting started.

"Famous opera singer," I answer flatly, knowing this will elicit another strong reaction. It usually does. I cringe in anticipation.

His eyes grow as round and wide as Katy Perry's. "GURL, ARE YOU FOR REAL? Your life sounds like a movie."

"Don't be fooled. It's more like a bad soap opera."

"Oh, come on. You can't be serious! It can't be that bad — Paris, Madame Grès, and a famous opera singer as a mom. My god, can your parents adopt me?"

I shake my head. My life is far from being a fairy tale. If only he knew the half of it. The truth is my family nearly imploded when my mother accepted a two-year contract to sing at La Scala in Milan a few years back and my father sought solace in the arms of his store's sales assistant. To make things worse, my mother began drinking heavily to calm her stage fright, and my father started taking painkillers to numb his pain.

Both of them stopped their nonsense when my mother returned home to Paris. Being the open-minded woman she is, she forgave my father's dalliance and quickly brushed it off. I suspect she wasn't a totally faithful wife while performing in Italy either. Everything was fine until she decided to hit on my boyfriend, Charles, last spring. Now ex-boyfriend, to be sure. She said she just couldn't help it; she has a thing for young men. It's still all over the European gossip mags. It was all so very disturbing and gross. That's why I had to leave home —

for sanity's sake. I needed a break from all the family drama. So I asked to transfer to New York.

"No, my parents can't adopt you. That would make you my half-brother and I'd have to pick fights, be rude, and boss you around. We can't have that. I much prefer having you as a friend."

"That's very presumptuous of you to call me your friend, Clem. But I like it. *A lot*. You and me, we'll rule the school."

"Sounds promising. I can see us now in the Sunday *Times*," I shoot back. The truth is I *can* see us making it to the top of our class.

"Okay, so what's your website's name?" Jake returns to our earlier conversation. He's all business now.

"*Bonjour Girl*. What do you think?" I've been mulling it over in my mind for ages. I hope he likes the French touch.

"Hmm, give me second." He places his hand on his chin, reminding me of Rodin's sculpture *The Thinker*. Although Jake is far from having *The Thinker*'s physique, he does have the same smooth skin and refined features.

"So?" I ask, worried he doesn't like it. We've only just met, but he's really growing on me. His opinion, strangely, matters to me.

"I'm thinking, I'm thinking," Jake says, biting the end of his pencil. "You know what, Clem? I LOVE IT. It's catchy with a French twist. I say go for it, sweetheart. I'll be your first reader."

"Really? Wow, thanks. That means a lot. Now you know *my* secret, so please keep it to yourself."

"Cross my heart and hope to die."

"We just met but I trust you, Jake, *just like a brother*," I tease. "And I really like you so please don't hope to die."

"Aww, that's so sweet. And you should trust me. I'm part of the fam now." He fist bumps me and I begin to laugh at his funny move when our teacher interrupts our discussion to continue her lecture.

She tells us that in this highly interactive world, it's imperative that we develop a strong visual identity for our personal brand, especially if we're to survive and thrive in the cutthroat fashion world. In order to achieve that, we must dig deep into our own past and explore our personal histories, which explains the exercise she had us do. I get what she's saying. This gives me a few ideas for my website. I'm taking notes when Jake nudges me in the ribs with his pencil.

"Hey, Clem …" he whispers.

"What? I'm trying to write this stuff down. It's important," I whisper back.

"Sorry, but someone's staring at you." He points to the door and I see Maddie peering in through the window. She waves and I wave back.

Phew. For a split second, I was worried it was that Ellie girl glaring at me. I need to get over her and work on my self-confidence. But it's not so easy when you've had a roller-coaster personal life like mine.

How long will it take for me to get over my mother's embarrassing indiscretion with my ex-boyfriend?

I hope it's sooner rather than later. It's time to put this behind me and move on.

Chapter Five

"WAS I DREAMING or did you look disappointed to see me?" Maddie asks as soon as I exit the classroom.

"Disappointed? Are you kidding? Why would I be?" Maddie probably picked up on my insecurity. I'm worried that my classmates will find out we're related; we've agreed to keep that under wraps, outside the faculty, to avoid any perception of preferential treatment. They already have enough details about me as it is. I don't want any more trouble. But I'm so proud to have such a stylish relative. I'd love to shout it from the rooftops.

Maddie looks particularly stunning today in a slim, black leather trench coat, a hot-pink cashmere turtleneck, black patent-leather boots, and large eyeglasses. She's accessorized her look with a colourful beaded necklace. Maddie reminds me of a young Iris Apfel, who recently, at ninety-five years old, took Paris Fashion Week by storm, stealing the spotlight from the top models. I think Iris and Cécile would have gotten along famously.

"So how did it go?" she asks.

"Great! Our class was super inspiring. I'm really happy to be here. I can't thank you enough for convincing my dad to let me come to New York," I whisper.

"I had very little to do with that; you did all the convincing. You're living the dream, girl. I'm so proud of you." She pats me on the back.

Maddie is my other muse. She finished top of her class in fashion school, received a scholarship for a master's degree in costume design from a prestigious college in London, was selected as a judge on the hit television show *America's Next Top Model,* and is one of the youngest professors at an international fashion college.

And you know what? She reached these professional heights not by stepping on anyone's toes, but with raw talent and hard work. She could've easily become the next Donna Karan, creating her own collection, but in a character-defining moment, she figured out her life purpose and chose academia over commercial success. Now, she proudly wears her students' collections around town and makes them (and herself) proud in the process.

That's who I want to be one day: a supportive, savvy, and stylish mentor to other women. With tons of clothes, international travel, and access to runway shows.

A girl can dream.

"I made a new friend today," I say, looking around for Jake. I wave and he saunters over.

"Jake, I'd like you to meet Maddie Laurent. She teaches fashion design here and she was instrumental in helping me with the paperwork for my transfer from France. I'm sure you'll be working together on some projects."

He stares her up and down approvingly. "Oh my gawd, THAT COAT!" He moves in close to inspect the details. "Hello, Maddie, it's a real pleasure. I've heard so much about you. Please forgive the drool but I've never been this close to a Dries Van Noten before."

"It's nice to meet you, too, Jake." Maddie flashes her elegant smile. "Welcome to the Parsons family."

"Thanks. Speaking of family, did you know that Clementine's great-grandma was famous?"

Maddie shoots me a sideways glance. I shake my head so she knows I haven't told him that we're related.

"Her family has probably been featured in *Paris Match*," he says loudly, swinging his large backpack over his shoulder. "I've asked for adoption and I'm waiting to hear back."

"Really?" Maddie responds coyly. "I had no idea."

He's right: my family *has* been featured in gossipy French magazines, especially after my mother was caught by the paparazzi leaving a Paris nightclub, inebriated, in the company of her daughter's boyfriend. I keep that to myself and know Maddie will, too. We don't need to spread the family gossip any further.

"Maddie's into vintage. That's why we get along."

"Right. I can see that. My family owns tons of vintage: piles and piles of stuff people dropped off and never picked up," Jake says. "Feel free to stop in at Fancy Free Dry Cleaners anytime and help yourselves to the merchandise. My father has no clue what to do with the stuff."

"Thank you, Jake, that's kind of you," Maddie says. I know she shops for vintage at fancy boutiques in Paris, London, and L.A., but she acts as if his offer is enticing. She's a class act.

"By the way, I signed up for your upcoming lecture and I can't wait," Jake says excitedly. "You're a true legend around here."

"Thanks, Jake. I look forward to seeing you there," Maddie says. It brings a sparkle to his eyes.

"I need to run; I don't want to miss my next class. I'll see you in the a.m., Clem."

I watch him saunter off, thrilled about having such a cool new friend. I'm already looking forward to seeing him tomorrow.

"What a charmer. I'm happy you met him," Maddie says. "The school does have a reputation for being competitive. Not all students make friends so quickly."

I want to say that I've already witnessed that first-hand but I keep it to myself. I don't want to sound like a child.

"When's your next class?" Maddie asks, looking at her watch.

"Not until after two. Why?" I ask.

"How about we go for lunch?"

"That sounds great. I'm in."

"Okay, follow me, *ma chérie*," Maddie says, as if she has something up her designer sleeve.

I don't know it yet, but I am about to be truly inspired.

Chapter Six

I WALK INTO LE MIDI, a charming French bistro on 13th Street just around the corner from Parsons, and it feels like home.

I look around the restaurant with its pressed white tablecloths and its long wooden bar where bottles of French wines are lined up. It reminds me of lunch dates with my father in the Saint-Germain neighbourhood of Paris.

To add to the excitement, Maddie seems to know everybody in this place. She waves and nods to every front table. I guess it's a popular hangout for the Parsons faculty. She introduces me around as one of her foreign exchange students. It feels really good.

We take a seat at a corner table overlooking the bustling street and I have to pinch myself to make sure I'm not dreaming. Today can't get any better.

"Thanks for your support, Maddie. It means a lot. I just hope I can meet Parsons' standards."

"Of course you will. I know how smart you are."

"Thanks. I'm ready to put in the hours. But enough about me. What about you? Any hot dates lately?" I ask.

"Well, if you want to know the truth, I dated that guy over there for a few months last year," Maddie whispers conspiratorially.

I discreetly turn my head and spot a man in his mid-forties wearing a crewneck sweater. He catches me looking so I quickly turn back around.

"What happened?"

"Nice guy, but really boring." She gives a fake yawn.

"You shouldn't have problems meeting fun-loving creative types around here," I say, putting my napkin on my lap.

"Right," she says nonchalantly. "Let's order some food. I'm starving." She picks up her menu, in part to hide a strange grin on her face. She's hiding something. But what?

"What do you recommend?" I ask, looking over the menu. I recognize all the traditional French dishes.

"Everything. I come here all the time; this place is like my second office. The organic chicken is delicious and so is the trout."

"I'll have the burger," I say. I'm in the mood for something American. "With a side of truffle fries. And I won't share until you tell me what's going on; I can tell you're hiding something." I know her weak spot.

She closes her menu and responds with a sly grin. Busted.

After we place our orders, she finally talks. "Clementine, I have some amazing news: you've been awarded a fashion scholarship." Maddie removes her glasses and her green eyes shine bright like a million sparkly diamonds. I sit back feeling dazed and confused, as though she's just told me I'm about to fly to the moon on a rocket with Karl Lagerfeld.

"I — what?"

Maddie sees my confusion. "You told me you wanted to launch your own website, right?" she says, looking for validation.

"Yes, totally. That's my dream."

"The school offers resources that can help students launch online platforms while they're still learning their craft. This scholarship is relevant to what you're doing, so I filled out an application on your behalf."

"Wow, thank you!" I can't believe my ears. It's surreal. "But what is it that made me … deserve it?"

"Well, you were eligible for several reasons. You have a strong academic record, and you worked hard as an intern for that magazine in Paris. Your writing skills are impeccable. Your resume did the job for you."

"That's amazing!" I jump from my seat, nearly knocking over my glass of water. I dive over the table to give her a giant hug. This garners a few awkward stares from the people nearby, especially her former flame. I don't care — it's not every day that a girl receives a scholarship to help launch her own business.

This news is so unexpected that tears of joy roll down my cheeks. I wipe them away with my serviette. "This is incredible, Maddie. Not to sound greedy but … how much is it?"

"Five thousand dollars. Not bad, right? It should cover your blog's start-up fees and pay for some graphic design and advertising to get your site off the ground," she says proudly.

I can barely sit still. I'm so grateful. I've already contacted a graphic designer to help me build the site. The timing couldn't be more perfect.

"Thanks, Maddie. This means a lot to me. You're already putting me up at your place, and now this? You're an angel."

She waves her hand dismissively and takes a sip of water.

The waiter brings our food and I dig into my truffle fries with gusto. Being psyched sure builds an appetite.

"It's too bad that I need to teach and you have class this afternoon, otherwise I'd order a bottle of red," Maddie says, sipping her sparkling water.

"A glass of Bordeaux never hurt anyone, especially when you're from France," a male voice says behind my back.

I whip my head around. A very good-looking guy has come up right next to our table. He's medium-tall with dark, curly hair, dressed in baggy cargo pants and a striped shirt, and carrying a large camera bag. I catch a whiff of his intoxicating cologne — it's an intense, smoky mix of sandalwood and leather and it throws me off a little. Um, I mean *a lot*. A hot blush covers my cheeks. And I haven't touched a sip of wine. But if this guy is offering some, I might just try it.

"Hello, Jonathan, it's nice to see you again. Jonathan's a freelance photographer who works with us on several projects," Maddie says, while I keep my eyes riveted to his attractive face. I'm relieved to hear that he isn't a Parsons student. It would be distracting to have him in any of my classes.

"This is Clementine, one of my foreign students. I'm advising her on a few matters."

Jonathan beams a megawatt smile that accentuates his dimples. *Mon dieu* — I'm turning into a puddle of sweat in my seat.

"Hey, it's nice to meet you." He puts down his black bag and extends a hand. Tattoos run up his arm. As soon as his hand touches mine, I can almost feel the electricity running all the way down to my toes. Thank god I'm sitting down, otherwise I'd probably keel over.

"Clementine. What a great name."

"Thanks," I respond nonchalantly while replaying the compliment at least a dozen times in my head. He runs his fingers through his hair and moves in closer. He smiles and I swoon.

"Are you French, too?" he asks.

"Can't you tell?" Maddie says, pointing at my outfit. "Clementine is one of the few at school not dressed in head-to-toe black."

"You *do* look European," he says, glancing at my dress. Whoever this handsome man is, he's just scored some points. "And you're the only woman here who isn't glued to her phone or tablet." He nods at the French novel sticking out of my bag.

"I'm old school when it comes to reading," I shoot back. "I mean, I do have a phone but I haven't activated it yet."

"My point exactly." He smiles wryly.

"Why don't you join us?" Maddie asks. Honestly, I'm not sure how I feel about that. I mean, I was just getting started discussing my blog and its upcoming launch and I was hoping to get some feedback from Maddie. And before I talk to this guy any further, I'd love to check whether I have anything stuck between my teeth.

"Okay, just for a few minutes," Jonathan says, taking a seat next to me. There's a sudden powerful heat that emanates from my solar plexus. Am I really that attracted to him? I try to control my heart palpitations. It's not easy. *Come on, Clementine, keep it together. You're not going to get thrown off by the first handsome guy that crosses your path in New York.*

"How are you enjoying the novel?" he asks. "There were great reviews of it in the *Times*. I can't wait to read the translation," he says, and this unsettles me even more. It's one thing to find him good-looking but to be impressed by his intellect — that's unexpected. I hand him the novel and while he elegantly flips through its pages, I catch another whiff of his cologne, and this time it sends all of my senses into overdrive. My heart pounds wildly in my chest. My cheeks turn the colour of my dress. This is embarrassing. I try to cover up my attraction but it isn't working. He must be able to tell.

I try to act cool as I reach for my glass of water. I wish Maddie would just say something but she continues to nibble at her salad, looking amused. I force myself to speak.

"It's really terrific so far," I manage to say. "The characters are well-developed and the setting is eighteenth-century Scotland. The author is particularly skilled at combining history with intriguing plot twists. If you like suspense and historical pieces, I think you'll love it." He looks impressed. Score.

"I always appreciate a little suspense," he says. He shoots me a mischievous side-glance, his eyes sparkling with amusement. My insides melt like cheese over pizza.

"Clementine just found out she's getting a scholarship," Maddie says.

For some reason, I'm uncomfortable with Maddie sharing this information. I guess I'm still digesting the news myself. This will likely bring more attention my way like I got in class this morning and I was hoping to avoid that.

"Really? That's great. Congratulations! This definitely calls for some wine. I'm ordering a bottle — it's on me."

My face turns bright red. But why? Is it the compliment or the fact that Jonathan seems interested in me? He's a fashion photographer and I don't look anything like the model types walking around New York. I think about my ex-boyfriend for a split second and have a flash of anxiety and doubt. His behaviour really affected my self-confidence and I'm still trying to recover from it all. I push those thoughts aside and tell myself to enjoy the moment and relax.

"Thank you, Jonathan, that's very generous of you," Maddie says. "Clementine, I hope you'll have a sip. After all, we're toasting you!"

"Okay then, twist my rubber arm," I say.

Jonathan responds by leaning into me and pretending to twist my elbow. Again his firm touch sends waves of electricity throughout my body. My insides are going haywire.

I feel hot. I feel cold. I feel I might just lose control.

Could this be a good thing?

"So, Clementine," Jonathan says, looking amused while making me squirm in my seat, "you must be really smart to get a scholarship. Good for you, I'm impressed."

The waiter shows up with the bottle of red and Maddie excuses herself to hit the powder room, leaving me alone to fend off the swirl of lustful thoughts swimming in the back of my mind. Never mind freestyle, we're talking

Olympic-level 100-metre butterfly here. It doesn't help that Jonathan brushes my arm as he pours wine into my glass.

"Thanks. It's not just about the brains, it's about the hustle," I say casually. I have no idea where that came from, but I blame Jake. That's something he would likely say.

I've only had two sips of wine but it has obviously gone to my head. I imagine my fingers running through Jonathan's thick mane of delicious I-just-got-out-of-bed hair while we sit side-by-side reading books on his living room couch. I'm clearly getting way ahead of myself here.

Having Maddie as a chaperone on this unexpected lunch date is a blessing. I feel more confident with her around, which is preferable when you're trying to flirt with a member of the opposite sex. Is that what I'm doing? I have no idea anymore. I'm clearly losing it.

All I can say is that I hope Maddie gets back to the table soon. Without her, I'd be a puddle of confused emotions, drunk by noon and stuffing my face with truffle fries. You see, just like my mother, when anxious, I tend to veer toward excess.

"How are you finding New York?" Jonathan asks before taking a sip of his wine.

"Can't complain," I say coolly. I try to hide my true feelings about the matter: I want to jump up and down and scream about how amazing New York has been so far. Especially right this second … but I talk myself out of looking silly. "It's been great so far. I've met some fascinating people and I'm really looking forward to diving deep into the fashion program. Parsons is top notch for what I'm interested in."

"And that would be?"

"Fashion journalism."

"Cool. I work with lots of journalists, especially those who cover Fashion Week. I can make some introductions if you'd like."

"Oh, thank you. That's very kind. But I'm looking to build my own platform and publish there. At least for now."

"You've got spunk. I like that." He winks.

"Thanks." I lift my glass, trying to remain calm so as not to shake or spill anything. He definitely has a powerful effect on me.

"Do you have friends in New York? People to go out with?"

"Yes, I've made a few," I shoot back. What I really mean to say is that I have one new friend, but boy, he counts for several people.

"Happy to hear it." He grins. "New York can be a lonely place. "So where are you staying? The school dorm?"

"No, in Brooklyn."

"Really? Whereabouts?"

I freeze in my seat. Maddie and I agreed to keep our living arrangement a secret. I just hope she shows up and comes to my rescue. In an attempt to deflect his question, I flick my hair back and wave the waiter over to order an espresso. I can't have any more wine; I may say things I'll regret later. Not that I need the extra jolt of caffeine, either. I'm already jumpy enough as it is. I try to use it as a delay tactic but it doesn't work.

Jonathan stares at me with a puzzled look. I guess he's still waiting for me to answer his question.

"In Williamsburg," I finally say under his watchful gaze. "With friends."

"That's awesome. I'm in Greenpoint. I know the area well. I lived there for two years."

Thankfully both the waiter and Maddie show up before he asks any more questions.

"If you like coffee, there's this new café that just opened. I could take you there on Saturday? I have a photo exhibit with other photographers at the Pratt," he says, with a glint in his eye.

"That sounds like fun," Maddie says, finally chiming in to answer for me. I can tell she's egging me on. I discreetly roll my eyes at her. I'm dying to gently kick her under the table to make her stop but I can't reach that far.

"Yes, it does," I finally respond. I feel ambushed — but in a good way. The truth is that I'm dying to accept — I just don't want the whole world to be in on it, that's all. "Sure, count me in."

"Fantastic. I'll let you two finish the lunch I so rudely interrupted. I gotta run but I'll catch you on Saturday. Here's my card. Do text me your number, and don't forget to activate your phone, Clementine." The way he says my name sets my heart spinning.

I watch him heading to the bar to pay for our wine. He catches me staring and winks. I look down at my shoes and when I look up again, he's gone. Through the tall windows, I see him walking down 13th Street on his way back to the school.

"Isn't he great?" Maddie asks with the tone of someone who's trying to fix me up.

"Mm-hmm," I respond, playing along. She knows that in Paris, dates aren't "arranged." You just hang out casually with friends until one of them finds the courage to ask you out. Anyway, no matter his intentions, I'm just thrilled Jonathan invited me to his exhibit.

"What?" Maddie lifts her hands in the air, as if claiming her innocence.

"Come on, don't tell me this wasn't set up. I'm much younger than you, but I wasn't born yesterday."

"Of course not. It was all very spontaneous," Maddie says, reaching for her bag. "But he sure is handsome."

"Whatever you say, dearest Maddie extraordinaire." I place my hand on hers. "All I can say is that you're definitely on a roll. You landed me a scholarship *and* the man of my dreams," I say in jest. It's still too soon to tell but Jonathan really is dreamy.

I grin. She laughs.

"You're right, that's a lot for one day." She grabs her trench and stands up. "I need to get back to work. I have a class to teach and a conference to prepare for."

In addition to being a terrific mentor, Maddie has a heart of gold. I feel so happy, my heart might explode. Before I can express my overflowing gratitude, she walks past me toward the bar.

"I'll be right back." She pulls out her wallet and her credit card and I can hear the waiter's response.

"No, *madame*. The young man paid for your lunch already." My heart skips. Jonathan is a real gentleman.

"Don't forget to stop by my office later to collect your cheque." Maddie squeezes my shoulder.

Honestly, it just can't get any better than this. We leave the bistro, and my mind goes into overdrive about Saturday: what should I wear, what should I say, and, more importantly, how can such an attractive man be into a girl like me?

Saturday can't come fast enough.

Chapter Seven

"HEY, CLEM, LOVE the outfit today. You look *flawless*," Jake says, standing next to me in the school cafeteria. We're waiting in line for our breakfast.

"Thanks." For my second day of class, I'm wearing palazzo jeans and a striped jacket I secretly "borrowed" from my mother's closet (*new with tags, never worn*, as they say on eBay), with a light-pink handbag and white sneakers. I'm also sporting a goofy grin on my face. Jake, on the other hand, has toned it down a notch. He's wearing grey jeans and a grey hoodie with the words *Justin 4 Ever* written across his chest. He catches me staring at it.

"I made an effort today, just for you. My standard school uniform is a onesie," he says. I'm not sure whether he's being serious, but imagining Jake in a pink unicorn one-piece makes me giggle.

"Great sweater," I shoot back.

"Oh thanks. It's by Supreme, the sportswear label. You know it, right?" he asks, looking concerned about my potential lack of inside fashion information. Even if I'd never heard of it, I would deny it — I have a reputation to uphold. I do know the brand and frankly I can't wrap my head around why anybody would spend an absurd amount of money on a big droopy sweatshirt with blatant branding. But I keep that to myself. He probably saved several of his hard-earned paycheques to buy it.

"Mm-hmm. Yes, of course."

"So are you going to tell me why you're smiling like goofball?"

I guess he can tell I'm daydreaming. I'm not sure how to respond. Should I tell him about my surprise lunch date with Jonathan yesterday? And the unexpected scholarship money?

Yesterday was by far the best day of my life. I met Jake, then Jonathan, then picked up my cheque from Maddie's office. I walked — um, I mean ran — to the nearest Apple store to activate my new phone. Scholarship money in hand, I also splurged on a pair of chocolate-brown boots to wear for my date Saturday. I don't know Jake well enough yet to tell him everything. But maybe just a bit.

Jake slides his tray in front of the cafeteria staff, waiting for his hot breakfast to be served. It looks as though he's ordered enough food for half the class.

"Well," I lean in and whisper, "I … met someone." I hate to admit it, but instead of doing homework, I spent the better part of last night thinking of about my incredible good fortune. The scholarship *and* the lunch — it was just too much for one day.

"Whaaat? When did that happen? In your sleep?" Jake frowns. "Don't take this the wrong way, pussycat, but that's a bad omen. You know how heavy the workload is around here.

This will likely kill your focus, your grades, and most probably, your future," he adds ominously, sounding a tad neurotic.

I shake my head and laugh at his over-the-top remark. "I think you're taking it too far. We've only shared one meal."

"You already shared a meal? Jeez, In New York, that *really* means something. Most people never make it past Joe Coffee," he says, referring to a small coffee shop on 13th Street. "So when's the wedding?" I ignore the silly question. "Listen Clem, we can't have you dating so soon in the school year, okay? I'm here to look after your interests and meeting men is not one of them," he finishes categorically, reaching for his coffee.

"Don't you want details? You're supposed to be my friend, remember?"

He sighs wearily. "All right, sweet pea, let her rip. Tell me everything."

I know he's just playing with me; he's dying to hear the details. Before I can say another word, he raises the palm of his hand in the air. "Wait! Let me guess: he's easy on the eyes, looks like Adam Levine with his tattoos, wears plaid shirts, is into music and the arts ..." His voice trails off as his breakfast arrives.

I stand in front of Jake with my hands on my hips. He nailed it.

"How d'you guess?"

"Oh honey, I'm sorry, but that was so predictable. You're like an open book. Don't get me wrong, I think you're charming and all — but I saw that coming from miles away."

"Are you saying I lack taste? Or originality?" I mean, doesn't he see my Claude Montana jacket from the 80s?

"No, that's not what I said. I just knew right away you'd be attracted to a certain type. It's a great type, make no mistake!"

"Okay, well, I hate to admit it, but you're right."

"Of course I am." He smiles triumphantly. "So, what's the story with this dude?"

"He's a freelance photographer. He likes to read novels and drink coffee and red wine. That's all I know about him so far. He's taking me to his photo exhibit on Saturday in Brooklyn. I'm really excited."

"A photographer? Oh come on, Clem, you should know better than that. They're notorious modelizers who can't keep it in their pants," Jake says, stirring milk into his coffee. "Haven't you heard?"

My stomach drops. My new friend is giving me a lecture before I've even had the chance to think this through myself. Modelizer? It's true that some photographers have a bad reputation. But Jonathan seems to be such a gentleman. I don't need Jake putting any doubts in my mind. I want to respond that what's on Jake's breakfast plate is far more dangerous for his well-being than me going on a casual date with a photographer is for mine, but I bite my tongue.

"What else do you know about this guy?" Jake asks, like the big brother he's trying to be.

I shake my head. The truth is that other than Jonathan's photography work for Parsons and the connection with Maddie, I don't know much about him.

Maybe Jake *is* right — I could have done some more research before accepting Jonathan's invitation. But Maddie had nothing but good things to say about him. It seemed safe enough to go for a coffee and to a gallery.

"It's just a casual flirtation," I respond defensively. "Nothing more. But you're right — I do need to focus on school. Thanks for reminding me. My father will be thrilled I met *you*." I give him a friendly nudge on the elbow.

"You can always count on *moi* to keep you in line, sweetie pie. I'd love to meet your dad. I have a feeling he and I would gel famously."

I nearly cough up my tea. He has no idea what my father's like. He's far from being relaxed and cool about stuff. He's the opposite: uptight, conservative, and sometimes a bit snobbish. Not exactly the kind of guy who'd want to meet up to share a slice of 99-cent pizza on an NYC street corner.

I watch him dig into his bacon, eggs, and sausage, but I'm distracted. I was so excited about seeing Jonathan on Saturday; now I'm more nervous than anything. I'll have to keep an eye out for troubling signs.

"Mind if I have a bite?" I ask, pointing at his chcocolate-chip muffin. I've learned that men come and go, but chocolate never disappoints.

I let the chips melt in my mouth and feel a gazillion times better.

"So, now that we've gone over the boy situation, I need your help, Clem."

"Oh? For what?"

"Shopping for Maddie's design class. I need to pick up some supplies, including some fabric for my first assignment. Are you free later? At lunch?"

"Oh, now you're talking my language. Absolutely."

"I'll meet you out on Fifth Avenue at noon. I have a few things to take care of, then I'm off. See ya in a few, my precious gabardine."

I smile and wink back. Photographers may love to chase models, but more than anything, I love to dress and adorn them. And shopping for fabric is one of the ways I get to do that.

And that's plenty to make me happy.

Chapter Eight

"HONEY, I'M HOME!" Jake sings as soon as we enter Ankara Designs, a fabric emporium on West 39th Street.

A young woman with blue hair standing behind the counter waves at Jake. He sends her an air kiss. He obviously comes here *a lot*.

I look around the store and it does feel like home. It's filled with bolts of fabrics of every colour and style including candy-coloured cottons, cool denims, luxurious silks, wools, funky plaids, polyesters, and tons of lace. There are buttons of every style and colour, loads of thread, zippers, patterns, and all kinds of yummy accessories. To me, it's like Disneyland, Dylan's Candy Bar, and MGM Studios all rolled into one. I could spend hours in here.

"This place is amaze-balls," I gush, inhaling the odour of fresh textiles. To some, it might smell like dust and mildew, but to me it's a fragrance that makes my heart sing. I'm like a bloodhound on the prowl for fresh game, except that I'm hunting silk shantung.

The place is packed with people of every age, style, and ethnicity. I recognize a few Parsons students from my class.

"In case you're wondering, I basically live here. It's my second favourite place in New York."

"What's your favourite?"

"Ah, that's a secret, but if you help me find what I'm looking for, you may just find out."

I look around the loads of fabrics. Unlike most fabric shops I've seen, the fabric bolts here are organized vertically so it's easy to look for patterns. If I were Jake, I'd want them all.

"So many styles, so little cash …" Jake sings. "How can I choooose?" He shimmies his hips behind a rack of velvets while humming the tune to "So Many Men, So Little Time."

He cracks me up.

"What do you need? Are you looking for anything specific?" I'm keen to help out.

"Maddie asked us to create an outfit with unconventional materials."

Hmm, interesting concept. "What about this?" I point to a bolt of gold lamé.

"Nah, sweetie. That's too *Golden Girls*, circa 1985."

"*Qu'est-ce que tu veux?* What do you want?"

"I need something a bit out there, but not too much. Crazy-cool but polished. Catch my drift?"

"All right, let me take a look and see what I can find." I'm not 100 percent sure I understand what he's looking for, but I'm up for the challenge.

I walk up to the second floor and let my imagination run wild. I imagine cut-out sundresses made from plastic flowers, shorts and midriff-baring tops made with silver and gold shoelaces, a cocktail dress made of feathers and tiny seashells. It's what happens when my creativity is cut loose. I'm enjoying every second of it.

Something catches my eye. It's a bolt of tie-dyed pink and white cotton. The material is also coated in plastic; it's known as oilcloth. The bright pink reminds me of summer picnics by the pool, gelato, and childhood vacations. The vibe is happy and sugary sweet. I think Jake could make something spectacular out of this. I grab the bolt and head back downstairs where Jake is inspecting some silver lace.

"What about this? The look is trippy ice cream truck gone wild. Or Lilly Pulitzer on acid."

"Wow, you've outdone yourself, Clem. I love it! It's Miami meets Cape Cod."

"You like it?" I ask, surprised. I'm happy that my instincts were on point. He gets me.

"Yeah, totally. I could make some palazzo pants and a sexy tube top. I could even accessorize the look with a beach umbrella and some ginormous white vintage sunglasses." I can tell the right side of his brain is as stimulated as mine.

"You nailed it. That's something I'd love to wear," I say.

"Clementine, you are my sunshine …" he sings, then moves in for a hug and spins us around. And right there in the middle of New York City's Garment District, our friendship is officially sealed.

I can't believe how excited I am. Can my time in New York get any better? Unfortunately, something brings my joy back down a notch. I can feel someone staring at me, as if their glare is boring holes into my back. The vibe is heavy and disturbing. I turn around and there's Ellie, giving us that weird look again. I wonder why? I nod and give her a tight smile. I'm not going to let some weirdo with bad energy and salty vibes get me down. I've worked way too hard to get myself here.

I decide to ignore her and follow Jake while he orders his fabric. He spends a few more minutes feeling the material with his fingers, and once he's confident it can be sewn into a wearable outfit, he orders several yards. The store employee cuts the fabric generously, which makes my friend giddy.

"I just love a store with generous cuts, don't you, Clem?" he says, batting his eyelashes at the woman helping us. What a charmer. I guess this is how he gets such good service.

After he pays for his load, he stares at me with a childish grin. "We need to celebrate this fabulous find with something sweet, my love. Follow me, it's my treat!" He hails a cab as soon as we exit the store.

"Where are we going?"

"To my favourite place in New York. It's named after the art of making happy discoveries. You know, like meeting you and finding my funky fabric."

"Huh?"

"Serendipity 3. It's an ice cream parlour for grown-ups. Haven't you heard of it? There was a movie made in its honour."

I shake my head.

"They serve stupid drinks like apricot smushes, big burgers, and towering sundaes. But the frozen hot chocolate will melt your heart."

I wrap my silk shawl around my shoulders and smile from ear to ear as I slide into the cab's back seat. I can confirm that thanks to my new friend, my heart has already melted several times over.

Chapter Nine

"ANOTHER DAY, ANOTHER slay," Jake says as soon as I take my seat next to him in class. I've shown up early so we can catch up. After our shopping trip yesterday, the two of us are joined at the hip.

"You bet. With that killer fabric, it's a slam dunk," I say with a wink.

"All thanks to you, love. I can't wait to start using it. Tonight after work, with the help of my mom's sewing machine, I begin my hot-pink masterpiece."

"Cool. I can't wait to see it. And thanks again for lunch. That hot chocolate was sinful."

"But totally worth it, right? Shopping can be such a gruelling exercise. It burns tons of calories," he says, pretending to flex his muscles.

"Whatever. I like you just the way you are, fit or not."

He grins. My comment makes him blush.

"Now that we've worked on one of my projects, it's time to work on yours. I don't want to pressure you, but have you thought about *Bonjour Girl*?" Jake asks, just as Stella, the former law student, walks by.

"What's *Bonjour Girl*?" she asks. "It sounds familiar. Is that a new French clothing line?"

I shake my head and glance over at Jake as if to say this topic is off limits. Even if Stella seems nice, I don't want her to know about it. I'm still working out the details in my mind.

"Oh, it's nothing. Just a French magazine I wrote articles for a long time ago. They've shut down since," I say, trying to change the topic.

"Oh, Clementine, don't be so modest," Stella says breezily. "You wrote for a French fashion magazine? That's amazing. You should let everyone know about it!" A few heads turn our way.

Oh man, here we go again.

"Thanks for saying that." I try to brush her off politely. She senses that I'm in no mood to talk so she walks back to her seat.

"Oops. Sorry," Jake says, looking embarrassed. "I shouldn't have mentioned it out loud."

"No worries. We're good."

"So what's your timeline for the launch?" Jake whispers, taking a sip of coffee from his *Namastay on the Couch* mug.

"Funny you should ask. I've started writing a business plan and creating a mock-up of the site," I whisper back. This takes Jake by surprise. I don't tell him about my scholarship and that getting it allowed me to pay for a graphic designer. I don't want to sound like I'm bragging — I'll bring it up when the time is right.

"No way! Really? Between running into fabulous men, dissing your detractors, and having a fabulous family, you've got it going on, girlfriend. Do you have any secret powers I should know about? And can you please be my manager? I could use a kick in the pants."

"Sure. I'll accept your funny comebacks as payment."

He smiles and goes back to his coffee. "That's a good thing, sweetness, 'cause I'm not exactly rolling in it. The Parsons tuition fees are killing me."

My face drops and I suddenly feel bad about receiving the scholarship money. Jake deserves it as much as I do. And if he's going to be my best friend, I should be able to tell him about it. I also feel torn between my pact with Maddie and my loyalty to Jake. Maybe I can convince Maddie that Jake *is* family and that the secret of our family connection is safe with him? Until then, I'll keep my mouth shut, but it's tough and makes me feel guilty.

"Parsons *is* expensive. And the cost of living in New York is through the roof. I'm on a budget, too," I say to commiserate. The fact of the matter is that I do need to watch my spending. My parents give me a monthly allowance and it's enough to manage but not much more. So far, I haven't felt the need to get a job but we'll see how that goes.

Jake remains uncharacteristically silent. My guess is that money really is a sensitive issue for him, so I decide to change the subject to lighten the mood.

"What about your secret collection?" I ask.

"I *have* been working on it," Jake whispers, raising his eyebrows, then wiping his lips with a napkin.

"Oh really? When?"

"At night, after work, and on weekends. I started a few weeks ago before school started. I don't sleep much." He takes a slug of coffee as if to make his point.

"What have you done so far?"

"I've collected some magazine clippings, patterns, interviews, and Instagram photos related to my concept. Inspirational stuff."

"Fantastic. I'm already feeling inspired."

"After I develop my design chops here at Parsons and then intern with an experienced designer, I'll be ready to launch."

"I know your design chops are strong already. You need to own it, my friend."

"All right, if you say so," he says pensively. "I do have a confession to make." He leans in to me, lowering his voice. "I have a new muse. She's been keeping me inspired late at night and lighting up my world. I've been drawing sketches like crazy."

Oooh, is he talking about me? My god, I'm so flattered. I've always wanted to be someone's muse but never felt like I was particularly captivating. I'm not sure what to say.

"Yes, I met her at a cocktail party last Saturday" — not me, then, I realize with a pang — "and she's the world's most delicious woman — after you, of course," he gushes.

I'm so silly. Why did I jump to conclusions? And why do I feel so jealous of this person?

"Who is she?" I ask in a fake perky voice.

"A fashion blogger from Russia who lives in New York. She's alluring and fascinating; you'd totally love her, Clem. She's the perfect muse for my collection."

"It sure sounds like it," I say, trying to show some enthusiasm.

"You see, she's paralyzed from the waist down. Terrible ski accident in her teens. But she's got an incredibly positive attitude and a love of life. She's totally amazing."

"Wow," I say, feeling underwhelming all of a sudden.

"She has a huge following — she's witty, stylish, and gorgeous," he says with much admiration in his voice.

"I guess like attracts like. What's her name?"

"Adelina," he coos. "I plan to use her as one of my models."

He pulls out his cellphone to show me her Instagram profile. She looks like a modern-day Grace Kelly. There are shots of her wearing a bright vintage coat, looking like a 50s movie star. In one photo, she has red lips and a matching sequined scarf. In another, she's sporting a colourful purple dress and vintage Hermès Kelly bag, just like the one Cécile used to carry. She also has the coolest vintage cat eye glasses I've ever seen.

"You're right. She *is* perfect," I say, biting my lower lip. Why do I feel so insecure all of a sudden? Why am I envious of someone I've never met? I try to shake out of it, but it's not easy. Was I expecting an exclusive friendship with Jake? It feels weird to admit it, but I guess I was.

"I plan to create designer pieces for people in wheelchairs, like her. It's high time the fashion world paid attention to people with physical disabilities." He's grown melancholic and I know he's thinking about his mom. "I plan on making Adelina famous, too, in the process," he says, with an air of determination.

"I don't doubt it for one second." I'm impressed by Jake's idea and his awareness. How many other young designers are concerned with representing physical diversity?

"What kind of features will your clothes have?" I ask, curious.

I can tell Jake's happy with my question. "Well, pants are usually too short for people in wheelchairs, for example. You need to remove excess bulk in the crotch area," he says, pointing at the crotch of his low-rise baggy jeans. "And add more room for the shoulders and arms to make movement easier." He clearly has done his research.

"This is super interesting," I say, my mind spinning fast. I'm taking mental notes. This is exactly the kind of thing I plan to cover on my blog. "I'm sure you could find some sponsors for your project." I bet lots of companies and organizations would gladly partner with him.

"Mm-hmm. But I'm not ready to launch yet. Far from it, actually. I need to save up some money and get some corporate experience."

This makes my stomach clench again. I know Jake could use my scholarship to launch his collection.

"I get it," I say, twirling a lock of hair, trying to come up with some ideas. Maybe I could share some of my money? Or invest in his concept?

"It's important I get it right," Jake says, lowering his voice while eying all the students around us, sizing up the competition. "It's a tough market out there, sugar pie. I need to execute my plan carefully."

He sees me frowning and immediately leans into me. "I'm sorry, Clem. I don't mean to monopolize the conversation with my business plans."

"No, no, Jake, please don't apologize. I think your concept is amazing. I'm just trying to think of ways to help you."

He smiles, revealing his dimples and the gap between his teeth. "Ah, thanks, honey. I'm glad I have a friend with such a big heart."

Ouch.

"Did you know Parsons offers grants, scholarships, and fellowships? The list is available on the school website. I bet you could find one to help with your project," I say, trying to be helpful without revealing too much. "I think there's even a scholarship for social innovation. You should check it out." The truth is I saw it when I collected my cheque in the administration offices yesterday.

His eyes grow wide with excitement. "Really? My god, Clementine, I knew you were special when I first met you, but now, I'm convinced heaven must be missing an angel …" He stands up and does a charming butt dance like Cameron Diaz in that old movie *Charlie's Angels*. His hilarious dance moves have the students in our class laughing out loud. A few even pull out their phones to film him.

I just hope Jake has the last laugh and finds some financing. He totally deserves it.

The question is, do I?

Chapter Ten

AFTER CHECKING MY new phone for the umpteenth time to make sure it *really* is activated and daydreaming about Jonathan during the greater part of the class, I decide it's time to kick some *derrière*. After all, the scholarship money is both an honour and an investment in my future, so I'm not going to let it go to waste. I know most students would kill for it, including my friend Monsieur J.

Hearing about Jake's project and new muse got my competitive juices in gear. It's called healthy competition when your friends boost your work ethic.

After class, I make my way to the library with my laptop to do some research.

What am I doing? Studying other bloggers. I'm looking for inspiration and I'm not leaving until I find a strong visual signature. I told my graphic designer I'll have this figured out quickly so he can finish my website. I'm also curious to find out how some popular bloggers do their thing — what angel dust do they sprinkle on their online presence to make it into the big leagues? I want to understand how they write and what kinds of content and pictures create the most engagement with their readers.

I jump from blog to blog, taking extensive notes, comparing styles, design graphics, bios, and outside links. I become entranced by this dreamy digital world that unfolds before my eyes in the form of countless pictures and videos — pages and pages of online beauty and style. These bloggers have become superstars in their own right, attracting media attention from all around the globe. I want to achieve what they have. I know I can do it.

I then spend time on their impressive social media accounts. All the heart-stopping images taken on exotic beaches and other fabulous locations around the globe take my breath away, too. And the selfies — my god, the gorgeous selfies — making it all look so effortless. But I know it's not.

I wonder how much time they spend on primping before taking these photos? And how many photos they snap before capturing the perfect one? And more importantly, how they can afford such lavish lifestyles? Many of these girls have closets more impressive than top fashion editors and Hollywood celebrities.

I'm not naive — I know many of the pictures are Photoshopped. I'm also aware that most of the fashion bloggers get freebies and get paid for their posts — with money, clothes, makeup, and travel. Many of them don't bother saying that their posts are sponsored, which is totally offensive. I also know how easy it is to manipulate your image, making it look as though you have a fabulous life when in fact the reality is far from it.

I was really impressed when Australian Instagram sensation Essena O'Neill publicly called out her own so-called "fake" Instagram life. The gutsy teenager with more than half a million followers suddenly quit after describing Instagram as "contrived perfection made to get attention," winning her praise from around the world, but also criticism. People didn't believe she was authentic. The social media world can be so harsh. People thought she was being fake when she quit *because* of how fake it was!

I never paid any attention to Essena O'Neill but I admire her bravery. She said, "Social media isn't real — so please stop worshipping me."

My reaction: I didn't worship her before, but I do now.

Ultimately, my own goal is to inspire, teach, and make young women feel good. To make my blog stand out, I'm thinking of sharing creative imagery with purpose — maybe I'll even add poetry and interviews with leaders in the fashion industry.

But more than anything, in addition to writing about diversity, I want to share my passion for quirky fabrics, vintage dresses, and colourful and bold designs; promote up-and-coming eco fashion designers; and do it all in a new way that involves collaborations with talented artists. Most of all, I want to make *Cécile* proud.

After I've looked at a dozen blogs or so, I decide to pick out colours and graphics. I'm leaning toward a blush pink and a modern design accentuated by vintage flowers. I play around with big black roses on an empty canvas for a few minutes, when, from the corner of my eye, I catch Ellie walking into the library. She's with a group of students from our class. No surprise, they're all dressed in black and grey. My bright jacket makes me an easy target for their smirks and condescending looks. I shrug it off and go back to the web. A few seconds later I get a tap on the shoulder. For some reason, I was kind of expecting it.

"Hey, what are you working on there?" Ellie asks, hovering over my shoulder. I quickly close all my windows. I don't want her to know about my plans and I don't want to give her any ideas.

"Nothing. Just browsing the web." I crane my neck to look up at her. She looks surprisingly feminine today with violet and purple eye shadow, a line of black liquid liner, and nude lips. It's not something I would wear — purple clashes with my complexion — but it works on her. But it's not enough to make her seem any less hostile.

"It looks like you've got a secret project or something," she whispers, staring down at me with crossed arms.

"Like I said, it's nothing. I just like to read fashion blogs."

"Really? My little finger tells me you're working on a project that involves Cécile." She cocks a groomed eyebrow and her eyes look right through me like two laser beams.

This conversation has to end; Ellie is giving me the creeps. It's not easy to keep my cool under such intense scrutiny, but I hold her gaze until she finally backs off. It reminds me of a scene I saw on the National Geographic channel of a woman interacting with a group of wild cheetahs. As soon as she stood up and stared right at them, they ran away.

She walks away looking strangely miffed, while mumbling something (probably nasty) under her breath. I just hope she didn't see my blog concept. I should've reacted more quickly when I first saw her come in. In addition to dealing with competition on the web, I need to watch my back for the school sharks. I've heard the stories. One student's design portfolio was stolen by another unscrupulous student, who sent in the stolen portfolio along with an internship application. The other student got the job instead of the actual designer, which created a scandal at school. I do my best to put it out of my mind.

After I open my laptop again, I see Stella sauntering toward me with a warm, ready smile. What a contrast.

"*Bonjour*, Clementine, it's so nice to see you again. How are you doing?"

"Great. I've met lots of interesting people and the school is amazing. I'm already sinking my teeth into some research."

"Really? So soon?" She stares at me quizzically. "What for?" She looks down at my computer and her eyes stop on the graphics I picked for my blog. She nods approvingly at my page. I grit my teeth in frustration. Why is everybody interested in what I'm doing? But I'm not worried about Stella. She's a former law student, after all. She must have strong ethics.

"I'm taking it easy this week and working on my personal stuff," she says. "I think we'll be inundated with class projects soon enough. Would you like to join me for coffee later? I'm meeting friends at the cafeteria downstairs."

I hesitate. For some reason, the invitation seems to lack sincerity. Or something. But I decide it's just me being paranoid again; not everyone can be as authentic right away as Jake. "Sure, why not? I'll see you there," I say, and I wave as she walks away. I'm thankful there are some decent people around.

I shake my head at Ellie, who keeps looking my way, and sigh, whispering to myself something Jake would say: *Don't worry, Clem. You got this.*

Chapter Eleven

"SO, WHAT ARE your big plans? Do you want to be a designer?" I ask Stella over a cup of tea that afternoon. She's sitting with her entourage. My question gets some strange looks from her friends and I lift my shoulders, wondering what the fuss is about.

"They're laughing because I already *am* a designer," Stella says confidently, tapping her red fingernails on the table.

"Oh really?" I feel silly for not knowing about this. Does she intern for someone famous? "Sorry, I didn't know. I'm from a different continent, remember?" I add.

She rolls her eyes. "Right. Well, my designs were featured in every major teen magazine, but it's nothing, really," she says with faux modesty.

"Wow, that's amazing. What is it that you do?" I ask.

"I create decorative stick-on patches. Like these." She pulls out her phone; its case is covered with stickers of stars, suns, emojis, unicorns, coffee mugs, flowers, and tiny avocados. I really like it; the look is fun and playful.

It only now hits me now that all of her friends have stick-on patches on their handbags and running shoes. I should have picked up on it sooner.

"Congrats. You're so imaginative."

She looks down into her cup of coffee. I hope I didn't say anything wrong.

"How long have you been doing this?" I ask.

"Almost a year. The concept really took off."

"You're an inspiration for the rest of us. I'll have to tell Jake about this. He'll be impressed."

"Right," she says, staring down into her cup of coffee again. That's odd. She looks uneasy about me telling someone about her idea. Maybe she and Jake don't get along. Who knows?

"Where do you find your ideas?" I ask, as if interviewing her for my blog.

She responds by staring down at her shoes. I guess she's being modest.

"I sketch the designs based on what my friends and I think are cool. I began by creating patches from draft sketches and adding them to my sneakers. It caught on like wildfire. Can you believe it?"

"Is that why you left law school? To pursue studies that match your business?" I ask. I am in awe of Stella's enterprise and, I must admit, a tad envious.

"Yes, you could say that I much prefer the creative side of things. I mean, as designers, we can hire lawyers, but we can't farm out the design of our business, right?"

"I admire your drive. Bravo," I say, before taking a last sip of tea.

"Oh, it's nothing. It's all worth it in the end," she says nonchalantly.

I wonder how she'll manage to run her business and keep up with her studies and class projects. She must work day and night.

"I saw that you have business plans of your own, am I right?" Stella asks.

"Don't we all," I say breezily, not ready to share too many details about my blogging plans. It's far too early in the process. Besides, I don't have anything set in stone yet.

I recall my father telling me about some famous writer who said that you shouldn't share any creative concept until it's fully executed. I tend to agree — that's great advice.

Stella squints, looking unhappy with my response, but I quickly change the subject.

"So where can I buy these patches? I definitely need that smiling avocado. And the timing is perfect — I just bought a new phone cover."

She smiles nervously. I'm not sure why. We're all good.

Or so I think.

Chapter Twelve

I SIT AT MADDIE'S kitchen counter while she makes dinner. I really lucked out; in addition to being a generous, fun roommate (who also has a great sense of style), she's an amazing cook.

I pop an olive into my mouth and look around. Her kitchen looks like the ones you see in interior decor magazines: modern appliances, a few antiques, touches of refinement peppered with pops of colour. Some exposed beams run the entire length of the ceiling, pots and pan's hang from a copper ceiling rack, and lots of greenery provides a fresh touch. The floor-to-ceiling windows overlook a courtyard where a wrought-iron bistro table and chairs nod to our French heritage.

Maddie looks much different at home. She dresses down. Today, she's wearing black yoga pants and a white cotton T-shirt, and her hair is pulled up in a casual ponytail.

"How do you handle the competition?" I ask, staring down at my nails. I'm doing my best not to bite them before my date with Jonathan. I just gave them a fresh coat of pale-pink lacquer.

"The what?" she asks, adjusting her glasses.

"You know — with colleagues?"

I asked the question breezily but the truth is I'm feeling uneasy about what happened in the library today. I'm tired of getting dirty looks and being followed around. Also, the fact that I haven't told Jake about the scholarship bothers me.

This idea that we need to compete for grades, internships, jobs, and money brings up complex emotions. It makes me feel insecure, afraid of overexposing myself and shooting myself in the foot. The struggle between these feelings and my ambition is real — and I'm not sure how to handle it.

Maddie turns away from her stove and gives me a concerned look.

"Why, Clementine? Is there something I should know?" she asks with a raised eyebrow. I know she's concerned about me and I know she's taking her role as my guardian seriously. And as a teacher, she's aware of the pitfalls of being my age: the bullies, the haters, and all those self-esteem issues. Oh, the joys of being nineteen.

"Don't worry, there's nothing to worry about. It's just petty nonsense," I say. I avoid telling her there's a woman at school giving me nasty looks — this will only cause her to worry and, frankly, it's just plain stupid.

"Oh? What do you mean?" she shoots back.

"It feels like there's a lot of competition at Parsons. That's all. Have you ever felt that way?"

"Of course, sweetie. Who hasn't?" She wipes her hands on her apron. "My god, I've dealt with pressure my entire life: to get decent grades, to get grants — you know my parents didn't have the money for graduate school. I also competed with thousands of candidates to become a judge on the TV show. I know it's challenging, but you need to adapt — that's just part of life. One way to handle it: don't worry about the others, just focus on your own path."

I exhale loudly. "It's not always that simple. People like to get in your way. And I hate the word *competition* — I prefer *collaboration*."

She senses my uneasiness and walks over to give me a warm hug. I feel better already.

"I know you do, you're a thoughtful person. But you need to find ways to relax and deal with the pressure. You just can't avoid it. But, if you handle it the right way, it can take you very far."

"You think?"

"Sure. When I created a collection for my master's thesis, there was tons of competition. And so much pressure. When I presented my pieces, the judges were so strict; the cut had to be impeccable," Maddie says, thinking back on her fashion school days. "And if there was any imperfection, you failed. The school, the program, and yourself." She points her wooden spoon at me as if to make her point.

"Ouf! I can't imagine that kind of pressure." I shake my head. "It's a good thing my future plans revolve around writing. Although I love designer clothes, I don't think I could handle the stress of putting together collections like that."

"You think being a writer or a fashion critic is easier? Think again, sweetie. There are lots of talented and eager writers out there."

"Right. Point taken."

I think of Jake, who'll be subjected to that level of scrutiny with his own collection. I haven't yet seen his sewing or execution skills. I just hope he makes the cut.

"Are you thinking about your friend Jake?"

She's obviously a mind reader.

"Yes. I really like him. We've only just met but already he's like a brother. But the thing is, I feel guilty about the scholarship."

"Oh, Clementine, I can tell he adores you. You know he'll be thrilled for you. It's your time to shine. You can't hold back now, that would be a terrible mistake. You've only just begun, and you show so much promise. Friends that matter will always support you, no matter what." She waves her spoon at me again, sending flecks of sauce my way. I duck to avoid them.

"You're right. I guess my insecurity comes from my mother, who taught me that if you get a part, you're taking it away from someone else."

"That's silly! You're not taking anything away from him! I'm not worried about Jake. He's got tons of charisma, passion, and drive. He'll do well. I can feel it … I'm clairvoyant, you know."

"Yes, and a good matchmaker, too, by the way," I say with a wink. Thinking about Jonathan puts me in a good mood. I start to relax a bit. "Those psychic skills of yours … do they explain why *you're* not seeing anyone? You can read men's minds and know in advance whether things will work out?"

"Very *drôle*. If only it were that simple, *ma chérie*. You know dating in New York isn't easy. It's enough to drive any woman mad … or to drink," she says, pouring some red wine into her glass.

Right. I hope that Jonathan won't add to my anxiety. I already have enough to deal with. Maybe Jake is right; dating while at Parsons is a bad idea. Only two days to go before our date. Not that I'm counting or anything.

"So what do you know about Jonathan?" I ask, remembering Jake's comment about photographers.

"How do you mean?"

"Do you know anything about his past? Any crazy ex-girlfriends? Drug abuse? Illicit activities?"

Maddie chokes on her wine. "Come on, Clementine, are you being paranoid again?"

She's probably right. I need to chill.

"I really don't think he has too many skeletons in the closet. I haven't seen him attend any of the Fashion Week parties. He looks pretty clean. I bet he's into yoga and meditation and is vegan," she says, placing the roast chicken on the kitchen counter. We both burst into giggles.

"Well, if that's the case, I have a bigger problem on my hands," I say as I dig into my dinner. Learning how to deal with your emotions sure builds an appetite.

Chapter Thirteen

"ARE YOU READY for your hot date with hipster boy?" Jake asks, sitting next to me in the school auditorium. We're here for Maddie's lecture. She's the moderator, and a few teachers, editors, and designers will act as panellists. Jake looks sleek today in a black turtleneck sweater, a grey wool blazer, and faux leather jeans. He accessorized his chic look with a matching black leather man bag that has me drooling. It's the first time I've seen him so dressed up and he looks fabulous.

"Mmm … yes, I guess so. I am a bit nervous and I definitely have butterflies. I guess that's a good sign, right?" Jake is rapidly becoming my confidant. He's so open about everything that I feel as though I can share things with him that I don't feel comfortable saying to Maddie.

"Don't worry, pumpkin, that's just excitement," Jake says, patting my knee. "I bet he feels the same way about seeing your beautiful face again."

His comment soothes me. Thank god I agreed to come here with him today.

The auditorium is buzzing with staff members shuffling around the room wearing headsets and carrying microphones and other technical gear. The crowd is getting denser by the second, and I can tell this event will be a major success.

The title of the conference is *Fashion & Diversity*, a popular topic these days in the media and within the industry. Issues of race on the runway, cultural appropriation of symbols by fashion designers, and diversity in employment and advertising are all on the agenda. Maddie told me that her lecture is part of a series featuring lively conversations on the intersections of fashion and culture, women and media. I'm thrilled that Parsons is forward-thinking enough to host such an event and I can't wait to hear her speak. She's been preparing for this for weeks.

I brought a new notebook to get all this insight down on paper. Maybe I'll write about this event on my blog.

All this talk about diversity reminds me of a runway show I recently saw on YouTube from Beijing Fashion Week. Chinese fashion designer Sheguang Hu sent seventy-nine-year-old Chinese actor Wang Deshun shirtless down the runway. Not only did he look dashing as he sauntered down the platform, he literally stole the show, smiling at the cameras and the crowd. That's the type of thing the industry needs. Diverse models that break the mould, that shake things up.

"This anxiety you feel about seeing Jonathan … it's totally normal," Jake says, munching on some peanuts while staring at a good-looking staff member wearing tight jeans.

"If you say so. Whatever it is, I'm definitely feeling it. I barely slept last night. Anyway, I'm looking forward to checking out that photo exhibit."

"Yeah, right. Photo exhibit my ass," he says, popping another peanut into his mouth. "Whatever you do, please avoid checking out other things — if you catch my drift. It's too soon. Unless you have little interest in seeing him again."

"I know *that*. Don't worry, I'll behave."

"Just play it cool, Clem. Everything will be fine. Be super chill about it all — but call me right after you get home, okay? I want *all* the details," Jake adds, smiling and revealing his dimples.

I chuckle inwardly. Jake acts like he isn't into my romantic prospects but I can tell he's totally into it, like a cheerleader on the sidelines of the Super Bowl just before the teams come out on the field. He's living vicariously through my dating, or so it seems.

"Did you look into those scholarships I told you about?" I decide to change the subject. I don't want to discuss going out with Jonathan anymore — it's making me super nervous.

"Are you kidding? Yep, of course I did. I could really use an inflow of cash. I even sent in all the paperwork. I worked all night to complete it. All I can say is that if I get it, I'm taking you out on the town to celebrate. Somewhere swanky, like the Carlyle. Just *toi et moi*." He puts on a posh French accent that makes me laugh.

"I'm really happy you did that. I have a feeling you'll get it. Your project is *so* on point. I mean, if anyone deserves financial aid, it's you. Speaking of which, I have something to tell you," I say, remembering Maddie's comment about how Jake would be thrilled for me. I move in closer so that no one else can hear. "I just found out I received a scholarship to launch my blog."

Jake whips his head around dramatically and his bag of peanuts falls into his leather satchel. I can hear the nuts dropping to the bottom of his bag one by one.

His eyes narrow and his face reddens. "Really, Clem? *You* got a scholarship? You really do have everything going for you, don't you?" he snaps. Out of nowhere his happy outlook has morphed into an angry one. I don't know what to say. I don't know what to do. His reaction takes me completely by surprise.

He brings his face close to mine. I freeze in my seat.

"Why would you need a scholarship? Won't your *papa* pay for everything?" he says with a snarl. "I have to work two jobs to pay for my tuition at Parsons. It sure would be nice if you could leave some crumbs on the table for the rest of us."

Ouch. My face drops, and there's a sharp pain in my chest. I want to run out of the room but my legs remain glued to the auditorium seat. I should have followed my intuition and kept my mouth shut. *Merde*, I'm such a loser.

Shame washes over me. He's right. I didn't get this money on my own; I had help from Maddie. I feel terrible for accepting it, cashing it, and worse still, using it to pay for designer boots. I'm disgusted with myself.

I look at all the talented students walking around the room, many of whom have taken out major loans to come to Parsons. Why should I be the one to benefit? I'm not about to ask my parents to pay for my blog launch, but I have my allowance and I know that if I ever have to, I can fall back on their support. My mind spins — it's not right. I need to give the scholarship back. I'll find another way to get some money. I'm a resourceful person; I'll find some alternative. I'll get a job.

Justin Bieber's song "Sorry" comes to mind. Is it too late to say it? Given my friend's reaction, I'd say the answer is most definitely yes.

"And you know what else, Clementine?" Jake whispers. He's on a roll now. "Because I'm so busy holding down two jobs on top of heavy schoolwork, I haven't had sex in over a year. Yeah, that's right. You heard me. Unlike you, I don't have the luxury of going out on dates with pretty boys who pay for my dinner." He turns away from me, biting his lower lip.

I begin to shake as I hold back tears. I want to say something but no words come out. I finally rise from my seat and rush out the door, bumping into Maddie at the exit.

"Where are you going, Clementine?" she asks, looking shocked by my sudden departure. "We're starting in a few minutes."

"I need to take care of something urgent. I'm really sorry. Good luck!" I know it's rude for me to leave now, but my reputation, friendship, and self-respect are at stake.

I rush out the door and let it slam behind me, remembering that Maddie made it through fashion school without any help from anyone in our family. If she could do it, so can I. And if I can't stand to look at myself in the mirror, how can I expect Jonathan or Jake to look at me with friendship or admiration?

I exit the Parsons main building and sprint toward Union Square, running past classmates walking in the opposite direction. I have something precious to lose; an important friendship is on the line.

I walk into the nearest Citibank, where my parents opened an account in my name. I want to get a bank draft to return the funds ASAP. And then I'll return the boots. My decision is final.

If Jonathan is real, it won't matter what I'm wearing on my feet tomorrow. What matters is what's in my soul and in my heart.

Chapter Fourteen

"WHY THE DRAMATIC EXIT, Clementine?" Maddie asks the next morning. I'm sitting outside on her terrace taking in some sunshine and fresh air, trying to relax before I meet Jonathan. I'm also trying to recover from Jake's hurtful remarks. I had a terrible time sleeping last night — I'm still upset about what he said and I'm not sure how to address it. Should I just call him? Send a text? Or should I take a step back, let him blow off some steam, and wait until Monday? I'm sad and raw and confused. Who knew friendship could hurt so much?

Maddie hands me a pink and white striped coffee cup with the words *Every Day Is a Fresh Start.* I take it gratefully and I take in the inspiring message, too.

I'm wearing my favourite pyjamas, made with the palest blue Egyptian cotton and decorated with navy piping, which belonged to my mother. She apparently received them as a gift from a secret admirer after a performance in Milan and quickly gave them to me to avoid making my father jealous. I do feel like a diva wearing them.

"I'm sorry I missed your conference, Maddie. Something urgent came up," I say, then bury my face in my cup of java.

"Oh? Are you going to tell me about it?" She takes a seat across from me in an iron chair. She doesn't look upset, but concerned. She's wearing the coolest Minnie Mouse PJs made of pure silk that she brought back from a trip to Japan. I hope to be half as cool as she is at her age.

"It's about this," I slide a white envelope in front of her. I know it's the right thing to do and deep in my heart, I know Cécile would approve.

"What's this? A cheque? But why?" She looks perplexed.

"It's my scholarship money. I'm giving it back. I just can't accept it, Maddie. Other students need this more than I do. I feel bad about it. Please don't be upset. I'm really grateful for what you did. I *really* am."

She looks disappointed and this makes my insides ache even more. "Please don't take it the wrong way, but I don't think it's fair to the other students, the ones working two jobs to cover tuition."

After a minute, her face brightens. She takes a deep breath, shakes her head, and smiles. "You know what? I'm impressed with your character. You remind me of my younger self, always looking out for your friends," she says, patting my hand. "It's a *very* mature gesture — I admire your sense of honour. Don't stop being that way, okay?"

"Don't be so quick to throw compliments my way. Jake is the one you should commend, not me. He told me off when I told him about the money yesterday. He was angry as hell and it really opened my eyes. He's the hero, not me." I get a frisson down my spine thinking about Jake's reaction again. He looked really upset and, although the words he used were harsh, he was right.

"Did you tell him about us?" Maddie asks.

"No, no. He doesn't know we're related. He thinks it was wrong of me to compete for the scholarship at all since my father is already paying for everything. When you think about it, he's right."

"If you say so." She tilts her head sideways and smiles. What a relief. It looks as though she agrees with what I'm saying. "Ah, *ce cher* Jake. I should have guessed he was behind all this. He has a lot of influence on you, doesn't he?" She reaches for her coffee and wraps her fingers around her cup.

"He's a great guy with solid values. He's struggling to make it like the rest of us. I suggested he apply for a scholarship to get his design project off the ground. I think he has a good chance of getting funding. His project is amazing."

"Oh? What's it about?" Maddie is quick to ask, her design instincts kicking in.

"I'm afraid I can't say. A promise is a promise." I wink.

"You're loyal and honest, Clementine, and I really do appreciate that. Just be careful. Not everyone out there thinks the way you do," she says before getting up and heading back to the kitchen. "Would you like some breakfast? I'm making an omelette."

"No thanks. I'm in the mood for granola and yogourt. Don't worry, I'll get it."

Before I head to the kitchen, I think about Jake again. Will this scholarship thing destroy our friendship? Then my thoughts move to Ellie. Would she give back the money if she were in my shoes? And more importantly, how will I find the money to fund *Bonjour Girl* now?

I begin to fret about my decision and wonder if I should cancel my date with Jonathan. This falling-out with Jake and my sudden reversal of fortune sends my morale into the dumps. Am I really in the mood for a photo exhibit? Or should I go hide under the duvet and spend the day feeling sorry for myself?

What to do?

My mind says cancel but my heart says go. We'll see which part of me is fiercest after I shower and do my nails. That always makes me feel better.

According to fashion designer Prabal Gurung, nails are the period at the end of the sentence; they complete your look. I'd add that they're like the rainbow after the storm. They make my day much brighter. And as long as this city doesn't do me in and make my heart as hard as nails, I should be fine.

Chapter Fifteen

"HEY, CLEMENTINE, WHAT would you like to drink?" Jonathan asks. We're standing in line at a hip café in Williamsburg while a barista takes our order. Thankfully, a steaming shower and painting my nails Urban Jungle pink by Essie with added tiny blue and pink glitter stars got me out of my funk. The nail colour aptly describes the city where I've landed and makes me realize I still have lots to learn about making friends in New York.

Jonathan and I agreed to meet at this popular hangout. It's filled with a youngish, hip crowd. There's a small patio in the back dotted with potted cacti that accentuate the *boho* vibe. Jane Birkin's voice booms from the speakers and I'm happy I dressed appropriately for this laid-back ambience. I chose a simple red and white peasant blouse, jeans, and tan sandals. My only true fashion accessory is a vintage red bag that belonged to Cécile.

"Regular coffee, black, thanks," I answer gratefully. I can't help but stare at Jonathan while he orders. He looks good in a relaxed pair of washed-out blue jeans, a white linen shirt, and blue Vans sneakers. I love everything about his look. Jake is right, I am totally predictable but I don't care. My taste in men is not up for discussion.

"No low-fat cappuccino or skinny mocha latte for you?" Jonathan asks jokingly. The way some Americans order coffee makes me crazy. I'm glad to see he seems to share my view. It's just not my cup of Americano.

"Um, *non,* I like to keep things simple. At least, most of the time," I say with a smirk. I'm not always that easy-going, and I do have some quirks and crazy hang-ups, but I'm not going there. I don't want to scare him off just yet.

"Good. I like that about you, Clementine," Jonathan responds, sending my heart into a tizzy.

"Would you like anything to eat? The granola parfait is pretty great and the vegan sandwiches are amazing," he says. I smile inwardly, thinking of Maddie's comment about Jonathan's lifestyle. It was pretty silly of me to worry. What a waste of energy.

"No thanks. I already had breakfast. Maybe next time?" I respond.

He winks. I'm in heaven.

"So, how's school so far?" he asks after we take a seat in a quiet corner.

"Good. I've made some friends. Well, at least that's what I thought until yesterday." My face drops when I say this. I still feel awful about what Jake said.

"Oh? Why? What happened?" he asks, and I immediately regret saying it. I haven't heard back from Jake after sending several texts and I'm really sad about it. I just hope our friendship will survive. I look up from my cup and see Jonathan staring into my eyes.

"I met the sweetest person in my class. His name is Jake and we really hit it off on our first day. And then he got really upset over something I said. I just hope we can fix this. It'll be the shortest friendship *ever*." I sigh and shrug my shoulders.

"Have you talked to him since?" Jonathan asks, looking genuinely concerned. I have to say that I feel totally at ease talking to him. I like that I can be totally honest and not feel judged. It hits me that I worried way too much about what I said and how I acted around my ex-boyfriend. Beginning today, that's a thing of the past.

I shake my head and stare at my feet. "I've sent him a few text messages but so far ... no response."

Jonathan takes a sip of coffee and a bite from his sandwich. I love the way he mulls things over and measures his words before saying something. "If he's the person you say he is, he'll forgive you. We all say and do things we regret," he reassures me softly. He's making me feel better and I'm grateful for it. And even more attracted to him, if that's even possible.

"You're right. I'm sure things will get back to normal once we clear the air," I say. Talking about it makes me feel better.

"I wouldn't worry too much about it. And just think about all the amazing things you have going for you. Like that scholarship." His eyes light up and this makes me want to bury my head in the potted plant. I worry he'll think I'm a total loser for giving the money back. I'm at a loss for words and, as I sometimes do in these kinds of scenarios, I begin to play with my nails.

"Oh, I'm afraid that didn't work out," I finally respond as evasively as I can.

"Really? What happened?"

"It's a long story, but it's my decision. I didn't think it was fair to take the money instead of someone under more financial hardship, so I decided to give it back to Parsons … on principle," I say, averting my gaze. When I look up, his eyes are nearly popping out of their sockets. That's it; he thinks I'm nuts. He wouldn't be the first to think so.

"You gave it back? Jeez, Clementine, I don't know a single person who would've done that. And on principle? My god, you are a rare bird."

A rare bird? He's comparing me to a strange animal. Oh well, I should have expected it. I am different and sometimes that's not such a good thing.

"An exquisite, rare, beautiful, winged creature, you are." He lifts his arms in the air as if flying. I burst out laughing. "You're interesting and different and I like that."

"I'll take that as a compliment. I thought you'd think I was crazy."

"Crazy, no. Supremely original, yes."

After he finishes his lunch and wipes his lips, he moves in closer and my heart skips a beat. I'm not sure if he wants to share a secret or kiss me but I'm okay with both. "I'm really glad we met," he whispers. "Are you ready to hit the exhibit? I can't wait show you my work!"

"Can't wait to see it!" I say, although I've already Googled him and seen most of his work on his professional website. A girl does *some* research before a first date. "Let's go!" I finish my coffee and stand up. The caffeine and heart palpitations have my blood pumping fast.

"I forgot to tell you," says Jonathan, as we make our way to the door, "there will be some journalists there. It's sort of like the exhibit opening for the media. I hope you won't mind — I may have to excuse myself for a little while when we get there for some interviews."

It's the exhibit opening for the media? I stare down at my casual outfit and feel underdressed. I am, after all, a Parsons fashion student and I should make more of an effort to look the part. I try to push these negative thoughts aside when it hits me that Jonathan invited me to this important event.

He takes my hand and gently guides me out of the café as we bounce into the streets of Brooklyn. I honestly don't know what happens for a solid thirty minutes after that. I'm so into him and into us and into this moment that I let my mind and heart wander as he leads the way.

On our way to the subway station to get to the Pratt, we make a few pit stops, including at a sweet candy store where Jonathan buys some old-style liquorice candy swirls I spot in the window; I tell him they remind me of my childhood. Afterward, he takes me to a vintage bookstore with creaky hardwood floors and antique bookshelves filled with contemporary and classic novels. He guides me to his favourite section, Russian literature, and points out some of his favourite books, including Dostoyevsky's *Crime and Punishment*. We huddle close together between the narrow bookshelves and every time his arm or his shoulder brushes mine, I feel more and more giddy. And with each new book he points out to me, I feel myself falling for him more and more. This is crazy; it's only our first date. But I can't deny how close I feel to him already.

At the Pratt, Jonathan leads the way to the exhibit. It's entitled *Suits, Ties, and Dresses*, and it's a series of portraits that capture popular New York City fashion mavens and artists: bloggers, designers, dancers, models, and fashion editors in their own stylish habitats.

As soon as we walk into the gallery, a journalist walks over and asks Jonathan a few questions. Before responding, Jonathan asks if I mind. The fact that he does this makes my heart sing. In addition to being hot, he's well mannered and classy.

Once the interview is over, he fetches two glasses of sparkling water with slices of lemon and introduces me around to friends and acquaintances. We clink our glasses before he wraps his arm under mine and leads me to the next room so that we can get a closer look at the photos. I can tell he's excited to show his work. If I were in his shoes, I would be, too.

"This woman is a total genius," he says, pointing at one of the photos. "Look at her eyes, and the way she stares at the camera — isn't she magnificent?"

He's referring to a Spanish woman who looks to be in her sixties wearing a crisp white shirt. Her lips are painted a bold red that matches her bold necklace. She has big brown eyes that are confident and wise. She looks amazing.

"Yes, she certainly is." I'd like to say *just like you* but I keep those words to myself. I'm not ready to say them out loud yet.

After we look at his portraits, he takes me to the next hall. "This is the garment photography section. I know you'll appreciate them," he whispers into my ear. I practically swoon.

"This cape is made with cutting-edge technology," he says proudly, pointing at another photograph with one hand while holding my hand with the other. He leans into me and I can smell his earthy cologne. It makes it hard for me to concentrate. "It's meant to respond to pollution and protect the person wearing it. Isn't that cool? It was created by a Parsons alum and I was asked to take its picture."

"That's really impressive," I say with a sudden touch of sadness, thinking of Jake. I know he'd love to see this. I make a mental note to send him a quick photo later. Maybe that will make him respond to me.

"And this fabric," he says, pointing to a photo of a dress in shades of yellow, "sheds layers with the temperature. Can you believe that?" His eyes are wide with excitement. He seems as fascinated about this stuff as I am. He places his hand delicately on the nape of my neck and I temporarily forget where I am. The dress disappears from view. I melt a little more inside. I don't want him to pull away.

"And finally, the *pièce de résistance* is this black dress. The feathers on its shoulders ruffle when you face North. Kim Kardashian should wear it!" he adds, referring to her daughter's name, North. I laugh at his joke and he brushes my neck with his fingers again. This time my knees turn to porridge. I try to make a comment about the photograph and the dress but it takes me a few seconds before I can speak.

"You're right, it is the most riveting piece so far in this room. That's exactly the kind of thing I'd like to write about on my blog." I take a picture with my phone and try to capture all the details. This is one of the reasons I came to New York: amazing designs and supremely innovative concepts.

As I'm taking notes on my phone, Jonathan grabs my arm, pulls me close, and kisses me softly on the lips. I forget my notes … I forget my name, where I'm from, and that I'm in a public place, and I kiss him back. We stand there in each other's arms for a long moment.

He then takes a step back, brushes my chin with his hand, and finally breaks the delicious silence.

"No, Clementine, the most riveting thing in this room is you."

Chapter Sixteen

IT'S TUESDAY AFTER Labour Day and I'm sitting in class, waiting for the guest lecturer to show up. It's intellectual property day and a renowned New York City fashion lawyer will be discussing the legal implications of protecting fashion designs. Although the subject really interests me, I'm distracted. I've got Jonathan's lips touching mine, and the dinner we shared at a quaint Italian restaurant, on my mind. And I'm nervous about seeing Jake again. He didn't respond to any of my texts, including the one with a picture of the magic cape from Jonathan's exhibit. Is it the beginning of one relationship but the end of another? I sure hope not.

I stare out the window looking over Fifth Avenue, getting lost in my thoughts. Instead of thinking of luxurious fabrics, international runway shows, and impressive cuts, I'm feeling out of sorts.

Our guest lecturer doesn't look anything like the lawyers I see on TV. No black suit, no stiff high-collared blouse. She's wearing sky-high Chanel stilettos with a large pearl on the front of each one. (I remember drooling over them in a magazine.) She's also wearing a bright-red blazer, slim black leather pants, a crisp white blouse, and giant chandelier earrings that sparkle in the sunlight flowing in through the window.

Maddie told me she's an adjunct professor of intellectual property at Parsons, and her bio says she represents many big fashion names, including Diane Von Furstenberg, Tory Burch, and Christian Louboutin. Her lecture should be interesting — if not distracting because of those shoes. Or is it my friendship woes that are distracting me?

"Hey," a male voice whispers behind me. I recognize it immediately: it's Jake. I'm not sure what to expect so I freeze up.

"Psst, hey, Clementine. It's me, Jake, the asshole. No, I mean the ginormous ass."

I'm so relieved that I practically jump from my seat. I turn around to get a better look at him. He looks pale in a black baseball cap, faded black jeans, and a matching silk bomber jacket with embroidered butterflies on one sleeve.

"Oh, Jake, please. Don't put yourself down like that."

"No, really, Clem. I'm so sorry about losing my cool. That was *really* stupid of me. And what I said — that was mean. I take it all back."

"You don't need to apologize. I'm the one who —"

Jake cuts me off. "No, I was lashing out for no reason. I felt like such a jerk and I was so embarrassed ... I couldn't do anything other than hate on myself all weekend," he says, staring down at his Adidas sneakers.

"No, I mean it, Jake, you were right. I shouldn't have accepted that money. It isn't fair. You deserve it way more than I do," I say, sounding like Adele apologizing to Beyoncé after winning the Grammy for album of the year.

Jake stops me midsentence and raises his hand in the air like a traffic cop. "Enough, girl. Just accept my apology, will ya?"

"Okay, okay, apology accepted." There's so sense in arguing with him anyway; he won't hear my side of the story.

"Phew. What a relief." He mock wipes his brow. "I thought you'd never speak to me again. And that would make me very sad, Clementine. I really like you. And of course, your great-grandma, too." He winks.

"The feeling is mutual." I rub his shoulder affectionately.

"And you, young lady, know all of my secrets. You're privy to all of my 'intellectual property.'" He uses air quotes while nodding toward the fashion lawyer standing at the front of our class.

"Don't worry, I'm not that kind of person. I'd never double cross you."

"I know you're not that kind of person, Clem. But do you kiss and tell?" he asks, sitting on the edge of his seat, obviously digging for some information about my date with Jonathan.

"No, I don't do that either," I retort, blushing cherry red, the colour of my leather handbag. He now has all the information he needs.

Our unofficial gossip session is interrupted by the guest lecturer, who introduces herself to the class. I turn around and start taking notes. After all, this could be interesting for my blog. After a half-hour talk on legal issues affecting the industry, she politely excuses herself for a five-minute break.

Both Jake and I nod approvingly at her outfit before we continue our chat.

"You're very discreet. I like that in a person," Jake says. Is that because he's not, I wonder? I hope not. I've been confiding a lot of personal stuff and I don't want it to get around.

"It's a rare quality in people these days." He cocks an eyebrow ominously, pursing his lips and crossing his arms while nodding toward the back of the class.

I have no clue what he's talking about.

"What are you saying?"

"I'm referring to the … you know … *the tweet*," he says in a hushed tone. "I'm so sorry. You didn't deserve that, Clem. There are serious consequences to what people write online … and bullies have no clue about the impact their comments have on others. Anyway, just so you know, I tweeted back in your defence. You have my total support."

I stare at him blankly and, within seconds, the glow on my face vanishes. My stomach clenches and I feel faint. Jake realizes I have no clue what he's talking about and lifts his arms in consternation.

"Oh, dear lord. You haven't seen Twitter."

I shake my head. It occurs to me that I haven't set up any notifications on my new phone yet. I extend my arm. "Let me see it."

Jake shakes his head in protest. He runs his fingers through his hair nervously. "Oh jeez, what have I done?" He puts his hands over his face. "Are you sure you want to read this shit? I'm not sure this is the right time or place."

"Well, if it's that bad, I *should* know about it, don't you think?" My stomach in knots, I brace myself for the worst. I have no idea who tweeted what about me but I know the message will hurt. I still feel the sharp humiliation of catching my ex-boyfriend kissing my mother. It still cuts to the bone and hurts like hell. Why is life so cruel sometimes? Just when I thought I was on top of the world, my house of cards comes crashing down. *Again.*

"All right, read at your own risk." He reaches for his phone, scrolls to the message, and holds it in front of my face. My jaw drops when I read the nasty tweet:

> @ClementineL, student @Parsons, received a scholarship because she's related to design teacher Madeleine Laurent. So UNFAIR!!

My stomach drops. I feel beads of sweat forming on my forehead. I take a look at the Twitter account, assuming it must be Ellie's handiwork. But I nearly keel over when I see it's not Ellie at all, but Stella, the failed legal eagle with the cute preppy outfits and funky decals. So much for being part of her entourage. I'm furious at myself for trying to befriend her. What a mistake — and what a frickin' mess. I hate myself even more.

Then it hits me: Jake knows about Maddie, and the fact that I kept it a secret. And yet he's still talking to me. He sees it dawn on me and pats me on the back. "Is it true, Clem? That you and Maddie are related?"

I stare down at my glittery Mary Janes. I'm embarrassed to admit it. I blush instead.

"You know you can totally trust me. Unlike some other people in this class," he finishes loudly.

"Yes, it's true," I whisper. "I was going to tell you but was waiting for the right time. But I didn't get any preferential treatment, I swear!"

"There's nothing wrong with being related, Clem. As a matter of fact, it makes total sense to me now: you both have great style, a French background, and all that jazz. I just wish you'd told me."

"I know, I'm sorry I kept it from you. But you need to believe that the scholarship was based on my academic performance and work experience — that's it," I add defensively. No wonder I've been getting more evil stares than ever this morning. How did this get leaked? I feel like I'm about to throw up.

"It's a dog-eat-dog world out there. Or should I say bitch-eat-bitch ..." Jake shakes his head. "Whatever it is, it's just plain rude. We need a strategy." He continues to stare at me expectantly. He's waiting for my response, but I'm speechless. I don't know how to reply to something so vile. Is revenge the best strategy? Or should I just take the high ground and ignore Stella's nonsense?

Jake points to his phone. "There are lots of retweets, likely by her *friends*" — he emphasizes the word to show his scorn — "in the back row. Tons of people saw this. Trust me sista, we need to plot revenge."

I turn and see Ellie staring at me from the other side of class with a strange look. Is she in on this, too? Is the entire class in on ganging up on me? But why? This really sucks.

I imagine standing up and giving Stella a piece of my mind in front of the entire class, something my hot-blooded French mother would probably do — bold and brash runs in my family — but I take a second to cool off and think it through. This is no time to mimic my mother's dramatic antics or her hot temper. It'll only get me in trouble just when I'm trying to find my place in this school. I'm dying to run out of class and snitch on these freaks but something keeps me firmly planted in my seat: self-respect.

Did Taylor Swift lose her cool when Kanye West burst on stage at the MTV Video Music Awards to snatch the microphone from her? No. She reacted gracefully. If she managed to keep her cool, so can I.

"Just when you thought Stella was your friend, SHE'S NOT! Welcome to New York!" Jake says, pointing his pencil at me.

The irony of Jake's words isn't lost on me, given that *we* just had a huge, almost friendship-ending fight after knowing each other for only a week.

I turn around and give Stella an evil stare but she turns away to whisper something to her friends. Her ignoring me makes me fume even more.

Why would she do this? I don't understand. Does she have her own digital plans in addition to her fashion collection? No wonder she left law school — she doesn't have a law-abiding ethical bone in her body.

"It sounds like this lecture about legal stuff may come in handy. You need to know your rights, darlin', so you can defend yourself," Jake says just as the teacher finally re-enters the classroom to finish her talk.

"Whatever." I roll my eyes. "Screw the rules."

"Oooh, that's more like it, love. I like that attitude. I am woman, hear me ROAR," Jake says, imitating some form of dangerous animal. It helps me calm down just a little. Deep down, I'm falling apart and breaking into a million little pieces. I'm dying to jump up from my chair and run out of the class, because despite my fake bravado, what I really want to do is disappear.

The question is, what will I do about this now?

"Come on, Clem. You can't let that she-devil get you down," Jake says to me over some delicious hot cocoa and a giant brownie. We're chilling at the Walker Hotel on 13th Street, just around the corner from The New School. Jake dragged me here after class to help me relax and get over Stella's vile tweet. As soon as I walked through the hotel's front doors, I felt better.

The decor is reminiscent of the Gilded Age, and it's the perfect hangout for an eclectic mix of New York writers, artists, musicians, and business travellers. And us.

It's a gorgeous architectural gem. We're sitting in plush half-moon-shaped red velvet seats, and there's a fireplace in the centre of the room whose warm glow makes me feel cozy and safe. Black and white photographs of the city hang above us. I find the room supremely romantic and, if I wasn't so upset and in need of comforting, I'd call Jonathan and have him meet us here. I guess that will be for another time.

"You know what the crazy thing is? I first thought it must've been Ellie who tweeted that stupid crap," I say, clutching my cup of hot chocolate. "I'm honestly shocked Stella would pull such a stunt. What a hypocrite. She tries to befriend me and then poof! Just like that, she stabs me in the back."

"I know! Stella looks all innocent and stuff with her pastel jackets and pink shoes. But she's the wicked bitch of the east draped in cotton candy," Jake says, taking a long sip of hot cocoa that leaves a trace of chocolate on his upper lip.

"How did she find out about Maddie? That's what I'd like to know," I say.

"Who cares? That doesn't give her the right to call you out all over the internet. This could be considered libel or slander," Jake adds, all legal-like.

"I'm not sure it qualifies. The information needs to be false or something."

"It *is* false. You got that scholarship because of your grades, Clem, not because you're related to Maddie."

"Right! I thought the fashion law lecture might help me, but it was too theoretical. Maybe I need the advice of another professional."

"Yeah, a top criminal lawyer — when I get arrested for punching Stella's lights out. Or better yet, setting the warehouse she uses to store her stupid patches on fire!" Jake says, hitting the table with the palm of his hand, making the water glasses shake and spill over — he's getting a bit carried away.

A bite of the hot fudge brownie soothes my nerves a bit. "I think success is the best revenge," I say calmly.

"WTF? Are you kidding me?" Jake drops his fork and gives me a quizzical look. He obviously wasn't expecting this kind of response, but his plans for revenge don't sit well with me. They're not realistic, anyway, even though I secretly wish I could make Stella suffer, at least a bit.

"Come on Jake, get real. You're not going to get arrested over some dumbass tweet," I say, sounding a bit like him.

"If you say so. But burning down her warehouse sounds like fun," Jake says with a devilish grin and a sweet moustache.

I move in closer and wipe away the chocolate. Friends don't let friends walk around New York with a giant brown 'stache.

"I'd love to teach her a lesson. And I think the best way to do it is by creating an amazing platform with a huge following. The problem is I no longer have any funding to start my business."

"What do you mean?" He whips his head around, looking confused.

"Well, I thought long and hard about what you said … and I gave the scholarship money back."

"Whaaat? Come on girl, are you out of your frickin' mind?"

"Maybe. I just want to do what's right, you know?"

"Um, NO." He waves his dessert fork at me. I back away to avoid flecks of fudge hitting my vintage blouse. "Am I responsible for this? 'Cause if I am, I'll never forgive myself." Some of the chocolate lands on the tip of my nose. I wipe it off. He doesn't even notice.

"No, it has nothing to do with you, Jake. It has every-thing to do with me. It's about appearances and karma. Besides, what's done is done," I say flatly.

"Well, look where this has gotten you: broke and humiliated. Listen, Clem, we've only just met and no mat-ter what you say, I know I'm responsible for this act of COMPLETE jackassery, but frankly you need to look out for numero uno. 'Cause Stella and Ellie sure ain't gonna do it for you, now are they?" He finishes, wipes his lips with the serviette, and drops a twenty on the table.

"What are you doing?" I ask, confused.

"It's my treat — I got a letter saying my scholarship application is under review. And god knows I ain't gonna turn it down if I'm so blessed. But no matter what, I feel like a giant scumbag." He stands up, whips his Burberry scarf around his neck, and slides into his trench coat. His dramatic exit is worthy of a Hollywood film star.

After a rough morning, Jake's flamboyance finally makes me smile. Jake isn't a scumbag. If he were any kind of bag, there's no doubt in my mind it would be a limited-edition Louis Vuitton.

Maddie is sitting on a tall stool in her kitchen reviewing class notes when I walk in to discuss the Stella situation.

I'm surprised to find papers strewn everywhere, empty coffee cups and colour-coordinated sticky notes all over the marble counter. Maddie is usually so neat; it's kind of reassuring to see a mess. It makes me feel like less of a scatterbrain.

I guess Maddie wasn't expecting me so early — I was supposed to get together with Jonathan after school. But frankly, with the nasty tweet weighing on me, the last thing I want to do is bring the man of my dreams down with my problems. It's enough that I told him about my temporary falling-out with Jake on Saturday. I don't want him to think I'm a drama queen.

I'd rather slip into my flannel pyjamas and take a hot bath. I text Jonathan and tell him I have an unexpected matter to take care of. I grab the half-empty bottle of red from the counter and pour myself a glass.

"Oh dear, I had a feeling something was up. Is it about the competition at school? It's a real jungle out there, isn't it?" Maddie says, still reading her notes.

"Jungle? No, I'd say we've moved up a notch from that. It's a shitstorm," I blurt out, pulling out the cork. Maddie gives me a curious look. I guess she's not used to hearing me talk like this or seeing me drink. Jake has a strong influence in the way I speak.

"Come on, Clementine. Is it really *that* bad?

"Yep, it is. It's that Stella girl, the one with the sticker business."

"Sticker business?"

"She started some fashion-decal business, stickers that attach to your sneakers and handbags."

"Hmmm, sounds familiar. I must have read about it somewhere," Maddie says, sounding intrigued. "What did she do?"

I show her the tweet and Maddie's jaw drops. "Oh dear."

"That's what I said. And she has a huge following. I just don't understand why she'd do such a thing. I mean, she can't be jealous, she's far more successful than I am. And to go through this after I gave the scholarship money back …"

"Well, um" — *cough, cough* — "not exactly …" Maddie says, looking at me sheepishly.

"What? What do you mean?"

"The finance committee that offered the money contacted me this morning. They won't accept your cheque. The representative was impressed with your forthrightness, but thinks you still deserve it. He even ran it by the school's ethics board. Since I wasn't on the committee, there's no conflict of interest. The money is yours, Clementine. You should use it. Do you think this Stella girl would give back the money? I think not."

"That's what Jake said. I don't understand how she found out in the first place."

"A written announcement was posted on the bulletin board in the admin offices. That's probably where she saw it, along with your full name: Clementine Laurent Liu."

"Oh shit." My mother gave me her maiden name as my middle name, which I always thought was kind of neat, but now it doesn't seem so great. Stella must have connected the name *Laurent*. "But she's making tons of money with her stickers. Why would she care about *this*?"

"Oh, there are so many reasons why people act out, Clementine. Competition, envy … maybe she's just an annoying spoiled brat."

I take another sip of wine. It helps me relax a bit. "You're right. I'm keeping the money. Here's to that, at least, at the end of a crappy day." I lift my glass in the air. I'm being supremely French tonight. We're all good.

Maddie lifts her half-empty coffee cup to meet my glass. "I thought you were meeting up with Jonathan tonight?"

"I cancelled. I was bummed out about the tweet, and I didn't want it to ruin our date."

"I bet you your scholarship money that you'll feel better if you go out and have some fun! It's New York!"

I look at her suspiciously. I have a feeling she's kicking me out of her place and there's a special reason for it. "You have a date?"

She blushes. "Why do you ask?"

"It's the first time you've tried to get me out of the house … on a Tuesday. You normally stay in and watch Netflix."

"All right, you win. Someone *is* coming over for dinner." She looks down at her watch. "And you have enough time to shower and change; he'll be here by seven."

"Oh, who's 'he'? I'm not sure I want leave now … I think I'll stay."

"Oh, no, you don't." She stands up and guides me to my room. I text Jonathan and put on Sia's "Cheap Thrills." Suddenly I'm in the mood for some fun. I twirl around my room to the beat and collapse on my bed thinking of Jonathan and his dreamy lips. I can't wait to kiss him again.

My phone buzzes with the perfect message.

See you in no time, sweet Clementine

Chapter Seventeen

"THAT WAS FAST," Jonathan says, sitting across from me at the Wythe Hotel in Williamsburg. It's true that I texted him, showered, and changed in record time. I was in a hurry to see him again and Maddie was in hurry to get me out of her hair. It was a win-win, especially given how sexy Jonathan looks tonight. I can't believe I almost missed out on it because of some run-in on social media.

This stunning hotel is housed in a historic, entirely refurbished factory on the Brooklyn waterfront. My jaw nearly dropped when I walked into the ultra-sleek white lounge decorated with minimalist couches and floor-to-ceiling windows overlooking the Hudson River. It looks like one of the bright, contemporary spaces on Garance Doré's Instagram profile. The view is amazing, both out the window and right in front of me.

Jonathan is dressed in a pair of washed-out blue jeans, tan leather boots, and a white Henley shirt that highlights his lean, toned arms. Seeing him and smelling him again gives me goosebumps.

I'm wearing a light-blue shirt, a green and blue midi skirt, and royal-blue pumps. I also threw on some chandelier earrings and painted my nails Blue Boy by Chanel to add sparkle to my outfit and, ironically, to get myself out of the blues.

Jonathan kissed me softly on the lips when I showed up and held my shoulders tenderly while looking into my eyes. It was the warm, affectionate welcome I was hoping for. So far, he hasn't disappointed me.

Jonathan sits across from me on the leather couch. He orders two fancy mixed drinks in martini glasses. "Ginger, vodka, and grapefruit. I hope you like it."

I take a few sips and revel in the gorgeous ambience. It feels like I'm on a movie set — except this isn't fiction, it's *my life*. Being here makes me forget the silly Twitter episode. I'm not going to let it ruin my evening or my social life. Stella isn't worth it.

"So, what made you change your mind?"

"All my issues magically disappeared after I texted you," I say between sips. "That, and my roommate made me leave the house. She has a hot date." I smile.

Jonathan hasn't said anything about it, so he hasn't seen Stella's nonsense on Twitter. I should probably tell him about Maddie. I don't like keeping secrets, especially from the man I'm dating. Before I can say anything, his phone lights up with a notification. It looks like a text message. He picks it up, reads what it says, then turns beet-red. He looks embarrassed and quickly puts his phone away. I wonder who it's from? The fact that his face reddened has me worried, but I brush it aside and take a sip of my drink.

"Um, I should probably tell you something."

"Sure." He cocks an eyebrow.

"It's about Maddie. She and I are related. She's my mother's cousin."

"I had a feeling that was the case, but I was waiting for you to tell me."

"Really? How so?"

"Mannerisms, similar facial and verbal expressions. I notice that kind of thing. I'm a photographer, remember? I tend to zoom in on details."

"Right." He's so easygoing about things. I consider telling him about the nasty tweet, too.

"I think that's awesome. Maddie is great. So, she's the roommate?"

"Yup. And a terrific one at that."

"I bet." He takes a sip of his drink and I feel relieved about having told him. Onward.

"Did your problem today have anything to do with your friend Jake?" Jonathan asks. "I hope you two are talking again. You seemed really bummed out about it."

I love that Jonathan remembers my spat with Jake. He's considerate and a good listener. And that hair — my god, all I can think about is running my fingers through it. *Okay, Clementine, you need to cut back on the liquor or you'll be doing things you might regret.*

"No, that wasn't it. The Jake thing was about my scholarship. We're good now," I say, fondly remembering my friend's apology.

"You mean the one you turned down?" Jonathan shakes his head and makes a funny face.

"Actually, not anymore. There's been a reversal."

"What? I can't keep up!" He throws his hands in the air. Then he waves the waiter over to order another round of drinks. We're going down a slippery slope here. I don't usually drink hard liquor; it doesn't sit well with me.

"The committee that granted me the money refused to take it back. They insisted I keep it. So, now I have money to start my blog after all." I lift my empty martini glass in the air again. This time, he clinks back and kisses me.

I feel the alcohol going to my head and it makes me feel anxious. For some reason, instead of loosening me up and making me feel good, it brings up all my old insecurities about the stuff with my ex-boyfriend, Charles. I guess that's what happens when you've been deeply hurt. I try to ignore it.

"You deserve to keep the money. We can all use a boost when we're starting out. I remember when I decided to go freelance, I struggled like crazy to make ends meet." Jonathan rubs his hands together and I notice how strong they look with those leather bracelets on his wrists.

"Did you get any help?"

"No, not really. My uncle helped out a bit. He let me stay on the couch at his apartment in Chelsea while I was chasing gigs. That's about it. The rest was all hustle and heart."

This makes me melt. I love a man who works hard to accomplish his goals. Not like Charles, who was a rotten spoiled brat.

"My family wasn't in a position to help me out financially," he continues. "That's just the way things are."

"And now look at you — your work is displayed in museums and galleries all over town." I touch his arm with a finger and make a sizzling sound. The electricity I feel is anything but fake, and he's not the one burning up — I am.

"Right, I'm just one of thousands of photographers covering Fashion Week in Manhattan, but I'll take it. I can't imagine doing anything else."

"I can see why. You're so talented. And respected by the press, too. I read that article about you in the *Village Voice*. Well done."

For some strange reason, a rush of sadness hits me. I stare into my martini glass. Maybe it's the alcohol getting to me, but talking about the media reminds me of Stella's tweet.

"What is it?" Jonathan asks. "I don't mean to pry, but … the problem you had earlier, is that … actually resolved?" He looks worried. I'm touched that he cares.

I sigh. "It's about this girl at school," I finally admit with the vodka's help. "She tweeted something nasty about me, but I'm over it now. It's okay," I lie.

"Are you sure? It doesn't look like it," he says, reaching for my chin and brushing it delicately with his fingers. "And that's *not* okay. What's on Twitter leaves a trace. What did she say?" He moves in closer, looking like a media strategist. I'm grateful he's looking out for me but I'm embarrassed to talk about this silly cat fight. It's making me feel weak.

I take a deep breath. This is humiliating. "Well, if you *really* want to know, she tweeted that I only got a scholarship because I'm related to Maddie."

"Say what?" He almost spits out his drink. "What's *her* problem?"

"I've asked myself that question a gazillion times. I have no idea."

"You can't just sit on this, Clementine," he says confidently. "You can't let this slide. Otherwise, she'll walk all over you. That's how bullies operate."

"That's what Jake said. I'm going to prove her wrong by becoming a huge success. That's my strategy."

"I'm not going to tell you what to do, but I think you

need a new game plan. This is New York. People are tough. She'll eat you alive if you let her."

"Jake said that, too. What do you propose?" I shoot back, taking a sip of my drink. I may be young but I'm not naive. I have my own ideas about how this should be handled. But I'll gladly listen to what Jonathan has to say. I know he's looking out for me.

"A gallery owner in New York once stole one of my Instagram photos, blew it up, and sold it for thousands of dollars without my consent. There are all kinds of dishonourable people out there online. But I learned my lesson and now I have some people looking after things. I know a lawyer who could help."

"A lawyer?" I'm surprised by his suggestion. Why would I retain a lawyer for some silly tweet? "I think that may be overdoing it. I don't want to spend all my scholarship money on legal fees; that's just not productive," I say.

"I have a good friend who has a small legal practice here in Brooklyn. She'll give you some good advice. Why don't you call her? She won't charge anything, I promise." He picks up his phone and texts me the woman's contact info. I smile gratefully. It can't hurt to have some backup advice just in case.

"Okay, I'll think about it. Thanks."

"Good — I'm glad that's resolved." He gets up from the white leather couch and comes over to my side. "Now we can move on to more important matters." He places his fingers on my chin and we kiss for a long moment. My thoughts drift away from the fact that we're in a bar, I'm under the legal drinking age, and most importantly, that I was harassed by Stella.

And I finally reach for that delicious hair.

Chapter Eighteen

"SO, CLEM, DID you get any sleep?" Jake asks me the next morning. We're sitting in the school cafeteria before class. He brought in a box of miniature cupcakes to help me get over yesterday's Twitter saga — he offered me the pink ones and kept the chocolate ones for himself. Not that I'm keeping score or anything.

"Yes, I did," I say confidently. I haven't told him about my dreamy date yet.

Jake's attending the design class with Maddie today; they'll be working with fabrics and patterns, and he'll be using the fabric we picked out together. He's dressed the part, looking dapper in a checkered shirt, dark denim pants, and a colourful bow tie that matches his brightly coloured socks. He's carrying an attaché case with peach and light-blue pockets. The look is preppy new wave with a twist and it suits him perfectly. I can tell he's excited.

After eating a cupcake and taking a sip of coffee, I look around. I'm getting funny looks from some classmates.

Actually, they're more like dirty or quizzical looks and frowns. One side of me, the sensitive side, wants to crawl under the table and sob. I guess they all think I'm a fraud. I can't believe how quick people are to judge me based on one tweet. But I decide to keep my head high and devour another pink cupcake instead.

"Stella didn't get under your skin. But it looks like lover boy sure did," Jake says, the corners of his mouth rising into a sly smile.

"What do you mean?" I know what he's talking about but I'm being coy.

"You have chafed skin under your chin, sweetie pie. It looks like a delicious carpet burn to me." He lifts his glasses off his nose to inspect my skin up close and I shoo him away like an annoying fly.

It's true that Jonathan and I spent a considerable amount of time kissing last night; first at the hotel bar, then on a park bench on my way home. His stubble rubbed deliciously against my skin and I enjoyed every second of it, until I woke up this morning with a sore chin and Maddie's pointed comments. She knew exactly what it was. She gave me some magic balm to soothe it, and then a hard time. I didn't get the chance to ask about her own date with her secret caller. We'll get to that later — a girl wants to know.

"Yes, we did make out, as you Americans would say. But it was very PG-13."

He smiles at my comeback and raises an eyebrow. "If you say so, love. Just make sure you don't let him get into your designer underpants too quickly. Like I said — he's a fashion photographer. These guys have a reputation."

I know he's partly joking and is only saying this out of concern … but it took me forever to get intimate with Charles, and now in hindsight, I totally regret it. What a mistake. I lost my virginity to a jerk, and he left me emotionally scarred. And I don't know about Jonathan's dating history yet. That's probably because I've been so caught up in my own drama. Do I think about having sex with Jonathan? Sure I do. And it's getting more intense every time we kiss. But I want to move things slowly, especially after getting hurt. I just want to avoid any more regrets.

"So did you think about your revenge strategy?" Jake asks before devouring another chocolate cupcake. I can tell these mini cupcakes are fuelling him. He's not going to let this go.

"Jonathan and I talked about it last night. Just like you, he thinks I should fight back. I still think focusing on my blog *is* the best strategy. I contacted a freelance web developer this morning and he's going to start building the beta version of *Bonjour Girl*. I also created some social media accounts for it on the weekend, and I'm registered to attend the Women and Technology panel at school this afternoon. It's hosted by the founder of *Free Fashion*." *Free Fashion* is a popular design hub that I love.

"Way to go, Clem. But you really should put Stella in her place before you launch your website. If you don't, she'll harass you again and could really hurt your image. I'm just sayin'," Jake says, reaching for another snack. "You need to watch your back, girlfriend."

Just as he says this, out of the corner of my eye I catch Ellie entering the café. She gives me a nod and a tight smile. I'm sure she's heard or read about the nasty tweet. I still have no clue why she keeps looking at me that way. It's so weird. I feel like the world is ganging up on me. I hate feeling so insecure.

"Jonathan suggested I talk to his lawyer. I thought it was a bit much at first but maybe it's not such a bad idea."

"Why not? It can't hurt. Besides, I'd love to see you sue her ass."

The truth is, all this unsolicited advice is actually making me more anxious and confused. I know I can look out for myself — I just haven't decided what I want to do yet. I try to imagine what Elizabeth Bennett, the main character in Jane Austen's *Pride and Prejudice*, would do about this.

"There is a stubbornness about me that never can bear to be frightened at the will of others," she said. "My courage always rises at every attempt to intimidate me." I mentally high-five Jane Austen. That's how I want to feel.

"How about you, Jake?" It's time to change the subject. I've had enough Twitter talk. "Have you made progress on your collection?"

"As a matter of fact, while you were busy swapping spit with pretty boy, I met Adelina, my new muse, for a nightcap. I was so psyched — we shopped for vintage fabrics and she agreed to model the new outfit I created out of that funky fabric you picked out for me."

"Wow, that's really cool. I'm not surprised she accepted. You're the best."

"Thanks, love. And that's not the half of it. After we left the wine bar, I took her to my parents' shop and we started playing dress-up. We made an impromptu runway in the shop's back store, modelling old clothes left behind by customers. What a hoot! Let me show you these photos we took." He pulls out his giant ice cream sundae phone and I chuckle. It's so anti-fashion that he somehow makes it look trendy.

As he scrolls through the countless selfies, I can't help but feel a pang of jealousy. The fact that he shared an impromptu fashion moment with another blogger who loves vintage as much as I do makes my blood run cold. Is this what they call girl envy? Am I *that* possessive of my friend? In the photos, I see the giant grins on their faces and the twinkle in their eyes and can only imagine the scene. I'm sure it was right out of the movies.

"My god, Clem, this woman is so funny, she had me in stitches. She doesn't have any French blood, but boy, can she wear a beret!" he says, pointing to a riveting photo of Adelina looking amazing in a black lace dress, funky tights, and a red beret. The fact that she's sitting in a wheelchair makes her look fierce and even more powerful. Compared to her, I feel like a wimp. I try to hide my reaction.

Why am I jealous of Jake's friend? Is it because he's showering someone else with so much attention? Besides, I was having an amazing time with Jonathan — would I have preferred to have been with Jake? A whirlwind of emotions envelops me and takes over my senses.

"You both look fabulous ... what an amazing duo you make." I excuse myself and rush to the ladies room as tears run down my cheeks. I have no idea where all these crazy emotions are coming from but I try to push them aside, at least for now.

Chapter Nineteen

"FOR AN AUDIENCE to truly engage online, there has to be a well-crafted story," the creative director of *Free Fashion* advises the crowd during his opening remarks at the Women and Technology panel late that afternoon. I love the way Parsons invites industry leaders to speak about current issues — there are four of them on this panel alone. I'm really looking forward to their perspective on what's going on out there and this puts me in a good mood.

I decided to show up early and sit in the front row. I know Stella will likely be here, too, with her squad. They typically sit in the back of the room. It makes sense, I tell myself — that's where they belong; they'll never be front-runners.

After I jot down some notes, I crane my neck to see if I can spot Stella in the crowd. She's not here yet. I take a second to close my eyes and imagine white light pouring over me to protect me from any negative energy, a trick I learned from Cécile long ago, when I was feeling anxious as a little girl. This fills me with strength and courage.

If Stella tries to pull another stunt, I won't let her get to me. I also try to imagine myself in a few years wearing a lovely dress and heels and standing at the front of this auditorium, telling Parsons students about the strategies I used to make *Bonjour Girl* a big success. This makes me smile and forget about the negative stuff.

"One thing you need to understand is that original content is *key*," Susie Lau (otherwise known as Susie Bubble, the founder of the famous fashion blog *Style Bubble*) says in earnest. She's here to discuss the power of storytelling in fashion. I admire her quirky style, her amazing website, and the way she speaks with confidence. She's a role model for me. I also love what she's wearing today: a bright-yellow and black long-sleeved dress with large peonies all over it. She has black patent leather Mary Janes and frilly white and yellow socks. The look is feminine and sweet without being over the top.

I get what she's saying; it's important to stand out. The most interesting websites and blogs are the ones that present the most original ideas. Case in point: Leandra Medine's *Man Repeller*. She built a popular platform with the idea that even if some fashion styles can be a turn-off to men, they're still fun to wear.

"Storytelling is just one component of the multi-faceted experience that today's consumers and readers expect from designers, bloggers, websites, and retailers. What's key is balancing this component with creativity to create a narrative that's unforgettable," says the CEO of *Free Fashion*.

I'm taking notes as quickly as I can when I hear a ping on my cellphone. I freeze in my seat. I turn my head as discreetly as possible to find out if Stella has made it to the conference. My stomach drops, my palms grow sweaty, and my mouth goes dry. *Holy crap, she has.* She's sitting at the back of the room and catches me looking her way. She stares back with a predatory smirk, like a hawk watching her prey. I imagine the worst. I slowly take my phone out of my jacket pocket and there it is, glaring at me in all of its bitchy glory:

> @ClementineL is a suck-up. Expect all content from today's event to be copied on her stupid blog. #bigyawn

I sink down in my seat, imagining the entire room bursting into laughter and pointing at me. I feel like such a fool. I begin to shake, imagining all of Stella's Twitter followers having a chuckle at my expense. I get why cyber intimidation and bullying can hurt so much. It makes you feel small, like really, really small, and terrible inside. Like you want to disappear from the face of the earth forever.

Tears well up in the corners of my eyes. That's it: I just can't take it anymore. I've had enough.

I need to stop Stella's efforts to destroy my reputation without doing myself in in the process. I text Jonathan:

Need to talk ASAP

He responds within seconds:

Are you OK?

NOPE

What's up? Wanna meet up?

YES. Please and TY

I'm at a meeting at Joe Coffee. Meet you out front in 10

Perfect xo

Relieved, I shut off my phone and let all the tweets and

retweets disappear into cyberspace. If someone wants to laugh at my expense, so be it. I have a gorgeous supporter waiting for me who'll defend my interests and make me feel good about myself.

I close my notebook and, after the panellists finish their closing remarks, I stand and stride confidently up the auditorium's main aisle. Just before I walk past Stella and her nasty entourage, I lift my middle finger into the air, throw my head back defiantly, and laugh out loud.

I always try to make my mother proud, and I'm sure Cécile would be delighted, too.

Here's to a lineage of strong and feisty women. I wouldn't dare disappoint my ancestors.

Chapter Twenty

"BEING FEARLESS ISN'T being 100 percent not fearful; it's being terrified but you jump anyway." Taylor Swift's words, which I read some time ago in a fashion magazine, echo in the back of my mind as I rush out of the Parsons auditorium and up to the main floor to meet Jonathan.

Was I scared to do what I just did in public? Of course I was. But more than anything, I'm exhilarated. Clearly, Stella's meanness knows no bounds, but my willingness to push back is pretty strong, too. I just wish Jake had been by my side when I lifted my finger; I know he would've howled with pride. I make a mental note to text him about it later. Right now, I have a far more pressing matter to take care of and it involves one smart and attractive man.

Elated by my brash move, I rush up the stairs, taking them two at a time in my suede boots. I see Jonathan waiting for me at the top and my heart nearly explodes when he waves. I walk up to him and grab his jean jacket, pull him close, and kiss him passionately right there in front of the school entrance. A few classmates give me side stares but I don't care. I'm done worrying what others think. It's a serious disease I'm not willing to contract.

"Wow, Clementine. I wasn't expecting you to be so …" His voice trails off as he stares at me incredulously.

"Thrilled to see you?" I say in jest after I take a step back. He pushes a stray wisp of hair from my face.

"Yeah, I guess you could put it that way." He gives me a curious look, cocks an eyebrow, and pulls me in. "Whatever it is, I like it." He kisses me again.

From the corner of my eye I notice Jake coming toward us. He makes a funny face and although I'm dying to introduce him to Jonathan and tell him about the Stella episode, he shakes his head, pretending not to see me. He then raises his thumb in the air as he enters Parsons' main building, thereby giving me his stamp of approval. Guess he hasn't seen the tweet yet.

I wish I could respond in kind but I just smile.

"So, how about we hit the town?" I ask Jonathan brazenly. I don't usually take the lead in this kind of situation, but something deep within me has been stirred. It must be that wild-child streak I get from my mother.

"What do you mean hit the town? What do you have in mind?" Jonathan asks, looking taken aback by my proposal.

"I'm ready to cut loose. I want to have fun," I answer. It's as if I'm having an out-of-body experience.

"Where? In a bar?" he asks, his hands in his pockets, looking sexier than ever.

I don't know why but I just nod. It's not like me to care about nightclubs or the city's nightlife. But I want to get out of this poisonous environment and forget about my classmates for tonight.

Jonathan stands in front of me, runs a hand through his messy hair, and puts an index finger to his lips, as if considering our options. He clearly wasn't expecting this kind of request. I wonder if he's well versed in the New York City club scene. Although Maddie likes to joke that he's a vegan homebody, something tells me Jonathan is, or at least has been, a man about town.

"All right, Clementine, your wish is my command." He reaches for my hand as we run onto Fifth Avenue to hail a cab. The sun has set on Manhattan and I can feel the pulse of the New York City nightlife beginning to buzz. If we're hitting the fabulous, fashionable club circuit, I'm underdressed for it in my high-waisted jeans, simple T-shirt, and blush-coloured leather jacket, but I don't care.

Once in the taxi, I pull out my phone, but quickly feel a lump in my throat when I see it lit up with countless notifications. Screw it — I throw it back into my bag.

"Are you okay?" Jonathan asks, looking concerned.

"Well, no, but I will be," I say. Despite my bold attitude, I'm still feeling the sting from Stella's second tweet. If I read it again or tell him about it, I'll likely lose it and cry.

"Please keep that phone in your bag. Tonight, it's just you and me," Jonathan says, then slides his fingers through mine. After he gives our driver directions ("Lower East Side, please"), I buzz with anticipation. I stare at him up close, the bristle on his chin, his liquid brown eyes, and his white shirt next to his skin. He rubs his palm against mine and I just know that tonight will be an evening to remember.

Just before the cab stops, he looks into my eyes. "All right, Clementine. Before we hit the town, we're going to get some food into you. No clubbing before you eat."

"That sounds perfect." I look up appreciatively.

The truth is, I do feel an appetite building from deep within. But it has nothing to do with food.

"That was delicious." I wipe my chin with my napkin, having finished my second zucchini cake. "Thanks for bringing me here. I love it," I say, looking around at the all-white modern space. I guess Jonathan has a thing for white spaces. That's cool — I love them, too.

We're at Dirt Candy, an award-winning vegetarian restaurant. It was the first vegetable-focused restaurant in New York and the first restaurant in the city to eliminate tipping and share profits with its employees. I love everything about this place, especially the company.

"So, where to now?" I ask, after he kisses my hand.

"Are you sure you want to go out? On a school night?"

I give him a naughty grin. The glass of red wine I had with dinner has put me in a party mood.

"Okay, then. Off we go," he says.

After a short walk, Jonathan leads us to Mehanata, a Bulgarian nightclub that's famous for wild parties, mesmerizing techno music, and a wicked vodka ice room.

"This place is a wild card. A lot of people on the clubbing scene overlook it," Jonathan says after we check our coats. It feels like we've just entered a totally different universe, far away from New York. I noticed Jonathan slipping a twenty to the club bouncer to get us in earlier. I doubt I would have been able to get in otherwise, since I didn't have fake ID. This clandestine behaviour fuels my excitement even more.

"This place is amazing!" I've never seen anything like it. The look is Eastern European party house. I'm dying to explore it further. "Great choice," I say into his ear.

"I'm glad you like it. Where else can you sit on swings at the bar, dance to punk and R&B, and travel to Bulgaria without leaving the city?" he shouts back into my ear. I get a whiff of his cologne that makes my knees turn to Jell-O. I feel intoxicated by Jonathan's sexy scent, the loud, thumping music, and the sultry downtown vibe. Now I see why New York is called the city that never sleeps. There's a raw energy here I've never experienced before. I could totally get used to this party scene. Despite my conflicted feelings about it, I now get why my mother loved it so much when she went on tour here.

Jonathan hands me a shot of vodka, the house specialty, and I swallow it in one gulp. Then the waitress hands us a second glass on the house. I know that if I drink this, I will likely do things I'll regret. It only takes a few seconds for me to decide to throw it back. I feel the hot, fiery liquid burn my throat deliciously and I grab Jonathan's arm and drag him onto the dance floor.

The throbbing music, the hippie vibe, and the wildly attractive people dancing around me all put me in a hypnotic trance that takes over my senses.

Jonathan and I dance cheek to cheek to the pulse of the music. He holds on to my waist and begins kissing my ear. I let my head tilt backwards as he kisses my neck slowly and deliciously. He then lifts the back of my shirt and runs his fingers up my spine and down the small of my back. His firm hand on my skin sends shock waves through my body. I pull him close and kiss him back in a way that I've never kissed a man before. There's a desire burning from deep within me. I follow his rhythm and slowly lose all my inhibitions. I lose track of time and forget there are people around us as we sway to the sensuous remix of DJ Calvin Harris's "How Deep Is Your Love." The lyrics hypnotize me and ask the questions that are swirling around in my head: *How deep is his love? Could it be like the ocean? And what devotion is he?*

I run my fingers down his back and hold on to him as we move to the sexy beat.

Something tells me that tonight will be memorable in more ways than one.

Chapter Twenty-One

I WAKE UP the next morning to a phone beeping, but I'm not sure whether it's actually happening or in my dreams — or should I say nightmares? I roll over and bury my face in the comforter to avoid facing reality. When I finally muster the courage to do so, I see that I'm in a strange bed wearing nothing but my pink camisole and men's pyjama bottoms. And my head hurts. *A lot.* I squint as I look around the room: I'm in an open loft with low, modern furniture, black and white photographs lining the walls, and clothes strewn all over the floor. *My* clothes. I assume the worst: in a moment of drunken *laissez-faire*, I lost control and had wild sex with a man I still know little about. I went against my own principles and all the advice Jake gave me. The sad truth is I don't remember much about the latter part of last night. After the vodka shots, it's a total blackout.

Shame washes over me. What have I done? It's not like me to do this. I've seen enough drama play out in my parents' marriage to understand the effects of not having any restraint, and it's not pretty. Is this what they call self-sabotage? It could be; it runs in my family. Maybe I'm just creating drama to avoid more pain. If so, that needs to stop.

Jonathan walks into the bedroom with two espressos in tiny cups. He's wearing jogging pants and a white T-shirt. His hair is massively dishevelled, making him look even hotter. I wish I could remember how it got that way. It feels like I'm in a TV ad for designer coffee, minus the elegant hairstyle and makeup. I haven't seen my face in a mirror yet but my guess is that I look as bad as I feel.

"Hey, beautiful."

"Hey." I guess he doesn't mind. At least there's that. I wish I could run to the bathroom to brush my teeth. I know I have morning-after breath.

I smile shyly. I cover my torso with the sheets. I am massively embarrassed.

"Something to help begin the day."

I take the cup and look away.

"Thanks. I need this."

He places the palm of his hand on my head then runs his fingers through my hair. Ouch, my throbbing head. But I don't dare tell him to take his hand off me; his caress is both gentle and soothing. I have flashbacks of us throwing back some shooters at the bar and dancing. Lots of dancing. And maybe some more shooters. The thumping sound still echoes in the back of my mind.

"You were on fire last night." He kisses the side of my head. I have no clue what he means by that. Is it a sexual reference or a partying one? I wait for more details while sipping my coffee in silence. I feel like a total lush. "You were a real dancing machine. The entire club was mesmerized by your moves, and so was I."

"Really?" I don't remember any of it. I want to escape this room, this conversation, and my skin.

"You don't remember the pole routine?" he asks incredulously.

Oh no. Please no. I begin to shake and nearly spill some coffee on the white sheets. Thank god, I catch myself before it happens. "The what?"

"They had this pole set up on the far end of the dance floor and well, let's just say you put on quite a show."

OMG. I can't believe I pole danced in front of Jonathan. I probably did that burlesque routine I picked up at dance school in Paris. My mother had wanted to experiment to add some spark to her marriage (*cringe*) and brought me along. We did have lots of laughs that day. I guess I inherited my mother's stage presence. Well, sort of.

"I hope I didn't embarrass you," I say quietly.

"Embarrass me? Oh no, you were the life of the party. Strangers were coming up to me asking who you were."

"Oh crap. I hope you didn't give them my name and number. I'm trying to launch an online business," I say, but trying to be funny is painful when you have a splitting headache.

"No, of course not. I wanted to keep you all to myself," he says and moves in for a hug.

"So … did we …?" I finally ask, my cheeks turning crimson red. This is so very embarrassing.

He grins, then shakes his head. "No, Clementine. We didn't have sex. But you definitely tried to get us there."

"I did?" I have no idea how to respond to that. Why do I feel like such a fool?

"We made out when we got back here but I made sure we kept most of our clothes on."

I look up gratefully. I was right about him: Jonathan is a gentleman.

"Okay, there was some groping. But minimal," he jokes, kissing my shoulder tenderly. "Are you hungry?"

"Huh, not really. What time is it?"

"Eight."

"Oh, dear god. Where's my phone?" I say, thinking of Maddie, who must be going out of her mind looking for me.

"I hid it. Somewhere over there." He points to the couch in the living room.

"You hid it? Why?"

"You were looking for it last night when we got here. You wanted to send Stella a nasty message. I didn't want to be responsible for any drunk texts." He winks.

It all comes back to me now, the nasty tweet in the auditorium. That explains all that drinking and acting up on the dance floor. I was trying to drown my sorrows and forget it ever happened. The truth is it now feels a *lot* worse.

"Thanks for saving me from myself in more ways than one." I extend my arm and he fetches my phone. "But I'm sober now — I can handle my enemies like an adult."

He looks up. "Is she at it again?"

"Mm-hmm. Yep. That's why I made such a fool of myself last night. I'll never forgive her or myself."

"Come on, Clementine. Don't be so hard on yourself. You needed to blow off some steam. We've all been there. Why don't you get ready and I'll make some toast. You can tell me about it on the way to class. I'll get a cab — I have a meeting there at ten."

I quickly send Maddie a text to at least let her know I'm fine. I can deal with the consequences of this immature behaviour later.

I get up from Jonathan's bed, give him a kiss on the cheek, and make my way to his bathroom and into the shower. The hot water pours over my head, shoulders, and entire body as I recall Stella's hurtful words. All that pain and all that shame. No wonder I craved an escape. Now I feel silly. In an attempt to forget, I only hurt myself more. Under the hot water, I vow to never let myself fall so low again. No bully is worth it.

After I towel off and comb my hair, I hear a ping on my phone. I cringe and my stomach drops — I feel nauseous and hold on to the shower door to maintain my balance. I fear it may be another cruel social media message. I hope not. I can't take anymore. I take a deep breath before I look and am relieved to see it's a text from Jake:

Hey Clem, SO sorry the bitch is at it again … Where are you?

I quickly respond:

You don't want to know

Oh boy. You ok? Are you in trouble?

No I'm fine. Talk to you later. Heading to Parsons now

OK. I want DETAILS and a side order of REVENGE!

I splash some cold water on my face, use some mouthwash to get rid of the lingering taste of vodka, and reluctantly slip into yesterday's outfit, ready to do the walk of shame, in more ways than one.

Chapter Twenty-Two

MY MIND WANDERS while the taxi drives us to Parsons. I stare at all the pedestrians rushing to work. They look totally energized, ready to face the day with determination. I, on the other hand, look like a melted piece of Camembert. Jonathan looks my way and smiles. I can tell he's trying to be kind and reassuring but frankly, I don't deserve it.

I try to stay positive and keep my head held high. The fact that I woke up at Jonathan's apartment with no recollection of what happened after we got there makes me sad. Time with him should be cherished, not forgotten in a drunken stupor. I also regret wasting a night; I have so much freaking work to do and I'm already falling behind in my homework assignments. Our workload is insane and so am I for not taking it more seriously.

I look down at my phone: I've received tons of messages from Maddie. I've texted her a few times to let her know I'm fine, but she's insisting we meet in one of the Parsons design studios. I know what to expect: a long-winded speech. This makes my head throb even more. Ugh.

After our taxi drops us off in front of Parsons, I kiss Jonathan and thank him for taking such good care of me, and we go our separate ways. I reluctantly head to the studio to meet Maddie. As soon as I walk into the deserted studio I know I'm in trouble. This is usually a hub of activity, so the fact that Maddie cleared the place to talk to me is a very bad sign. She puts her hands on her hips and shoots me a death glare. Given the angry look on her face, I should probably jump on social media to create the hashtag #prayforclementine.

"Where the hell were you? You look terrible," Maddie snaps. She rarely raises her voice so I know she's super upset. Uh-oh.

"I'm sorry, Maddie. I should have called you earlier."

"Earlier? Jeez. Where have you been?"

I look down at my feet. This is embarrassing but I have to tell the truth. "I went out … clubbing," I finally admit, trying to avoid any eye contact. I know my answer will make her even more pissed off. As expected, she gives me a look of disbelief.

"Are you kidding me, Clementine? Clubbing? On a weeknight? I've been going out of my mind!" she says, making dramatic arm gestures, just like my mother. I guess it runs in the family. "Do you know how worried I've been? Didn't you get my calls? I promised your parents I'd watch over you, young lady. And I didn't think you were the clubbing type. What got into you, anyway?" She finally pauses.

"You mean other than a few vodka shooters?"

Maddie rolls her eyes. "Were you out with Jake celebrating something?" she asks hopefully. I detect wishful thinking. Too bad I'm about to burst her bubble.

I stare down at my feet again and shake my head.

"No. I was with Jonathan." I have a feeling this won't go over well.

Her mouth hanging open, she stares at me in silence.

We hear a pin drop, literally.

"Oh no," she covers her mouth with her hands. I know what she's thinking, and she's right to be worried. I almost did what she thinks I did. Except I didn't.

"Don't worry, Maddie. It's not what you think. Nothing happened. Well, not much, anyway."

"Clementine. You've only started dating him. It's a bit early for sleepovers, don't you think?" she scoffs. I can tell she's royally pissed off now. Like calling-my-parents pissed off. I just hope she has mercy on me and doesn't do that. My days at Parsons would be numbered. Like I said, #prayforclementine.

"I just slept at his place — that's it. Don't you trust me?" I ask, my voice shaking. The sad truth is that after what happened, I don't really trust myself, but I refrain from saying it out loud.

"Come on, Clementine, put yourself in my shoes." I look down at the gorgeous pair of pink loafers she's wearing. I'd very much like to be in her Miu Mius right now. But that's beside the point.

"Of course I trust you but this is New York and lots of crazy stuff happens here. My heart nearly stopped when I saw your empty bed this morning."

"I'm really sorry, Maddie," I say, trying to offer her some comfort.

"Do you want to talk about it?" Maddie asks, softening. She pushes a strand of hair back from my face.

"I'm not sure what happened. I guess I needed some kind of escape from school and Jonathan was willing to come along. It's not his fault, I pressured him to go out," I admit.

"*You* pressured *him*? You know you're under the legal drinking age, don't you, dear?" Maddie asks, trying to drive her point home. I want to respond that I've been going to bars since I was sixteen but don't dare bring that up now.

"Yes, I know that but it slipped my mind. In Paris, I never got carded."

"Okay ... so why the need to escape?" she asks. "Are you still stressing out about school? Don't put too much pressure on yourself, Clementine." She pats me on the back gently. "Everything will be fine."

"Nope, that's not it." I look away and hold back tears. The lack of sleep combined with the string of nasty comments on Twitter is making me super emotional. I'm about to lose it. But I don't.

"What is it, then?" she asks quietly.

I shrug and after a long, awkward silence, I pull out my cellphone and scroll down to Stella's tweet.

As Maddie reads it, her eyes nearly pop out of their sockets and her lips form a tight pucker. I imagine steam coming out of her ears. "You could have Stella before the student conduct board for this," Maddie blurts out, throwing her arms high above her head.

"Really?" The thought brings a smile to my face but it vanishes just as quickly. I know lodging a complaint against Stella would make me look like a tattletale and feel like a fool. Things would have to get worse before I'd go down that road.

"Thanks, Maddie, but I need to fight my own battles." I think back to the scholarship saga and the drama it created with Jake. "I'd rather deal with this on my own. It's time I faced the world like an adult."

"All right, if you say so. But I brought you something from home. I think it might come in handy," Maddie says, handing me a small hardcover book. It has a French title, which translates to *How to Be a French Lady*. I can tell it's old; its pages are yellowed and frayed and its cover design looks vintage. The cover has a *pied de poule* background like the old Dior perfume boxes my mother collects on her vanity. On its cover, there's a small, round image of a young woman with the air of a young Audrey Hepburn. She's wearing white gloves and a hat. It's the kind of book I love to shop for in flea markets in Paris.

"What is this?" I ask, puzzled.

"It's an etiquette book. It belonged to your great-grandmother. I read it often; it has come in handy many times in my life. Cécile would want you to have it now." She smiles.

"Wow, thanks, Maddie." This is a total surprise. Instead of reprimanding me, she offers me a gift.

I open the book to a random page and translate the chapter title in my head: "How to Maintain Grace Under Pressure." I begin to laugh. With Jake pushing me to get back at Stella, me making a fool of myself in front of Jonathan last night, and my feeling insecure at school, this book is exactly what I need.

I wish I could skip class, curl up with Cécile's book, and read it in one sitting. I have a feeling it'll help me make better decisions. With the help of this treasure, things can only get better. I put it in my bag and start walking toward the door but Maddie grabs me by the jacket sleeve.

"Here, you should wear these. I found them in the studio." She hands me a funky blue and white striped blazer and ultra-slim black cigarette pants. The look is futuristic and avant-garde. It's not my cup of tea but I can tell my wearing it would make Maddie happy. "A student's collection from last year. To avoid dirty looks from your classmates," she says, and I know I have little choice but to wear it. I want to say that wearing this Star Trekkish outfit will probably have the opposite effect but I keep my mouth shut.

"Right." I take the ensemble off its hangers and head behind a flimsy curtain to change. I immediately feel better. This *was* a great idea; it's totally refreshing to take off yesterday's smelly club clothes. And it's comforting to know someone has my back. I give Maddie a warm hug.

I'm so grateful for my thoughtful relatives, both past and present.

They sure know how to live, and they sure know how to dress — two of life's precious treasures, right?

Chapter Twenty-Three

A LADY, LIKE EVERYONE ELSE, goes through challenging times. Where others would scream, cry, or hurl objects, the lady keeps her head held high and does not crumble under pressure.

These words from Cécile's book jump from the page. I'm sitting with a hot chocolate in the far corner of the school cafeteria after my first class to avoid prying eyes. I try to turn the pages as carefully as possible to avoid tearing the book's delicate paper. Just like my reputation, I need to protect this family heirloom.

I close my eyes and try to let these words of wisdom sink in. My great-grandmother was a wise woman who always kept her composure, even after my great-grandfather died. She may have showed her sadness to close friends and family, but not for long. She never crumbled under pressure when the family business went through tough times. Like Jake's mother, she mended dresses and skirts as extra work on the side and had designer friends help her put together a fabulous wardrobe by giving her free samples. It's not that she didn't suffer — *au contraire*. I think she did, but she built up her courage and didn't show it. She accepted the difficult periods with grace, knowing they would eventually pass.

I turn the pages and another passage makes me cringe:

> A lady may cry or act out to expel her pain
> but she shouldn't do it in front of an audience.

Oops. I think about Stella's intimidation tactics and how I reacted rather ungracefully in front of a large group of students in the school auditorium. And my cheeks blush with embarrassment when I think about myself being unladylike on the dance floor last night. I flush with shame at the thought of Cécile, with her impeccable manners, seeing me gyrate my hips and slinking around on a pole in front of countless strangers. What was I thinking? And throwing myself at Jonathan — the whole thing is mortifying. I wonder whether Cécile ever did anything like that when she was my age. I have a feeling she probably cut loose in her own unique way. This makes me feel better.

The book is just so on point that I keep reading.

> A lady is the embodiment of *strength, courage,* and *hope*. She believes she can get over any situation or hardship and learn from it. While some people take pleasure in wallowing in their misfortunes, a lady stands tall and continues on her path.

Voilà! That's it. That's the message I was looking for. I close the book, relieved and satisfied. I mentally thank Cécile for leaving this treasure behind for family members to read.

I stand up from the chair, smooth out the creases in my borrowed black pants, and tie my hair up in a pony-tail. I apply some lip gloss and decide to head to class with grace, hope, and renewed optimism. I'll respond to Stella in a way that would make my great-grandmother proud. No more wallowing.

It's time to stand tall, take action, and find closure and satisfaction. A few students turn around and watch me leave the cafeteria with renewed self-confidence. I can already feel a shift in their perception of me that reflects how much stronger I feel inside.

Chapter Twenty-Four

"HEY, PRINCESS, I'VE BEEN looking all over for you. What's up?" Jake arrives at the cafeteria just before class.

He's wearing grey jeans, a grey sweater, a grey beanie, and a white T-shirt. He's also sporting grey studded high-tops and a skull-print scarf. It looks like the school's student colour palette has rubbed off on him. But hey, who am I to judge? I'm wearing clothes borrowed from the design studio that make me look like a character out of a sci-fi movie.

Jake doesn't seem to mind my look.

"Whoa girl, you're looking sassy," he says, staring at my outfit approvingly. I respond with a nod. I can't bring myself to tell him I borrowed these clothes from school to avoid the walk of shame. At least not yet.

"So where were *you* this morning? And more importantly, what are you hiding from me, young lady?" he asks, holding his iced coffee in one hand and pointing to my handbag with the other. He saw me slip Cécile's precious etiquette manual into my bag as he approached, but I've decided it's off limits.

"I'm not hiding *anything* — it's just an old textbook I picked up at the library," I respond dismissively. "And if *you must* know, I was at Jonathan's this morning when I texted you." I look around to make sure no one can hear.

"JESUUUS. You slept with him already?" Jake says loudly while taking a seat next to me. This makes me want to crawl under the table. "I can't believe it, Clem. I mean, he's attractive and all, I'll give you that, but what did I tell you? It's not the best way to proceed." It's like he's giving me advice on how to buy tickets for a concert at Madison Square Garden.

"Shhhh." I put my index finger against my lips. No thanks to Stella, I already have a reputation for being a fraud. That's enough for one week. "No, I didn't sleep with him, at least not in *that* way," I whisper. "We went out clubbing and I slept over at his place but we didn't have sex. There. If that's what you want to know."

He shakes his head while cutting his muffin into small pieces, as if he's thinking this through carefully. "Okay, so how did *that* happen? The last time I saw you two, you were kissing in front of the school entrance. What led to this complete *déchéance*?" Jake asks with a faux French accent that usually makes me laugh. Except that he's talking about my reputation so it's not funny.

"Nothing worth gossiping about."

"Oh, I'll be the judge of that, pussycat. I'd say so far, you're totally off base. This story is as juicy as it gets." He raises both eyebrows mischievously and pops a small piece of muffin into his mouth.

"We went out for dinner, had some wine, then went out for more drinks at a bar downtown. I was tipsy so Jonathan let me sleep over to make sure I didn't get into any trouble —

that's all there is to it. We didn't even get to second base, as you Americans would say. No need to fuss," I say, taking a sip of my black coffee. Thankfully, the stuff is keeping me awake.

"You know I'm only looking out for you, Clem. I don't want to see you get hurt, that's all. A lot of men in New York are 'players,'" Jake says, using air quotes.

"Right, so you said ... but Jonathan isn't one of them. He could've taken advantage of me but he didn't."

"All right, whatever you say, darlin'. I just don't want to be picking up the pieces of your broken heart," he says, before finishing the last piece of his snack.

He sees the quizzical look on my face. I've never seen someone cut muffins into so many small pieces.

"Don't ask — it's a trick my mother taught me. Cutting my food this way helps to curb my appetite. She thinks I should lose a few pounds. But you wanna know what I think?"

"Of course."

"I prefer to follow the wise words of *Oprah*, one helluva smart woman: 'They say getting thin is the best revenge. Success is much better.'"

"Right. If you say so." I somehow doubt the effectiveness of his mother's well-meaning advice after he finishes his third mini muffin. Oh well.

"Enough about the boy. Let's talk about Stella," Jake says, wiping his fingers with a napkin and taking a sip of coffee.

I take a deep breath and exhale slowly. I want to follow the advice in Cécile's book, though I know my approach may not go over too well with Jake. But I need to stick to my guns. I'm committed to being a lady at all costs — my family history and reputation are on the line.

"To be honest, Jake, I don't really want to talk about it anymore. Stella's made her bed by spewing vicious rumours about me and I've decided not to engage with her on that level."

"My god, listen to you…. Did you join some spiritual cult or something?"

"No. It's just common sense. *C'est tout.* Don't worry, I'll find a way to get back at her — but on my own terms. Besides, I think revenge is overrated."

He stares at me as though I just said I'm wearing a flannel shirt to a black-tie dinner.

"I know it's hard for you to understand, but it's the best way to handle this."

"All righty then, sunshine. If you say so. This case is closed." He pretends to drop his gavel on the table like a judge. "Now that we've resolved two very important matters, it's time to talk about this." He places a piece of paper on the table in front of me. I already know what it is.

"OMG. You got the scholarship!" I say, my eyes wide with excitement.

"Oui," he says, and tears of joy well up in his eyes. He likes to play mister tough guy about Stella, but deep down he's a total softie. "Yup. I did. All thanks to you, Clem. Thanks for the tip. I owe you big time."

"No, you don't owe me anything, Jake. You only have yourself to thank for this. I only supplied the information."

"You're a major part of this, kiddo. I'm a bit nervous, though — there are a few conditions attached to it."

"Oh? Like what?"

"I guess my collection concept clinched the deal. They

loved the idea of me creating something for people with disabilities. Now I have pressure to execute my plan."

"It's all positive pressure, right?"

"You bet it is."

I'm really thrilled for him. This reminds me of my own personal project. I need to stop worrying about Stella and move on. Maybe I can write something for my blog later?

"I wish I could go out to celebrate but I've barely slept in the last twenty-four hours," I say.

"That makes two of us. But not for the same reasons, Clemmy." He wags his finger at me jokingly and gives me faux naughty bedroom eyes. I poke him back.

"Can I count on you for some support? I'm freaking nervous about this. I'm only starting out and they're expecting me to show my collection in front of the entire Parsons faculty, for god's sake! I won't sleep or eat for the next six months."

"Yeah, right," I respond jokingly, pointing to his empty plate.

"Ouch, *touché.*"

"You can count on me to help out. If I remember correctly, Jonathan mentioned he was the official photographer for the Parsons student showcase event. Is that the one you're talking about?"

"Yup."

"I'm sure he'd be willing to take some pictures for you for free. He also has lots of contacts that could help you get organized."

"In that case, I take back any negative thing I ever said about him." He pats me on the shoulder affectionately.

"I'll try to arrange something so you guys can meet. Maybe dessert at Serendipity?" I wonder how Jonathan will react to meeting Jake in such a girly setting. I can just see it now: Jake flirting with my boyfriend and giving him sweet eyes over hot fudge sundaes. In terms of entertainment, that could be the red maraschino cherry on top.

"That would be awesome. You're the best, Clem. Listen, we'll talk later 'cause I gotta run!" Jake gives me a peck on the cheek as he stands up from his chair and grabs all of his stuff, then saunters out of the cafeteria, looking excited.

I remember some wise words from Cécile's book: "A lady understands that being a good person is a choice you make over and over." And that's how I roll.

Just as I'm about to leave, I spot Ellie across the room, and she's staring my way. She's giving me a nasty look again. Why does she keep staring at me that way? What have I done to her to merit this? Honestly, I'm far too tired to deal with this nonsense. I stare back at her defiantly before heading to the cafeteria to get what every lady needs to maintain her composure: another strong caffè Americano.

Chapter Twenty-Five

I'M STARING OUT THE WINDOW of Joe Coffee looking at NYU and New School students walking by. I wonder if any of them have also gotten into trouble lately. They say misery loves company, and I could sure use some support.

I asked Jonathan to meet me here after his work meeting. The café's vibe is hip and airy. I order a chocolate croissant. And some sparkling water. I don't need any more caffeine.

I feel bad about what happened last night. After talking to Maddie, it really hit me that I made a serious mistake; I should have gone home instead, and it's been on my mind all day. Now I just want to talk things over with Jonathan to see if we're still on the same page.

I peer down at my out-of-character outfit. It feels odd to be wearing these clothes. I try to ignore it; I have more important things to worry about, like whether Jonathan still wants to date me after I made a complete fool of myself.

"Hey, beautiful." Jonathan kisses me on the side of the head. "Cool jacket."

I'm not sure if he means it but his compliment makes me feel like gold and pulls me out of my funk. I hope it's a sign I haven't ruined my chances with him.

"Everything all right?" he asks, putting his backpack on the seat next to me. I look down sheepishly; that's exactly what I want to know.

"Yeah, well, um, I guess. *Is* everything all right?"

"Sure it is, Clementine. There's nothing to worry about, okay?" He grabs my hand.

"Okay, if you say so. I just feel awful for acting like a complete ass." I've done stupid stuff before, like accidentally shaving off an eyebrow after watching a YouTube tutorial about how to shape them. But pole dancing in public — never.

"That's not what I saw. You looked great, Clementine, full of raw energy, getting creative on the dance floor." He runs his fingers through my hair soothingly.

I'm floored. This guy really is special for seeing the art in my dancing instead of the messy drunkeness. I'm falling for him hard. I just hope he feels the same way.

"Oh come on, you're just saying that," I say, still holding on to his hand.

"No, I'm not. You should stop being so hard on yourself. We've all done something we've regretted. It's no big deal," he says, taking a sip of the coffee I ordered for him. He looks as sexy as ever with his shirt sleeves rolled up and his eyes full of compassion.

"You think?" I give him a quizzical look. "You've done stupid stuff, too?"

"Of course, back in college … I've also had too much to drink on a few occasions. Especially after some of those

Fashion Week parties. They can get pretty wild." Jonathan looks out the window.

A red light goes off in my head as I recall Jake's warnings about dating a fashion photographer. I try to stay calm and tell myself it's all part of the job. There's no need to worry about the parties, the booze, and certainly not the gazillion attractive women. But I have a hard time focusing. Questions pop into my head unbidden, including whether or not we're dating exclusively. Of course, it's way too soon to even consider it (even though I'd happily make it official right now). I decide to play it cool. This is no time to lose it and become insecure and needy.

"Right. I imagine those parties can get *pretty* crazy," I say nonchalantly, as if I know anything about them. But I don't, at least not yet. I sure aspire to, though — I'm hoping Jake invites me to some.

I get a blank stare and a nod.

It's not exactly the response I was hoping for. I was hoping he'd just say that he only attends parties with clients or colleagues and goes home early every time. But he doesn't, so I take a deep breath and try to ignore my discomfort.

"I have to work on my portfolio tonight and tomorrow. But let's get together tomorrow night. How about we catch some live music in Soho?" he asks in a comforting tone. I'm relieved. He does want to see me again after all. Thank god.

"I'm not sure going downtown again is a such good idea. I tend to lose all self-restraint down there," I shoot back jokingly.

He moves in close, his shirt pressed up against my borrowed blazer, and looks into my eyes.

"Wherever I go, I lose all restraint when I'm with you."

And then we kiss. This makes my heart thump and my mood skyrocket into the stratosphere.

I push away my snack with my hand. I don't need any more sugar or artificial stimulants — my life is already pretty sweet.

Too bad it doesn't stay that way.

Chapter Twenty-Six

MADDIE IS OUT WITH her mystery man tonight. She told me he was taking her to some film premiere in Tribeca. I can't wait to meet him to make sure he's up to snuff. In the meantime, I'm happy to have her place to myself.

I've been working on mood boards, which I create for inspiration. I've got stacks of magazine clippings, scissors, sticky notes, and coloured pens everywhere. But my conversation with Jonathan plays on repeat in my mind. Some questions remain unanswered: Is he a party boy? A player? Maddie says I could be a role model for other girls because of my inner strength but Jonathan turns me into a puddle. Why am I filled with self-doubt?

Am I scared about dating someone new? Hell yes. Especially after what happened in Paris, and after what Jake said. But I need to snap out of it. For my own sanity and peace of mind. Jonathan seems to be into me despite my silly blunders so this is no time to get cold feet.

To build my self-confidence, I decide to focus on my blog. I need to be more like Maddie, an independent and successful woman. My graphic designer sent me a link earlier today for review, and it's perfect — exactly what I had envisioned. Now all I need is content.

I pull out my laptop and set it on a pillow on my bed. I'm so lucky to be working here. My room is bright, modern, and feminine, just like the website I'm trying to build. Thanks to Maddie, it's decorated with scented candles (clementine, of course), crisp white sheets with a touch of French lace, vintage necklaces, and art posters bought in Europe. There are fashion books — tons of gorgeous books, including Cécile's — on the shelves and on my nightstand. I guess fashion and its history run in my blood. So does a love for pretty things. And then there's my lucky cat, a porcelain souvenir from Japan that my dad gave me and that I take with me for luck wherever I go.

A passage from Cécile's etiquette book says a lady's surroundings should match her state of mind and be clutter-free. It's a far cry from that right now; thanks to my earlier homework blitz and collage session, my bedroom has turned into a war zone. That's okay, it makes me feel productive.

I begin some late-night reading. I thought I'd be asleep early tonight after last night's nightclub escapade, but somehow I have a ton of energy. I come across an article about a teenage fashionista who suffers from a rare illness that causes her hair to fall out. Her name is Amy.

Amy uses wigs of different styles and colours to match her moods and her clothing. I find her story so inspiring that I send her an e-mail at two in the morning. Also a night owl, she responds immediately. We chat on Skype until three and I ask her questions for my first *Bonjour Girl* feature. I'm excited. Amy is the kind of woman who leads others by overcoming her own challenges.

She sends me pictures of herself wearing wigs of different colours with funky matching outfits. Her bright and cheery personality makes her a perfect subject for my first blog post.

I download the photos, type up the notes I took during our chat, and add some of Amy's most inspiring words in large, bold print: "I have found self-respect through living with a severe chronic illness. Now I want to show the world who I truly am."

After I read this for the third time, I feel silly for being so insecure about dating Jonathan. I honestly need to get over myself. Am I going to spend all my precious time and energy worrying about a guy's past? Nope.

Instead, I reread Amy's second inspiring quote: "I tell everyone to just be themselves. With a positive outlook, you can have all you want out of life."

This amazing quote from Amy gives me the courage to write my first blog post. I feel a mix of excitement and worry pulsing through my veins while I type, my blue nails clicking on the keys as words come pouring out of me. I'm making it happen — not without some anxiety, especially when I think of what Stella might say or do after I publish this. But then I think of my new friend Amy and all the challenges she's overcome. I also think about the humiliation she may have endured along the way and I tell myself: to hell with Stella. This is my moment of truth. I'm not going to let anyone get in the way.

I finally press the publish key.

I share my first post on all my social media platforms, including Twitter — bullies and haters be damned.

Once it's out in cyberspace, I turn off my computer, lie down on my bed, and think as many good thoughts as I can about Amy, my blog, and all my future readers. Maybe I can send some positive energy into the world this way. I also thank Cécile for sending me her precious book. She's been a strong influence in getting me here. I read a few pages of her book, then fall into a short but deep and satisfying sleep.

We'll see what tomorrow brings. *Bonne nuit.*

Chapter Twenty-Seven

OMG. I CAN'T BELIEVE IT. Is this for real? I press my hands over my mouth like I've just won the lottery.

The number of people who read and shared my blog post overnight is astounding. The reaction is so overwhelming that I shut down my laptop and reboot it, just to make sure I'm not hallucinating. This is way better than getting scholarship money. It's lifting up my self-esteem — and that's priceless.

The clock indicates that it's ten a.m. I overslept but I guess it's a non-issue since I have no classes until this afternoon. My guess is that Maddie purposely let me sleep in. I make my way to the kitchen and brew myself a quick cup of tea. While I wait for the water to boil, I wonder if this is a dream. Did *Bonjour Girl* really take off this quickly? With my vintage coffee cup from Euro Disney in hand, I sit down again in front of my computer and wait for it to reboot. When it finally does, what I see makes me want to jump for joy: there are thousands of reads, shares, likes, and retweets from people in Europe, the U.K., and America. I raise my arms in victory.

Holy crap. This is one of the most exciting moments of my life. The lyrics to Alicia Keys's song "This Girl Is on Fire" play in the back of my mind.

How did this happen? Was it sheer luck? Magic? The blog fairies? I'm not sure. All I know is that Amy shared the article I wrote about her with her own followers. I made sure her story was told as authentically as possible and I guess it touched people's hearts.

I feel proud, like really proud. For following my instincts and for not letting anyone's nasty remarks stop me from moving ahead. I take a soothing sip of tea ... but after a few minutes, I begin to fret. What if Stella sees this and tweets something hurtful that makes the sudden interest in my blog disappear? And what should I write about next? I mean, coming across Amy was a lucky break, so where will I find more content like this? My mind begins to dive into negative thoughts.

This needs to stop. I shut down my computer again and get in the shower to calm down. Afterward, I get dressed and text Jake. I need his help to figure out my next move.

Can you meet up?

When?

Like, right now???

You mean TOUT DE SUITE?

Yes. Need to talk to you. URGENT

Boy trouble?

No ... business expansion! HUGE!

Oh! YAAAY! Jake at your service! Meet at deli in an hour?

Perfect. You're ZEE best

Of course I am

xx

Out of breath, I show up at the deli across from Parsons. It's one of those food emporiums that has a salad bar and a juice bar and everything else under the sun. Jake seems quite at home here. He's picked up things from every aisle: he's ordered his regular egg sandwich and piled on the bananas, energy bars, and cold drinks. I open my laptop to show him the warm reception I received from thousands of strangers overnight — for me it's the creative equivalent of going to a buffet.

"That's my girl! This is freaking awesome, Clem. *Bonjour Girl* is a major hit!" He puts down his sandwich and scrolls through my blog post with his sticky fingers. I'm so excited, I don't care. "I knew you'd score big, girlfriend. You see, you just had to put yourself out there."

"Mm-hmm. I guess so. I was scared to publish that first post but I'm really happy I did," I say, still staring at my screen. "I guess I'm on the right track …"

"Right track? Are you kidding me? You're a rock star! And so is this Amy. What a sweetie. I dig her style, too — she's fly. I'd love to have her on my team when I present my new collection," Jake says. I can tell the cup of java has his wheels spinning.

"I knew you'd be impressed with her," I say. And then, still inspired by the Parsons conference I attended about creating online content, I get a flash.

"I just had an idea. How about we collaborate? You present your design ideas and I blog about them?"

"Oooh, that would be a fab collab. I like the way you think." He winks.

And just like that, after throwing his empty coffee cup in the trash, Jake takes me by the arm. "Let's get started, then."

"Right now? Where are we going?"

He whisks me toward the door. "The design studio. I'll show you my latest work-in-progress. Maddie says my sewing skills are impeccable."

"Of course they are."

"We're gonna make Cécile proud!" Jake says, pulling out his phone. He launches into a lengthy texting session. I'm not sure who's on the receiving end of these messages, but my guess is that I'll soon find out. "Just give me an hour to get organized. I'll meet you in the design studio."

I sure hope to make Cécile proud, because so far this semester, I've only given her reason to cringe and worry. But with my popular blog post, it feels as though my big break is finally here. May lady luck continue to be on my side, at least for a while.

"So, where are your precious darlings, darling?" I ask as I saunter into the Parsons design studio where Jake's been working on his collection. My eyes dart around the room, looking for Jake's first pieces. I know they're in here somewhere. He's been working late every night this week and I know I'm in for a treat.

Jake's face lights up like the Ferris wheel at the Place de la Concorde in Paris.

The large space is filled with sewing machines, cutting tables, and mannequins. There are a few pieces of clothing that catch my eye, including a light-blue dress covered with embroidered eyes and lashes. The look is modern and playful and I can totally picture myself wearing it, especially on a date with Jonathan.

"A lovely Bulgarian student made that," Jake says, seeing me admire the piece.

"It's beautiful."

My friend places his finger over his mouth, floating around the room while the silk scarf around his neck flows gracefully behind him. Despite Jake's unhealthy eating habits and occasionally unglamorous ways, he possesses the charm of Truman Capote, the author of *Breakfast at Tiffany's* and a popular, well-dressed man about town.

"No, dear one. You won't find my precious pieces lying around the studio or just hanging on a mannequin. I keep them all in a special hiding place." He wags his finger exaggeratedly.

He saunters toward a large metal chest in the back of the room and opens it ever so carefully. I have no idea what he's doing, but the suspense is killing me.

There's a knock on the door. I can't believe my eyes when a gorgeous creature sitting in a wheelchair enters the room: it's Adelina, the blond Russian blogger. In person she looks ethereal with her sculpted cheekbones and perfect eyebrows. She wheels toward us, periodically raising her arms high above her head to dance in her chair, looking like a total rock star. She's dressed in a simple blue and white striped ensemble, full of simplicity and glamour, looking like a character out of *The Great Gatsby*, accessorized with a red beret and matching lips. She's holding a canvas bag with the hilarious inscription *Why Go to Therapy When I Can Just Live in NYC and Be Weird?*

Her allure and panache leave me speechless. She exudes such self-confidence that she makes me want to emulate her radiant, happy vibe. I now get why Jake loves to hang out with her; I'd love to follow her around, too.

"You must be Clementine. I'm Adelina." She reaches out to shake my hand. I'm in awe of her raw beauty and style. "Jake told me all about you, sweetie. Love what you're wearing. That vintage dress is superb. Where'd you find it?"

"Artists & Fleas at the Chelsea Market," I say. I picked it up while shopping with Maddie the weekend before I started school.

"Oh, really? That's my second home. Can't believe you snatched it before I did," she adds in perfect deadpan. I begin to laugh and Jake looks on proudly, seeing that his two besties have similar taste in fashion and are getting along famously.

"I love what you're wearing," I tell her. "So elegant and chic."

"That would be *moi*," Jake chimes in.

"Wow, this is amazing work, Jake. Now I know why you got that scho—"

He cuts me off. "Shhhh!"

"Right, sorry."

"It's okay, Adelina knows. She can totally be trusted. It's the other students I'm worried about," he adds, looking around. There's no need to worry, though; there's only one other student in the room right now, sewing away behind a noisy machine.

Looking at Adelina's ensemble, it's obvious that Jake was meant to do this. He's got talent up the wazoo.

"Adelina looks amazing."

"Doesn't she, though?" Jake walks toward her, kneels down, and gives her a big hug.

"It's stunning. You are so talented, it's crazy!" I gush.

"Why, thank you, madam," he says with faux modesty and a flourish.

"You two make quite the pair," I add, trying not to get jealous of their friendship again.

One thing's for sure. My friend has found the perfect person to wear his clothes. Great design, savvy sales, and marketing skills clearly run in his genes (or jeans?).

"Do tell me more about your collection, sir," I say playfully.

Jake puts on his best TV-interview voice. "It's a line of fashionable and functional clothing created to make wheelchair users look and feel great. I've only created a couple of pieces, four to be exact, but I have plans for many more."

"What are the key features of your collection?" I ask, pulling out my notebook to take notes for my blog.

"Our clothing has cuts and styles for a seated body, which fit better, look nicer, and feel more comfortable than standard mainstream clothing and don't interfere with wheelchair mechanics." He points to Adelina's chair.

"Very impressive. Anything else you'd like to add? About the textiles, perhaps?"

"Ah, yes," he answers, adjusting his hipster glasses. "We use quality fabrics selected for stretch and durability. Take a look: there's much more here than meets the eye, with details like wrap-waist palazzo pants, an open-snap back, and an easy zipper. Our clothes are not only easier to get in and out of, but they also take ease of movement into consideration."

"That's for damn sure!" Adelina chimes in, throwing her hands in the air again while dancing in her chair. I don't know what kind of music is playing in her mind but my guess is that it's some kind of upbeat disco.

This is fantastic; Jake's research and execution are flawless. And the print placement is impeccable. But more than anything, his idea of making attractive clothes that are wheelchair-friendly warms my heart.

"Wow, Jake. Can I be honest here? I'm really impressed. Like, big time."

"I'm glad you like it, sweet pea. I also plan to donate 5 percent of our sales toward accessibility initiatives and social programs. Whaddya think?"

"I'm floored, *très* floored. What can I say? You rock, my friend."

I'm clapping my hands above my head to show my support when the studio doors open and Jonathan walks in with his large camera bag and a huge grin on his face. I do a double take.

"We need a photographer to take pictures of Adelina for your blog, right?" says Jake.

"Mm-hmm …"

"Well, I found our man for the job, then. Sorry, I mean *your* man."

Wow, another big surprise. I'm thrilled about Jake's idea. I wish I'd thought of it first.

"I love to help out when I can," Jonathan says, looking good in a denim shirt and washed-out grey jeans. This is a great surprise. He walks over to me, kisses me on the cheek, and shakes Jake's hand, then Adelina's, like a true gentleman.

Looking as excited as a child on Halloween night, Jake pulls out the entire contents of his chest: a shirt, wide-legged pants, and a wrap dress in blue and yellow cotton and silk. All of his pieces have the most exquisite details — a touch of lace here, a pearl button there.

"All right, let's get to work and shoot these babies before the rest of my design classmates show up. They like to hog the place; it's a miracle we have this studio all to ourselves right now." Jake claps his hands, ignoring the lone student in the back, who hasn't looked up from his machine once since we got here.

"Yeah, baby! Let's shoot!" Adelina exclaims in a loud, rambunctious voice. We all burst into giggles. She really is a hoot. "Let's get this photo session started. My Bloody Mary is waiting for me at the hotel bar," she adds. She winks at Jake and he winks back.

"You're welcome to join us for lunch later. I promised Adelina I'd take her out to thank her for her time here," Jake says, looking at Jonathan and me.

Can this day be any more perfect? I think not.

There's an Irish proverb about friendship: "A good friend is like a four-leaf clover, hard to find and lucky to have." I'm learning that not only can I share my friends, I can make fabulous new ones in the process. And that is an important lesson to learn. I lift my (imaginary) glass to that.

Chapter Twenty-Eight

"I'M IMPRESSED, CLEMENTINE. What you and Jake are doing to promote diversity in fashion — I think it's really progressive and smart," Jonathan says, reaching for my hand. He runs his fingers through mine and I feel all tingly inside. My heart pounds a gazillion beats per minute. I'm on a major adrenaline high and I don't want to come down. Like, ever.

"Thanks, that means a lot."

We're at Le Midi, the French bistro where we first met through Maddie. We thanked Jake for his generous lunch invitation but let him saunter off with Adelina. We didn't want to impose so we decided to come back here. It's like a reunion of sorts, but just the two of us this time — without Maddie as a chaperone. There are lots of Parsons teachers sitting around us so I try to act professional and limit my displays of affection, although I fantasize about pushing the bottle of Perrier out of the way and making out with Jonathan right here, right now.

"I wasn't expecting you to drop in this morning. It sure added excitement to the moment," I say.

"I had so much fun taking photos of Adelina. She's a riot. And you really got into it, acting as Jake's assistant, didn't you?"

"Yes, I loved playing his number two. Isn't he awesome? I think Jake is super special."

"Absolutely. Just like you," Jonathan says, and I want to melt in my seat. He runs his fingers softly along the inside of my palms and I am burning up inside. I find myself falling for him more and more every time we meet.

My romantic thoughts are interrupted when Jonathan nods toward the back of the restaurant.

"Friend of yours?" he asks. I turn around and catch Ellie staring at us from behind a large textbook. When our eyes meet, she looks away. Not again. What's with her? A part of me feels frustrated by our lack of privacy and wants to stand up and leave. The other, more rebellious side decides it's better to stay. I'm not going to let my classmates get to me more than they already have.

I decide to take a different approach and tell Jonathan I need to use the ladies room. I need to find out why Ellie keeps popping up everywhere I go and looking at me that way. I can't take it anymore; it's getting way too creepy. I stop beside her table.

"Is there something you want to tell me, Ellie?" I ask, gritting my teeth. "You're not one to hold back, so don't be shy."

"Um, no. Why?"

"Every time I turn around, there you are, staring. In the fabric store, in the cafeteria, and now here. Are you stalking me? What have I done to you?"

"Nothing. It's just a coincidence, I swear," she says sheepishly. I detect some insincerity in her voice, but it's clear that's all she's going to say.

As I walk away, I focus on Jonathan's remark about our project being progressive. It reminds me of an article from the *New York Times* that my father had me read before I left for school. It was called "What's So Scary About Smart Girls?" The writer's answer holds a dear place in my heart: "There's no force more powerful to transform society." I just wish girls would act with more civility and respect toward each other.

Once in the ladies room, I wash my hands and forget about Ellie. I look in the mirror proudly. It's such a great feeling to be involved in the evolution of fashion, to become an agent of change. Although the fashion industry is evolving slowly, things are moving in the right direction. I'm happy to be here and a part of it all.

"I'm ready to do it again if you guys need me to take any more pictures," Jonathan says as soon as I take my seat. "Working with Jake was a real treat. I wish other fashion brands would broaden their perspectives and hire more models like Adelina. I think he'll be making a huge impact on the business and I'm happy to contribute any way I can."

"Really? That's amazing. I'm sure he'll be thrilled and grateful."

"Just name the time and place and I'll be there. If it's important to you, it's important to me." He pokes my nose playfully. "Besides, this will be fantastic for my portfolio," he says, reaching for the pepper. "Should we order some wine to celebrate the launch of *Bonjour Girl*?" he asks, and I hesitate. The truth is I'd love to spend all afternoon with him drinking wine, but I have lots of homework to do.

"Thanks for the offer, but I'll stick to sparkling water. I have lots on my plate."

He points to my barely touched roast chicken. "You sure do," he says jokingly before digging into his steak frites.

"I blame *you* for that. You make me hungry for something else," I say, reaching for a french fry.

He laughs.

"So, did you contact my lawyer friend?" he asks between bites.

"No, not yet. I'll call her if I need to. So what time are we meeting tonight?" I ask, trying to change the subject.

"Oh, right …" he says, looking out of sorts. He looks away.

I feel uneasy *and* queasy … what's that about?

"I'm really sorry Clementine, but I have to work." He reaches for my hand again but this time I don't let him get to it so easily. I'm disappointed.

"Did something come up last minute?"

"Yes, it's Fashion Week, remember? I didn't have that many bookings, and finally something came through just now. I'd ask you to join me but it would be distracting and counterproductive. I hope you understand. Let's get together on Sunday. There's this quaint French restaurant in the Village with a roaring fireplace I'd love to take you to. It'll be just perfect."

I try to keep things in perspective. *Come on, Clementine, don't overreact. It's just a change of plans.* I'm about to accept his dinner invitation when I hear the faint ping of my phone. Here we go again. I peer discreetly at my cell, which I've placed on top of my handbag, and I immediately regret reading it.

My stomach drops, my face turns as white as the tablecloth, and I begin to shake. I'm going to lose my french fries. I want the floor to swallow me up right here in the middle of Le Midi bistro.

> @ClementineL's blog, Bonjour Girl, is a total fake-ass disaster. Don't bother reading it. It's a waste of your precious time.

OUCH. That really hurts. I feel a sharp pain in my stomach; it's a combination of embarrassment, shame, and fear. I should have seen this coming. I change my mind. I need to a) have that glass of red wine, b) contact Jonathan's lawyer friend, and c) find a way to stop the cycle of hell.

Fashion school is full of glitz and glam and much hoopla. But sometimes it has a dark side. And I'm about to go to war against it.

Chapter Twenty-Nine

JUST BECAUSE YOU'RE ANGRY doesn't mean you have the right to be cruel. A lady is never cruel ...

This is one of the pearls of wisdom I read in Cécile's etiquette book. The truth is I want to respond nastily to Stella, say something really harsh because I'm hurting inside. When will her cruelty end? Should I file a harassment complaint? All I know is that my heart can't take this anymore. I feel depleted and weak.

I show Jonathan the tweet. I need help deciding what to do.

His eyes bulge. He looks really pissed off and he pounds his first on the small bistro table, making our neighbours stare.

He grabs my phone from the table and takes a screen shot of the tweet. "Evidence ... you'll need it."

"Right." I'm glad he thought of it. I'm still too much in shock to even think about these things.

"You can't let this go on, Clementine. I'm not going to sit here and watch Stella destroy your reputation. You need to consult with my friend. It's non-negotiable. I want you to call her today."

I respond with a tepid half-smile. "Okay." I was so happy about all the positive feedback I got on my blog in the last twenty-four hours, and then our shoot this morning — now this feels like a bucket of ice-cold water. But what I am supposed to do with a lawyer? Sue Stella? The news will spread like wildfire at school and make *me* look like the villain. I feel trapped.

"Stephanie might have some ideas. She's super smart," Jonathan says after taking a sip of water. The way he says this makes me feel uneasy. I'm feeling really insecure right now and I hate this feeling.

He notices the sadness in my eyes. "You can't let Stella get you down. What you need to do is get *her* where it hurts …" he says, his voice trailing off. I can tell his mind is spinning. "Doesn't she own some kind of business?"

"Uh-huh. Fashion decals. It does brilliantly well apparently," I say, showing him Stella's company's Instagram profile with close to a hundred thousand followers. I'm disgusted.

"Maybe she uses unethical business practices to get clients and followers. Have you thought of that? It sounds as though she's capable of anything."

"I guess …" The thought of doing research about my nemesis's business makes me want to gag. "I'm not sure where to look."

"The beginning is always a good place." He winks.

"What do you mean?" I ask, confused.

"Maybe *she's* guilty of the exact thing she's accusing you of …" he says, like a private investigator with a hot tip.

"Wow. I never thought of that. You're brilliant!" I say, grateful for the advice. This man really does have everything.

I move in closer and our noses practically touch now. I lower my voice to match his whisper. "The investigation is officially under way. And it'll be conducted with tact, class, and style." I slip on my Ray-Bans and look down over the top of them to add a faux air of mystery and Jonathan laughs at my silly move. He pokes my nose playfully. I stare at his lips — those luscious lips. For a brief instant, I forget about the bullying.

Just when we're about to kiss, a booming voice I recognize comes through from the street. I turn my head and see Jake standing at the restaurant window holding his iPhone high above his head. There are drops of sweat trickling down his forehead and both sides of his face. He looks flushed and out of breath and he's using his purple silk scarf as a *mouchoir* to wipe his face. I already know what this is about. I guess he interrupted his own lunch date to come and alert me.

"OMG, CLEM, THE FREAKING BITCH IS AT IT AGAIN! Can you believe this crap?" he shouts, and I want to run into the kitchen and hide. Now the entire bistro knows about my predicament and every customer's appetite has been killed. *Au secours.*

"What are we going to do about this?" Jake is still shouting across the room.

I can feel the awkward silence fall upon the room as dozens of eyes stare at me, including Ellie's. Mortified, my face turns a deep burgundy. This is quite *à propos*; my French heritage kicks in and I turn to Jonathan to ask the only logical question under these circumstances.

"So, where's that glass of red you offered?"

> Being a lady is a state of mind. A lady is calm and never loses her cool. This is the direct result of her inner confidence. Confronted with a stressful situation, she always tries to maintain a state of grace …

Maintain a state of grace? After being bullied by Stella and embarrassed by Jake in the middle of a room filled with Parsons faculty? Nice try, Cécile, but it isn't working.

I signal at Jake to stop shouting. I wish he'd be more discreet. But I remind myself of his intentions. I know he means well and it's comforting to have a friend who cares about me so much.

Jonathan waves Jake over to our table and orders him a sparkling water with a twist of lime so my friend can cool off.

"Where's Adelina?" I ask after he takes a seat.

"She's at the restaurant. I had to run here and see you. This is more important than lunch!"

Given that food is at the top of his priority list, I'm grateful he interrupted his lunch date for me.

I share our strategy. Within seconds, Jake's face lights up like the Christmas tree at Rockefeller Center.

"Oooh, I like it! Let's get on this investigation, pronto! I'm sure you'll dig up dirt on that douchebag of a girl," Jake says, looking ready for action, but he needs to calm down.

"Not so fast. We need to think things through. We don't want to lose our scholarship money, now do we?" I cock an eyebrow to drive the message home.

"Right. Good point," Jake responds. I know he doesn't like to be told to tone down his enthusiasm but I need to make sure things don't get out of control.

"I think we should get ahold of her school records. See what we can find in there," Jake says, rubbing his hands together. "How about asking Maddie for some help?"

Hmmm. I'll admit that the thought *did* cross my mind but I hesitate to involve her in this. She'll tell me to lodge a formal complaint against Stella, and that's the last thing I want to do.

"I'm not sure we should get Maddie involved."

"If you say so, Clem," Jake responds, but I'm not sure he gets it. He's really taking these Twitter slights to heart. Jake did admit to being the butt of some hurtful jokes in high school. That would explain why he's taking my battle so personally.

"How about using your charming persona to get some info from your pals at school?" Jonathan asks Jake. "I'll do some online sleuthing on my end and let you guys know what I find. Don't forget to call Stephanie, okay?" He looks at me and I know he means it.

"I'll call her. I promise."

"I have to go." Jonathan stands to leave. "Sorry, I have a meeting. Let's talk later." He bends down for a quick kiss and throws some money on the table. I can't believe this supposed romantic lunch turned into a strategy session for investigating Stella.   .

Jonathan disappears into the busy street and Jake watches him go.

"What a catch. He's totally dreamy, Clem," Jake sighs.

"I know. I have to pinch myself. My problem is that I worry it won't last, what with all the gorgeous women running around campus. And with all my personal drama …"

"Oh stop that! Who put those terrible thoughts into your head?"

"YOU DID!" I say, punching him on the shoulder.

"So, who's Stephanie?" Jake asks, switching to Jonathan's seat.

"A lawyer friend. He thinks she can help me."

"A lawyer? Really? Wow, he's taking this to the next level. I like it. Let's call her now."

"No way! Not from here! I'll call her later from a quiet place," I say. I refrain from telling him that he's one of the main reasons this place is so loud.

"It sounds like it means a lot to Jonathan that you call her. He wants to help, Clem. And so do I."

"I know. I *really* appreciate that. I really do. I'm just bummed out about the negative publicity this will bring my blog, and just as it was starting out so well."

"You know what they say …"

"No such thing as bad publicity?"

"Right on, kiddo." He dives into my remaining fries.

"You can have them all. Stella killed my appetite."

"Don't mind if I do."

"I'll just sit here and watch you eat and think about what to do next."

Jake slips on his large vintage shades while finishing my lunch, looking the most intriguing of us all.

Chapter Thirty

I ENTER MADDIE'S office quietly. She's on the phone so I tiptoe discreetly around her desk and take a seat in one of the two visitor chairs in her office. I reach for a jar on her desk and pop a sugar-free gummy bear into my mouth. It's late afternoon and I guess I'm hungry after all, since Jake ate my lunch.

The space reflects her style: whimsical sculptures acquired during her trips abroad, fashion runway photographs, piles of books, sketches of fashion collections — some her own and some her students' — carefully hung behind her desk, and lots of fresh flowers in pretty Murano glass vases.

A love of things retro runs in our blood. She owns one of those vintage phones with a rotary dial and a spiral cord in bright cherry red. She's sitting in her white leather chair facing the windows looking out to Fifth Avenue, twirling the cord with her index finger. I feel a pang of envy. She's made it to the top. I hope I do, too. It's the reason I'm here: to protect my interests so I can move on gracefully with my project.

She turns to face me. My visit comes as no surprise; I texted her after leaving the bistro to let her know I'd be dropping by with questions. She smiles and winks conspiratorially while she finishes her call. She's wearing a gorgeous barrette in her hair that contrasts nicely with her green eyeglasses. The numerous bracelets on her wrists make a tingling sound while she plays with the phone cord.

Maddie has no clue why I'm here. Although I don't want to drag her into this, aside from Jake she's the only person on campus I trust. I'll admit it feels wrong to try and dig up some dirt about a classmate, but I finally caved in and told Jake I'd ask. Apparently, it's for my own good.

"So sorry, Clementine. It was the dean from a sister school in Europe. We're trying to organize an exchange program for some of our top students next year. It's taking a lot of convincing but we'll get there."

"That sounds like fun." Maybe I should apply. It might be my only option for getting as far away from Stella as possible.

"So, what's up?" Maddie asks, making her chair twirl as she talks.

"Remember when I told you about Stella, the girl who tweeted nonsense about me?"

"Of course. Don't tell me she's at it again?" She lowers her stylish glasses to the tip of her nose and stares into my eyes.

I look down at my shoes, embarrassed to admit it. I feel helpless. Should I deny it? Pretend like nothing happened, brush it under the carpet? Under Maddie's unflinching gaze, I have no choice but to admit the truth. I can tell she already knows the answer.

"Yes, she keeps tweeting about me. And now it's about my blog," I admit, holding back tears. It's not easy to act as if it doesn't matter when it really does.

"Really? Okay, Clementine. That's enough already. I'm calling her into my office for a meeting. This needs to stop."

"No! Please don't do that. It's not why I came to see you. I'm no tattletale. I just want some information ..." I say vaguely. I know it sounds ridiculous and now I regret coming to her.

She looks at me with her big eyes, puzzled, and raises an eyebrow. "What kind of information?"

"I'm trying to find out whether Stella's done something like this before. Or worse ..."

Maddie shakes her head. "What are you up to, young lady? I hope you won't lower yourself to her standards. You know that two wrongs don't make a right, right?" I can hear my father's voice echoing in the back of my mind, giving me the same speech. I know my mother would approve of my sly sleuthing tactics, though. She'd be all over Jonathan and Jake's revenge plot. She might also be all over Jonathan, period. I brush these negative thoughts aside; it's no time to think about that.

"I'm sorry, Maddie. I shouldn't have asked you for anything. I just want to understand why she keeps attacking me like she does."

Maddie takes a deep inhale, then sighs. "You know I can't share personal student information with you. All student records are confidential. I could lose my job, Clementine." She looks offended and I feel terrible for putting her on the spot. "All I can say is Parsons is very strict about its code of conduct. We expect nothing but exemplary behaviour from our students." I don't have Cécile's etiquette book with me but I doubt a lady asks a relative to conspire with her to commit an illicit act. What was I thinking?

"This is a terrible mistake. Forget I asked." I stand up to leave.

"Wait, Clementine, I have an idea." Maddie softens, seeing the distraught look on my face. "How about this: I'll ask around to see whether other teachers have dealt with her before; they might know something."

I smile gratefully. "Thank you. That means a lot." Since we're behind closed doors, I give her a hug. "Don't worry about me. And whatever you do, don't tell my father. He'll send me back to France!"

Maddie laughs. "Okay, I promise." She crosses her heart. "I'll let you know what I find out."

As soon as I leave Maddie's office, I nearly run into Ellie, who's standing in the hallway. Her looming presence startles me.

"Hey," she says.

"Hello, Ellie," I say flatly. This can't be a coincidence; she's clearly following me around.

She looks around the empty hallway before nodding for me to come over to her side. I hesitate; it feels like we're involved in some kind of drug transaction.

"I have what you're looking for," she whispers.

"What? What do you mean?" I'm not sure what she's getting at but I feel a tinge of both fear and excitement.

"About Stella. I know something … that could take her down."

My eyes become as big as saucers. I stare at her incredulously for a few seconds before I crack a half-smile. This is interesting. "Really? What do you know?"

"Follow me."

"Where to?"

She doesn't answer. She just stares at me with those heavily made-up eyes. Can I trust her? I have some doubts, major ones. But I need to decide in a split second whether I'm prepared to play her game and take a risk.

I replay Maddie's words in my mind: *In this school, we expect nothing but exemplary behaviour.* I may be putting my future at Parsons on the line by following Ellie but for some reason, my inner rebel kicks in. This is New York City and it's time to live dangerously. I have risk-taking in my lineage, particularly on my mother's side. Besides, my self-respect demands it.

"Okay, Ellie. Show me what you've got. Let's go."

Chapter Thirty-One

AS I FOLLOW ELLIE down the hall, it hits me that she's not only mysterious, but mesmerizing, too. Today she's wearing a shimmering purple caftan made of gauzy, ethereal material over skinny black jeans, with biker boots, black liquid eyeliner, and hot-pink lips. The look is disco witch and I admit she wears this funky style well. She's an unlikely mix of danger, aloofness, and zen attitude all mixed into one.

Perhaps I was wrong about her. Considering my recent indecent behaviour at some nightclub downtown, she may be more of a lady than I am. The fact that she's looking out for me makes me wonder even more if I've misjudged her.

I follow Ellie up two flights of stairs and through numerous doors and hallways. I can tell we've reached a different department of the school's administration and can't help but wonder where she's taking me and what she has up her designer sleeve. One thing's for sure: I'm intrigued by her audacious ways.

Ellie walks quickly and I have a hard time keeping up. Once we've raced through one last set of doors, she looks around before entering a room. She nods for me to follow.

Instinctively, I know we're in a space students are forbidden to enter. I'm not 100 percent sure, but from the filing cabinets lining the walls, my guess is we're in the room where all of Parsons' student records are kept.

I get a chill down my spine at the thought of being caught in here — I know Maddie would never forgive me for this. I shake my head and point toward the exit but Ellie swiftly grabs my wrist and stares into my eyes with her deep, penetrating gaze.

"What's wrong?" she whispers under her breath. "Got cold feet?"

"We shouldn't be in here. We should leave. I have too much to lose."

"Excuse me? And I don't?" Ellie retorts, her eyes bulging. She looks menacing and I don't know what I fear most: Ellie's wrath or Maddie's scorn. I'm in serious trouble now.

"Listen, Clementine. I know what I'm doing. I know this must be hard, but you need to trust me. This is no time to back down, okay?"

She turns around briskly and puts her index finger to her mouth as we hear footsteps on the other side of the door. I get more chills down my spine — but this time it's not fear. It's more like exhilaration. I guess Ellie is right — it's no time to back down.

After a few seconds, she reaches into a tall metal filing cabinet and pulls out some folders with the ease of a secretary in a legal office. Clearly, she knows her way around.

My mind spins. Has she gone through my personal files, too? What information has she uncovered about my family that could leave me exposed and vulnerable? I start to panic. *Again.*

"What are you doing, Ellie?"

"Shhhh. Let me find it first." She waves me away.

I imagine the worst: Parsons calling my parents to let them know I've been expelled. Me on the streets of Paris, begging for euros with a paper cup. The image is too much to bear.

"We shouldn't be in here, Ellie. These files are confidential. I've changed my mind. I want out of this plan of yours."

"Really? I don't think you do," she mutters while flipping through some files. Her eyes stop on a particular folder while I just stand there, hands on my hips.

The suspense is killing me. I'm tempted to open the cabinet myself to see what she's looking at. But something deep in my gut stops me.

"So, what is it?" I ask.

She sighs loudly, her dark bangs fluttering over her wide forehead. I read somewhere that large foreheads are a sign of great intelligence, which would mean Ellie knows what she's doing. But does she? More importantly, what the hell am *I* doing?

Ellie looks exasperated by my lack of confidence. "If you need to know, these are students' final projects, collections, and presentations from the last five years. Along with all the teachers' comments and final grades," she adds nonchalantly without lifting her head.

Oh man. My mind races. I frown. I'm about to tell Ellie again that I'm leaving when we both hear a door opening and footsteps coming our way. She shoves the folder back into the cabinet.

My heart in my throat, I hide with Ellie behind a tall bookshelf. We stare at each other in silence, trying to keep out of sight of the small window in the door. We're so close I can feel her breath on my face. She looks right at me, and I'm pretty sure I recognize honesty in those heavily made-up eyes. I exhale from deep in my belly.

When whoever made the footsteps is out of earshot, Ellie rushes back to the cabinet and pulls out a manila folder. She opens it up and hands it over to me with a glint in her eye.

"Why are you showing me this? It's empty."

"My point exactly. *Voilà.*"

"What do you mean, *voilà*?" I ask, getting impatient. Is this a joke?

"Take a look at the name on the folder. Then look it up on your phone. You'll have all the answers you need."

The name on the file is Brian Kim, and underneath his name it says *Foreign Student – South Korea.* I take a deep, exasperated breath and type his name into the tiny browser on my phone.

My eyes nearly jump out of their sockets. I can't believe what I'm looking at: the young Korean is selling a collection of cool decals to accessorize sneakers, handbags, jeans pockets, phone covers, hats, and other fashionable accessories.

There are numerous photos of his work in neon colours and links to fashionable Asian blogs and magazines. From what I can read on his website, it looks as though he was a finalist for a prestigious prize, too.

The work looks identical to Stella's collection. Or is it the other way around?

"Wow. So why is the folder empty? When was he studying here?"

"He was here three years ago. As for the documents, take a wild guess."

It's got to be Stella. I can't believe that Jonathan was right on about this: she's guilty of the very thing she's been accusing me of: being a fraud.

I high-five Ellie and she smiles for the first time since we met — a gorgeous, riveting smile. Never mind lady, Ellie just made it to the status of queen in my book.

The question is, what will I do with this new information?

Chapter Thirty-Two

I SHOULD BE on cloud nine.

I just uncovered some dirty deets about Stella that will put me in the driver's seat. The tables are about to turn. No more putting up with her bullying. I also did some more online research this weekend about Brian Kim. His business is more than thriving in Asia — it's on fire. He sells his patches online to clients all over the world. This is reason enough for him to want to shut down Stella and her copycat business. I take a sip of sparkling water and grin at Jonathan while he peruses the menu.

I'm sitting across from him at La Ripaille, one of the oldest restaurants in the West Village. According to Jonathan, its owner scours local markets for the freshest produce, choosing the day's specials based on his finds.

The restaurant itself is beautiful, with a lovely terrace and a fireplace in the back. Candlelight at each table accentuates French posters on the walls, and there are fresh flowers throughout the room. In one corner, an antique clock from 1846 is set to the opening time of the restaurant. I find it all super charming.

But even the best plans are subject to unexpected twists of fate. Our idea of a romantic dinner changed abruptly when I told Jonathan and Jake what I discovered in the student archives.

Jake wanted to discuss the matter *tout de suite* after I texted him and Jonathan the details. We couldn't get together immediately since Jonathan was busy at work, so Jake invited himself along to our Sunday-evening dinner date. He's sitting right between us in front of the roaring fireplace. I can tell Jonathan is a little annoyed, but, ever the gentleman, he's playing it cool for my sake. This makes him an even sweeter guy in my eyes.

I look at Jake digging into his plate of foie gras, and it makes me chuckle. I can tell he's excited, but whether it's about the food on his plate or what I told him about Stella, I'm not sure.

"So, when are you going to tell the whole world that Stella is a freakin' fraud?" Jake asks with a wry smile. I know that if he were in my shoes, he would've sent out a press release about Stella by now.

I pick up my glass and take a long sip of Perrier.

"I'm considering my options carefully. I don't want any of this to reflect negatively on *Bonjour Girl*."

"Whatever you say, madam girl-boss," Jake says jokingly. The truth is that finding out about Stella has made me even more determined to succeed in my new online venture. I know I have an original concept that showcases talented and creative people who shine from the inside, unlike Stella. And it's something the world needs right now.

Pumped up by my discovery, I spent all of yesterday and last night holed up in my room, searching for fascinating people to interview for my blog. And boy did I find a gold mine, including a young woman who creates handbags made from Pakistani cotton woven by local artisans.

I sent her questions via Skype and she answered them by the next morning. I uploaded my new post as soon as I finished it and the feedback I've already received today has been amazing. I even got a message from an eco-conscious fashion brand offering to send me samples. I just can't believe my luck.

"Ellie sure did a one-eighty on us, didn't she? Can you believe that girl? What a badass," Jake says, taking a sip from his sparkling water. He isn't drinking any wine either — he's heading back to school later to work on his collection.

"You can say that again," I say. "She's on our side. I guess it took a while for her to show her true self."

"But what's her motive?" Jonathan asks, reaching for a piece of bread. He doesn't seem as willing to trust Ellie as Jake and I are.

"What do you mean?" I ask. "She's one of the good ones. I was wrong about her."

"Pfft — you don't actually believe she's doing this out of the goodness of her heart, do you?" Jonathan asks, frowning at me. I guess he thinks I'm being naive. This is disappointing. Why can't we all be on the same page?

"Yes, I honestly do. I know it's crazy after how weird she's been but I trust Ellie now. I think she's trying to help." I don't like my intuition being called into question.

"That's not what you told me when she made fun of your outfit in front of the entire class," Jonathan says. "You need to watch your back, Clementine. It could be a trap."

"You've got it wrong, Jon. I actually think Ellie changed her attitude toward Clementine when she heard about Cécile," Jake says in a loud whisper.

Jonathan stares at me quizzically. "Who's Cécile?"

I shrug. I guess I've been too busy complaining about my classmates and my parents to get to the older generations.

"My great-grandmother. She was kind of popular in certain Parisian circles," I say, trying to downplay the whole thing.

"Certain circles? WTF, girl? She was a muse to Madame Grès, one of the greatest female designers of all time!" Jake shouts, making me want to crawl under the table. People sitting nearby turn around and stare while the waiter rushes to our table to find out what's going on. I try to make Jake tone it down a notch by handing him a fresh piece of baguette but he ignores me.

"Really?" Jonathan looks at me, puzzled.

"Yes, it's true," I finally respond — deep down, I am proud to admit I have a fabulous ancestor. She gives me mental fortitude and inspiration.

"Why am I not surprised?" Jonathan says, shaking his head. "So that's where you get it from — all that style, elegance, and class." Jonathan reaches for my hand and I feel on top of the world again.

Jake rolls his eyes. Being the third wheel isn't easy.

I decide it's time to share some secrets with my two favourite boys. "Oh, and Maddie recently gave me a gift: Cécile's etiquette manual. It's filled with tips about being a lady."

"Oooh, I need to read that!" Jake coos.

"I've been following some of them lately and they've been working for me. So I've decided to apply some of them to Stella."

Jake puts down his fork. "So, what's the book suggesting you do now, darlin'?" He leans in conspiratorially.

I take a deep breath before responding. "To act with grace, tact, intelligence, and class."

"Pfft, that's it? That's a bit boring, don't you think? What else does the book say?" Jake asks.

"Well …" I say, trying to determine whether I should quote passages from the book. I decide against it; it's best to keep it simple. "Yeah, that's it. I have all the necessary resources to settle this with tact."

Jake shakes his head again. He's not pleased about this. At all.

"Jeez, Clem, I was expecting way more from you and Cécile. This kinda blows."

I can tell he's disappointed. He wants me to fight back, and hard. We've gone over this a gazillion times. It's getting exhausting. I'm losing my resolve to argue with my friend. Maybe Jake *is* right? Before I can say anything further, he gets up from the table, walks over to the waiter, and hands over his credit card in a huff. "What about self-respect?" he calls out from the front of the room. "Didn't Cécile teach you anything about *that*?" He makes a dramatic exit and runs off onto the street.

Jake's bold move leaves both Jonathan and me speechless.

Perhaps my friend is right and I should consider alternative points of view. We'll see which option I choose after consulting with the lawyer in the morning.

Chapter Thirty-Three

I WALK INTO the office of Jonathan's lawyer friend, Stephanie, and feel a sudden tightening in my chest. I can't explain why, but I do.

I really have no idea why I'm feeling this anxious. After all, I had a wonderful dinner with Jonathan yesterday. We were the last ones to leave the restaurant after the waiter politely indicated they were closing for the night. We stood outside the restaurant kissing for some time before hopping in a cab back to Brooklyn, where I insisted we go our separate ways. After the embarrassing club scene, I'm trying to cultivate an air of mystery and fan the flames of desire. I'm happy to report it's working.

Stephanie's lobby looks like the inside of a Ralph Lauren store. It's so refined; I wish I could crash here permanently and call this place my home.

Black and white photographs of runway shows and exclusive publicity campaigns cover the walls. These must be Jonathan's photographs — I recognize his signature style. That's how they know each other.

There are also lots of hardcover books lining the walls in an impressive display. I walk over, pull a copy of *The*

Great Gatsby off a shelf, and finger its gold-leaf pages. It reminds me how much I love to read and how little time I have for my favourite pastime these days. I sigh, remembering that this phase of my life is temporary and I'll get back to reading novels soon.

I try to remain cool, remembering that I'm also launching a fashion business and one day soon, I hope, I'll be in a position to afford my own chic office and my own legal advice. Until then, I need to be grateful for the freebies I get along the way.

I check in with the receptionist and take a seat in one of the low, modern chairs. I try to relax. After all, I'm here for a friendly legal consultation about a silly Twitter fight, not some major lawsuit. In the grand scheme of things, it's only cyber intimidation and I'll survive. Or so I hope.

One side of me feels terrible about digging up dirt on Stella. Is this the right way to fight back? I also feel bad for her — the fact that she doesn't have the wherewithal to find her own fashion concept makes me cringe. How could Stella not think that Parsons would find out sooner or later?

I wonder what kind of advice I'll get from Stephanie. Will she recommend that I send a formal demand letter to make Stella stop? Or that I just let things slide?

My thoughts are interrupted when a tall, slender young woman enters the room. She has long, dirty blond hair and the longest legs I've ever seen, and she's wearing a tartan dress, a black motorcycle jacket, and matching boots. She looks like a supermodel. This is not what lawyers typically look like.

I feel out of place in my bubble-gum-pink blouse and funky pineapple-print skirt, with a blue bandana in my hair. And I feel short — really short. I repeat a mantra I read in

Teen Vogue, "My body doesn't define me," over and over in my head as she struts my way. The mantra is supposed to help with my self-esteem issues. So far, it's not working.

"Clementine? Hello! It's so lovely to meet you!"

I nod. "Yes, thanks for meeting me. I really appreciate it." I shake her hand and it occurs to me that I probably look like a five-year-old next to this glamazon. I may as well be getting legal advice from Gigi Hadid. In other words, it feels weird. I know attractiveness doesn't cancel out brains but this creature is making me feel insecure again. Big time.

My body doesn't define me … My body doesn't define me …

"Jonathan told me all about you!" She flashes a megawatt smile.

All about me? Hmmm. What did he say? That I'm the victim of some silly cat fight on Twitter? Or that I made a complete fool of myself while dancing at some nightclub? I feel ridiculous and so very small. I want to hide underneath her expensive coffee table.

I follow her into her office and my heart drops again. The space is spectacular, with a view of lower Manhattan that most people only get to see in movies. She takes a seat behind her designer wooden desk, fresh cut flowers on either side of her. There are bouquets of white peonies and stacks of beautiful books everywhere.

I have hair, office, wardrobe, and flower envy. I try to remind myself of the lyrics to "Scars to Your Beautiful," Alessia Cara's song about self-image and loving yourself.

I try to push away my insecurities but it's hard. Why do I feel so worthless next to this woman? Is she triggering issues from my past? Most likely. And god knows, there are tons of those. Issues with my parents, especially my mother, who was so overbearing and competitive, and being betrayed by my first love. The list goes on.

My body doesn't define me … My body doesn't define me …

Come on, Clementine, you need to keep it together. Stephanie's doing you a favour and there's nothing to worry about. Is there? My mind fills with dark thoughts: she and Jonathan share similar taste in decor, fashion, and books. Who is this mystery babe and how did they meet?

"I hope you didn't have too much trouble finding my office. I know you study in the city," she says, flipping her hair back and leaning back in her chair. She's twirling an expensive Montblanc pen with her delicate fingers. I try to guess her age — she can't be much older than her mid-twenties. How could she have such an enviable legal practice so young? She must be super smart on top of it all. This woman totally won the gene-pool lottery.

My body doesn't define me … My body doesn't define me …

"It was no trouble at all. I live in Brooklyn," I respond coolly.

"Ah, that's perfect, then. So, what can I do for you?" Stephanie stares at me intently.

I freeze in my seat. I guess Jonathan didn't tell her my story. Now I regret coming here. The reason seems so juvenile. I feel a lump in my throat and I reach for my neck.

"Are you okay?" she asks, looking worried.

"Um, I think so. My throat is scratchy. It's nothing. I'll be fine."

"Let me ask my assistant to get you some water." Stephanie rushes out the door. I stand up and look out at the breathtaking view. Maybe this will help me calm down.

I take a deep breath and tell myself to be more confident — after all, Jonathan cares about me. He introduced me to his fabulous friend in order to help and I should be grateful, not act like a child. I need to follow Cécile's book and embody tact, elegance, and grace. Not so easy.

Staring out at the view, I cross my arms and try to imagine what it would feel like to reach this kind of success. I've heard of a visualization technique that helps you attract your deepest desires. I try to take a mental snapshot of the amazing view in my mind in order to attract it. I imagine *Bonjour Girl* employing a team of smart and talented women in a similar office. After a few seconds, I open my eyes. Unfortunately, what I see is far from desirable.

Sitting on a console by the window is a large paper agenda. I can't believe my eyes. Under tomorrow's date, in bold, red ink, are the words *dinner with Jonathan*.

My hand flies to my mouth. The room spins. My stomach clenches and my mouth goes dry. Scenes of my doomed relationship with Charles flash through my mind like the lights on a pinball machine. I'm going to faint. I grip the side of the console.

Stephanie walks in holding the glass of water and I take it from her, slug it back, and hand her the empty glass. And then I do what any sensible, classy lady would do in these circumstances.

I rush out of her office to call Jake.

"What's the matter, princess?" Jake says when he picks up. I don't know how he's guessed something is off, but he has.

He must have a sixth sense. I'm standing on the sidewalk outside of Stephanie's office, barely keeping it together. After the bullying, now this.

"Are you okay?"

Silence. Tears. Tight knots in the pit of my stomach. My heart jackhammering in my chest.

"Clementine? Are you there?"

Silence. I can't utter a word. I feel lost and confused.

"HELLLOOO? *Girl, talk to me!*"

More silence, muffled tears, and a lump in my throat.

The dinner date marked in Stephanie's agenda has completely thrown me. Is Jonathan dating her, too? Are they sleeping together? More importantly, what am I to him? A silly game? A cute side project?

All the self-doubt and pain caused by my ex and my parents' extra-marital affairs, and all the damage it caused our family, comes flooding back. The disagreements, the fights, the screaming matches — all left me feeling scarred and bruised. And all that baggage is coming back to the surface.

"Jake, um" — *sniff* — "can we … meet? Something came up with …"

"Let me guess. Pretty boy?" His tone is flat. I can feel the *I told you so* between the lines and this hurts even more because the reality is that he did tell me so.

"Mm-hmm."

"What happened? Just yesterday you guys looked like the only two people on earth."

"It's a long story. I'd rather tell you in person. There's room for interpretation."

"Interpretation?" I can tell I've piqued his curiosity.

"Yes, the situation is murky … and I need your advice. You're good at making sense of these things."

I can feel his smile across the line. He's happy to feel needed and is pleased with my compliment.

"I was on my way to a runway show. Why don't you join me?" he asks. "I promise it'll make you feel better."

I totally forgot it's New York Fashion Week. Jonathan told me he'd be busy shooting some of the runway shows. Now I know what other activities are keeping him busy this week.

I imagine him with her, dressed to the nines, attending the most sought-after fashion events this week, and it makes me sad. Honestly, Fashion Week is the last place I want to go to right now.

"That's not a good idea. Jonathan might be there — he's a fashion photographer, remember? I don't want to see him before I talk to you."

"Oh, stop it. He won't be. It's a runway show for plus-sized underwear. Trust me darling, this ain't his kind of gig," Jake responds, and I finally smile. He knows how to cheer me up. And there's a sliver of hope: I might find some interesting material for my blog.

"Okay, where is it?"

"Milk studios in Chelsea. I'll meet you there in an hour, pussycat. I'll save you a spot in the FROW."

"The what?"

"Oh, sorry, hon. In fashion-land, FROW is an abbreviation of 'front row,' which is just one too many syllables."

"All right. Got it. Thanks."

"Don't be late — you don't want to miss that sexy view."

I shut off my cell, hoping my mood won't be a total buzz kill for the cool FROW vibe.

I walk into the impressive white loft and my mood darkens again. The tall, white columns and concrete floors remind me of Jonathan. I try to push my negative thoughts aside to avoid ruining a big moment: my first New York runway show. I want to take it all in.

I text Jake and, with the help of a PR intern, find my friend at his seat. We're sitting in the FROW thanks to Jake's budding friendship with the talented plus-size designer. Apparently this collection celebrates women whose sizes fall outside of the fashion industry's typical size range. Beauty from outside of the mainstream is sweeping the runways; the time for massive change has come. Despite my broken heart, I'm thrilled to be here.

Jake went all out today: he's wearing a shiny black bomber jacket and black jeans, and has accessorized his look with oversized red glasses and a polka-dot man bag. The look is playful. I just wish I was here under more positive circumstances; it's the kind of event I've dreamt of attending for years. And here I am with my heart in my throat, ready to burst into tears — not the best timing.

I look around and recognize some familiar faces: famous editors, bloggers, and some celebs. This kind of show is refreshing. When it comes to anything beyond a sample size, the fashion industry still has a long way to go, and the fact that some famous bloggers are here sends a hopeful message about body positivity. I plan on being part of the revolution. Once I've resolved my personal issues.

"So, what's up, babe?" Jake asks as soon as I take a seat. "Tell Uncle Jake everything."

"Well, um, remember the lawyer Jonathan wanted me to meet?"

"Yup. Trouble, I assume?" Jake says casually while flipping through the show program. I can tell he's excited about this collection and I know why: the designer is a Parsons MFA alum who won many prestigious prizes and received the same scholarship as Jake for social innovation.

"Indeed," I say, keeping my eyes locked on my cellphone. Jonathan has tried me calling me a few times, presumably having talked to Stephanie. The last thing I want is to talk to him right now. "I think Jonathan is dating her."

"WHAT?" He swivels his head toward me. "Are you joshing me?" But for some reason, his reaction doesn't seem authentic. Does Jake know something I don't?

"I came across a note in Stephanie's agenda about them having dinner plans tomorrow night. Jonathan never mentioned anything. It's just plain weird. And upsetting. She looks like a Victoria's Secret model, for god's sake."

"Ohhh."

Silence, more doubt, more stomach cramps, and more inner turmoil. My mantra has lost its power. I've stopped reciting it.

"Listen, maybe she's an *ex*-girlfriend and they're just friends now?"

"I doubt it." I shake my head.

"Why would he want you to meet her? That *is* weird." Again, his response seems understated. Usually Jake goes for way more drama. This time, I wish he would.

"I don't understand it either. How could he be so insensitive? It doesn't jibe with his personality. He's been so thoughtful to me. I'm sad, Jake. Especially after Stella's bullying, too. Is the whole world ganging up on me? What should I do?"

"First of all," — he brushes his fingers softly against my cheek — "I'm here for you, munchkin. So never forget that. Secondly, you should probably ask Jonathan about it before jumping to conclusions. And the good news is that you can do it now because he's standing right in front of you." I turn and see Jonathan, looking haggard, his creased linen shirt falling out of his jeans. His hair looks wild and his complexion pasty. Beads of sweat run down the sides of his beautiful face. "I've been looking everywhere for you," he says.

Jake gets up from the bench, nods to Jonathan, and waves for him to take his seat. Instead of bitching about my boyfriend and taking my side, Jake is in cahoots with him. *Merde*, what is going on?

Jonathan and I lock eyes for a moment and mine well up with tears. I want to fall into his arms and have him tell me what's going on but the lights go down, the music begins to play, and a voice over the loudspeaker tells us to take our seats. The show's about to begin.

"Clementine," he whispers. "I need to —"

He gets yanked away by an aggressive PR lady just as the music begins to play. I guess he was blocking the view.

I could run after him but I have no idea where he's gone and I'm in no mood to make a scene. I sit alone in the FROW as the lights go down. The models begin to strut their stuff in revealing black lingerie to David Bowie's

"Fashion," showing off their beautiful, curvaceous figures, but my mind is elsewhere. I want to know what's going on between Jonathan and Stephanie. And why did Jonathan contact Jake, or vice versa — how did he know to find me here? And where did they both go?

I pull out my cellphone and try to discreetly text Jake. I get no response. I try Jonathan. No response either. Within seconds, I feel a tap on my shoulder — it's the overzealous PR lady who, in no uncertain terms, tells me to turn off my phone. She stares at me menacingly so I put it on vibrate and shove it in my purse.

Although the show is entertaining and the pieces are breathtaking, being forced to sit here for more than twenty minutes feels like a lifetime. It's excruciating.

There must be a logical explanation to all of this. I imagine myself back into Jonathan's arms, lying on his couch, listening to jazz while he delicately plays with my hair.

My reverie is interrupted by the buzzing of my phone. It's a phone call from Jake. I look around to make sure the aggressive PR lady is out of sight, then answer the call under the watchful gaze of my seat neighbour, who looks worried for me.

"I'm about to jump off a frickin' bridge. Come find me now."

"Where are you?"

"Front entrance. This is urgent, kiddo. Future is on the line. I need you now."

He hangs up. Oh man, this is serious.

Just when I thought I couldn't endure any more drama. What the hell is going on?

I put my phone back into my pocket, take a deep breath, and straddle some knees to make it to the end of the bench. What could have happened to Jake in the last fifteen minutes?

The PR lady grabs my arm and shows me some teeth.

"How dare you get up from your seat before the finale?" she whispers loudly, making more of a scene than is necessary. "And *who* are you? I'll see to it you never make it in this industry!"

"Ha! Lady, that's just fine because at this point, I want nothing to do with it!" I retort and pull away from her tight grip.

I rush to the elevators but they've stopped on another floor. There's no time to waste so I rush to the far end of the building and down the stairs.

I make it, out of breath, to the lobby, where I find Jake sitting on the floor looking like a complete mess. For the first time since we've met, he looks sullen. He's taken off his hipster glasses. He rubs his eyes with his knuckles. It looks as though he's been crying.

"What's wrong?"

"It's gone. All of it."

"What is?"

"My collection."

"What do you mean?" I can't believe my ears.

"Someone stole it from the studio after I left to come here. I just want to fucking DIE."

"What? How'd you find out?" I ask, completely beside myself. I start to mindlessly bite my nails — never a good sign.

"One of my pals from the studio texted me just after the show started. She looked everywhere for my stuff. I had left it on some mannequins. But it's gone. ALL OF IT! FINITO! *TERMINÉ!*"

"This is horrible!" I pace the hallway frantically. I'm trying to make sense of it all while I try to pull myself together. "Who would do such a thing?"

"They took everything, Clementine. Including my mother's sewing kit and the costume jewellery I borrowed from a supplier." His face falls into his hands and he begins to bawl his eyes out.

I feel helpless. Then I remember something my father used to say: *When you reach the end of your rope, tie a knot in it and hang on.*

"I'm calling Maddie."

"Wait! Stop!" Jake places his glasses on the tip of his nose and gets up off the floor. At least I got him to stand up and move. It's something. "I don't want any trouble! Or to lose my scholarship!"

"What? Why would you? Maddie has clout at Parsons. We need to get to the bottom of this."

He looks grateful that I'm offering to use my contacts but nods for me to put my phone away.

"Before you set off any alarms, I need to check out the studio myself first. To see the damage first-hand." He sounds like a hurricane survivor. I guess a violent storm has just passed through his heart.

I have a terrible feeling Stella has something to do with this. If she does, we'll make sure she gets what's coming to her. Her nastiness has to stop.

One thing's for sure: I don't need a fancy lawyer to help us find out. With Jake, I have all the audacity and courage I need to figure out this mess at my fingertips. Like my father would say, *just hold on, Clementine, hold on …*

Chapter Thirty-Four

I PUT MY PHONE back in my handbag. This whole thing has gotten ridiculous and exhausting — all the texting, the tweeting, and living in a digital universe. I know my career ambitions revolve around an online project, but the truth is I need a digital break. Real life involves interacting with real people and having real conversations. And despite the dread I feel about doing it, I'm about to have the conversation I should have had ages ago.

I put on my coat and head outside to grab a cab. With more determination than I've felt in days, I say, "I'm going to resolve this matter personally."

"What? What do you mean? Are you insane?"

"Yes, I may be a little bonkers, but I'm going to find out who stole your collection. No more lying, hiding, or backstabbing."

He looks taken aback by my sudden self-confidence.

"You sound like a total badass." He arches his eyebrows quizzically. "Okay, girlfriend, I'm following your lead. Let's do this."

We share a cab back to Parsons, holding hands the entire way. Jake doesn't say a word, which worries me a little. I pray we find out who took his collection quickly; I know how much this project means to him. Before we arrive, Jake finally admits that Jonathan called him after I ran out of Stephanie's office. Jake agreed not to tell me that Jonathan was coming to the show, knowing I would not have shown up. I nod gratefully but don't ask any questions. I can only deal with one thing at a time.

Once on campus, I suggest that Jake go find his studio buddy to get more detail about what she saw. I, on the other hand, am on a mission to find Stella. Most afternoon classes start in a half-hour, which gives me just enough time to locate her royal nastiness and find out whether or not she's behind this. Either way, we need to chat.

I walk through the basement cafeteria, where I see a few senior students and teachers, but there's no sign of her. I breeze through the library, study lounges, and secret reading corners — there's so sign of her there, either. Where could she be?

I then recall that she's into watching *Project Catwalk*, which is occasionally filmed on campus.

I decide to head to where they normally shoot. What have I got to lose? I walk briskly and approach the crew, and there's Stella in all her glory, wearing a pink and white gingham suit jacket, tight blue jeans, and towering heels. Her wild mane of jet-black hair bursts from the top of her head. It matches her temperament perfectly.

She's standing in the middle of her entourage, chatting away. I bet she's gossiping and spreading more vile rumours and negative vibes. I have no idea how she manages to have so many friends, what with her nasty mouth and unethical spirit. I give a loud, exasperated sigh.

She catches sight of me coming her way from the corner of her eye. She's obviously not happy to see me.

I zero in on her like a hawk. She stares at me and I nod for her to follow. I expect her to stick out her tongue or do something else super childish, so I'm surprised when she walks over, as though she never tweeted that gibberish about me.

"Hey," she says coolly, crossing her arms.

"Hey to you, too." I cross my arms to mirror her. I can tell she doesn't like it.

There's a long, awkward silence.

"So … is there something you want to talk about?" Stella asks, lifting her nose at me, clearly disturbed by my stoic presence.

I'm enjoying this moment immensely, seeing her squirm while I just stare. As a matter of fact, I'm getting a real kick out of it, so I stare some more. I resolve to hold back from referring to the Korean designer; I fear that might just finish her right here on the spot.

"Well, I should ask *you* that question, right?" I say finally. "You're the one who blasted me on Twitter. What did I do to deserve *that*?"

She pinches her lips. I can tell her mind is spinning. With what kind of nonsense, though, I have no clue.

"Oh come on, Clementine…. Don't take *me* for a fool. I know what you're up to. You want to make me look like the bad girl when in fact *I* caught *you* red-handed."

"Oh? Doing what?" I retort, hands on my hips. I can't believe she's spewing this delirious crap.

"You think you have such an original, highbrow concept for your blog, but the truth of the matter is that it's far from unique, girl. Your concept is *so* unoriginal," says Stella.

How dare she? She's the one lacking originality by copying another student's designs. This makes me fume with anger. I try to calm down, but it's not easy.

"Anyway, it seemed like you were taking yourself too seriously so I wanted to bring that to your attention," she says petulantly.

"So you thought you'd send me a little reminder," I say sarcastically. Her guile is beyond shameful.

Before I can say anything further, she pulls out her cellphone.

"Tsk, tsk, tsk. And I know what you're going to say about me and my business. But too bad for you, 'cause I have this." She shoves her cellphone in my face.

I can't believe my eyes. It's a picture of me going through the student records. It shows me hunched over a manila folder reading student files. The very file that shows that Stella is the fraud. I stare at her phone and want to throw up. She must have been the one we heard outside the room, waiting to take the photo as soon as Ellie got me into position. Then, I want to tear every strand of her hair out. Not very ladylike, I know.

"Is that legit behaviour? I don't think so," Stella says with disdain in her voice while wagging her finger at me.

This is beyond disturbing. Jonathan was right again. This was a frickin' setup and I was naive enough to fall for it.

I am consumed with anger. Ellie double crossed me and I was played for a fool. I'm so upset and tongue-tied I forget to bring up Jake's collection.

I decide to back off. Instead of sending her phone crashing to the ground, I remember Cécile's precious book and hand Stella her phone back, first and foremost to protect my own sanity and self-respect. There's simply no other option.

And then I walk away. Just like that. Because a lady cares more about maintaining her self-respect than about being right at all costs.

Chapter Thirty-Five

I'M SPEECHLESS, DUMBFOUNDED, and angry. I want to cry but no tears come out. I feel foolish for taking Ellie's bait and sad that she double crossed me. I thought I had finally seen the real Ellie. I sincerely thought she was on my side.

What a mistake.

What worries me the most is that it feels like my intuition is off base.

I decide to take the back stairs in case I turn into a blubbering puddle of tears on my way down. I've already suffered enough embarrassment as it is; I don't need any more. I need to stay strong if I'm going to survive this ordeal. I try to steady myself on the railing as I head down to the basement.

I guess both Jake and Maddie were right: New York is a ruthless place. And I feel knocked down. I had such high hopes of graduating from Parsons and becoming a renowned fashion writer. And I thought Jonathan would be my ally. Together, we'd travel the world, take fabulous photos of interesting people and fascinating places. My passion project would turn into a lucrative business, providing me with the creative freedom I so dearly crave and the ability to see the world with fresh eyes.

Despite its early success, I doubt my blog will go anywhere, especially if Stella keeps up her campaign of hate and lies. Maybe I should just give up.

I can't even imagine how I would tell my father. I managed to convince him to let me apply and to help me out financially, and now I'm going to give it all up? He'll think I'm a terrible daughter. But still, all I can think about is calling him so he can bring me home.

The effects of cyberbullying are really painful. Being on the receiving end of it has made me feel lonely, sad, and ashamed. But now I'm sure that Jake's been dragged into it too, and I can't imagine why anyone at school would do something so hateful to such a kind soul. I'm afraid to even face him and tell him what happened with Stella. He'll think I'm weak.

As I go down each stair, it feels as though cold, hard cement has been poured into my shoes. I think of a poem my father shared with me, one of his favourites by Emily Dickinson:

"Hope" is the thing with feathers –
That perches in the soul –
And sings the tune without the words –
And never stops – at all –

And sweetest – in the Gale – is heard –
And sore must be the storm –
That could abash the little Bird
That kept so many warm –

I've heard it in the chillest land –
And on the strangest Sea –
Yet – never – in Extremity,
It asked a crumb – of me.

I need to hang on to these words right now. I open the stairway door and see Jonathan sitting at a corner table near the cafeteria entrance. He looks completely distraught. My heart sinks seeing him looking this way. I approach him slowly and he turns to face me. He drops his large camera bag to the floor, rushes to my side, and scoops me up in his arms.

"Oh, Clementine." He caresses my hair and tears run down my cheeks. All of my sadness and anger come gushing out.

"Shhhh, please don't cry. Let me explain. It's not what you think, I promise …"

And with those comforting words, I feel a glimmer of hope come rushing back.

Chapter Thirty-Six

"WHERE DID YOU RUSH OFF TO? I looked everywhere for you after the show," Jonathan asks, holding my hand.

We're huddled together at the back of the school amphitheatre. We sneaked in here to find some privacy and I'm relieved we're finally alone. I probably look like a complete mess with my face stained with tears and mascara, but Jonathan doesn't seem to care and, frankly, right now neither do I. He gently caresses my face and brushes a strand of hair aside.

"Where have I been? What happened to *you* at Milk studios?" I ask, before getting to the real question I'm dying to ask, the one that may break my heart. I'll stall as much as I can. I don't want to feel more pain.

"I was thrown out on the street," Jonathan says, staring at his shoes. I haven't ever seen him look this beaten. I guess we're both in the same state of mind.

"By that wicked PR witch?" I ask. Her angry features are still engraved in my mind.

"Yeah. She was *totally* wicked," he says, nervously running his fingers through his sexy, messy hair. I'm dying to do that, too.

"I wasn't registered as an official photographer for the event so they threw me out. I couldn't even retrieve my bag from the coat check. I totally freaked out. I mean, my entire livelihood is in there."

"How did you get it back?" I point to his black bag on the floor.

"I had to beg for it. It was a real nightmare but I finally managed. Then I went back inside to look for you but you were gone." He takes off his jean jacket and there are traces of sweat on the sides of his shirt. I can tell he's had a rough day.

"Anyway, it's just a camera and a few lenses — it's not the end of the world. What's more important right now is telling you how much you mean to me, Clementine. I feel like such a jerk. I was worried sick I'd lose you."

My heartstrings are pulled in a million directions. Does he really mean it? Or is he saying this to make *himself* feel better? Before I can ask any questions, he moves in closer, stares into my eyes, and kisses me softly on the lips. My heart flip-flops and bangs hard against my chest. Instead of pushing him away and demanding answers, I let his soft, luscious lips linger on mine for a moment longer.

"I know what you saw in Stephanie's office," he finally says, breaking away but still holding my gaze. I try to look away but he keeps gently holding my face.

"The truth is that Stephanie has been helping me resolve some legal issues of my own."

This comes as a complete surprise. "Oh? What kind of issues?"

He sighs loudly and nervously runs his fingers through his hair. "Issues I've been ashamed to tell you about." He lets his face fall into his hands. "I met this model, Julia, on a photo shoot in Paris several months ago. We spent a week working together, and she turned on me. She became aggressive and demanded more money than I could afford to pay. When I refused to increase her fee, she became nasty toward every person working on the shoot and poisoned the work environment. It became so unbearable, I had to terminate her contract."

It's the reverse of what Jake warned me about. Jonathan isn't really a modelizer, he's just being harassed by one. I can tell this is really painful. I rub his shoulders gently. It sounds like we're facing similar issues.

"Since Stephanie and I share some clients in the fashion industry, she offered to represent me *pro bono*. She's doing me a favour. There's nothing going on between us, I swear. Just occasional meetings to go over things," he says.

"Why didn't you tell me? It's not your fault."

"I was worried you'd be upset with me. Who wants a crazy model suing her boyfriend for breach of contract? And what if your family finds out? Your mother is a famous opera singer in Paris and your family has connections in the fashion industry. Word gets around — it already has in some circles." His eyes are filled with tears.

I exhale a long sigh of relief and my entire body relaxes, as if I've taken off a pair of uncomfortable shoes. He's not dating her. He even calls himself my boyfriend. We'll get over this; we'll be all right.

I remain silent for a moment longer as thoughts swirl through my head. We're both the victims of bullying and manipulation. I let myself fall into his arms as a few tears run down his cheeks. I am genuinely touched by his earnest display of emotion.

With tears in my eyes, I decide it's time for me to admit my own dark secret. If he's being honest and vulnerable, then I should, too. I take a deep breath and break the silence to tell him about what's been eating at me for months.

"I'm sorry I jumped to conclusions so quickly. I shouldn't have assumed anything. I've been feeling insecure and heartbroken a lot in the last year. I faced a major betrayal that scarred me deeply."

"Really? What happened?"

I feel a big, giant lump in my throat. What I'm about to share is so painful that my mouth goes dry and I begin to shake, just like I did back then when I saw them together. It's the kind of traumatic memory that gets frozen in your cells and triggers the same painful reaction each time you think about it. I tried discussing this with a therapist but it didn't help much. Leaving for New York was the best option for me to escape the pain and trauma.

"Whatever it is, you can tell me," Jonathan says, caressing my hair and squeezing my hand.

I try to look away again but he delicately places his fingers on my chin and forces me to look at him while I tell him everything.

"It's pretty horrible. I caught my ex-boyfriend kissing my mother in our own home. Or maybe it was the other way around. Anyway, I was still with him at the time. It hurt like hell. I haven't been able to get over it or forgive either of them."

"Oh man, I'm so sorry, Clementine." He holds me while I continue to weep. It feels good to let it out. "He kissed your mom? What a jerk," he says.

"Mm-hmm. But it takes two to tango. My mother has a reputation for creating that kind of drama. He's not the only one to blame in this mess."

"Did you talk it out with her?"

"We tried. She said it was an innocent flirtation, just a 'momentary lapse of reason.'" I use air quotes. It still cuts to the bone just thinking about it.

"She sounds like quite a character."

"She is. Thankfully, my father is more grounded and mature. He's managed to keep the family together. Apart from an affair with his employee a few years ago."

"Wow, your family's been through a lot. Does he know about your mother and your ex?"

"No. I haven't been able to tell him. It breaks my heart just thinking about it. I broke up with Charles and I've been trying to move on. It's not easy."

Instead of asking more questions, Jonathan squeezes me close and holds me tighter. His embrace is soothing and it brings me peace. We stay like this, cradled in each other's arms, until my phone makes a pinging sound. I don't look at it. I already know what to expect: more crap.

I finally get up from my seat and reach for Jonathan's arm, and we leave the auditorium holding hands. It's time to show the world what we're made of. No longer will we be fearful, easily manipulated, or weak.

Chapter Thirty-Seven

I MEET JAKE DOWNTOWN at Sigmund's Pretzels on Avenue B, one of his favourite New York hangouts.

It's renowned for its impressive handcrafted pretzels made from organic flour. According to Jake, the best flavours are cinnamon, truffle, and cheddar. Personally, I prefer French baguettes and pastries but I'm willing to give the pretzels a try.

I can tell Jake is heartbroken — he has three giant pretzels in front of him with a gallon jug of iced tea.

He sees the look of concern on my face.

"Churro pretzels with raspberry jam are my new therapy."

I crack a half-smile, taking a seat next to him and patting him on the back. I get it, I really do. I've done it, too. In my case, it involves eating an entire box of macarons or a giant Toblerone. Our vices kick in at the worst of times.

I'm dying to tell Jake that Jonathan and I made up, that his dinner with Stephanie was strictly business to solve a legal issue, but this isn't the time to mention it. Jake wants to talk and I'm here to lend an ear.

"Have you told the Parsons faculty about what happened?"

"Nope. Not yet. I was hoping to handle this myself. I've searched every corner of our campus, Clem. I swear. I didn't say anything 'cause I don't want to lose my scholarship. What if Parsons asks me to give the money back? I really can't afford to ... I spent all of it on fabrics and accessories and my new website."

"Why would they do that? Honestly, I doubt the school would hold you accountable. It's not your fault they have thieves on campus," I say.

"Right." He tears off a piece of pretzel and pops it into his mouth. Clearly, I haven't managed to calm his anxious mind. "But the school might think it was negligent to leave my things unattended."

"Unattended? Don't you keep everything under lock and key?"

"Nope, not this time I didn't. I was late for the runway show so I left my work on the mannequins. I guess someone happened across the unlocked door and took it all. I'm so pissed off at myself for doing that. You have no idea."

"What about your studio pal? Could she have taken it? Do you trust her?"

"Yes, I do. She's far more talented than I am. She'd never take my stuff. I just regret telling anyone about my concept. I was so excited about the idea that I told people in my design class. I should have kept my big freaking mouth shut."

Listening to Jake talk about his predicament, it hits me that this is also what harassment does to you: it plays tricks on your mind and makes you think *you're* at fault when in fact you're just the victim. It's hurtful and damaging and detrimental to your self-confidence and mental health. It just sucks.

"I made some progress on our investigation. Nothing substantial yet, but I think I'm on the right track," I say.

Jake drops his snack on the counter and wipes his fingers with his napkin. "Really? Whose ass is getting kicked?"

"She didn't admit it outright, but my gut tells me that Stella is behind this."

"Pfft, same shit, different day. Now *there's* a frickin' surprise!" His plump cheeks turn a deep burgundy red and I imagine steam coming out of his nostrils like a bull about to charge. "Do you have any clues?"

"My hunch tells me that she didn't do it herself. She's too much of a wimp for that. She likely got somebody to do it for her."

"Okay. What makes you think that, Ms. Agatha Christie?"

"She's trying to blackmail me."

"WHAAAT?"

"She has a photo of me snooping through the school archives. It was a trick, Jake; Ellie wasn't trying to help me. She's on Stella's side." How could I have let myself get caught up in this silly game?

"This shit is bananas. You're kidding me, right?"

"I wish I were." I reach for a piece of pretzel and dip it into the jam. The flavour explodes in my mouth. It makes me feel a little better.

"Stella has a huge entourage of mean girls that eat out of her hand. They'll do anything for her. She's a ruthless, conniving bitch. So if she's capable of rallying Ellie to her side, she's capable of stealing your collection."

"If you say so, darling. Ellie, though? That's a real downer."

"Yeah, tell me about it. I'm so angry at her for manipulating me. What a fool I was," I say, going for another bite of pretzel. These flavours are starting to grow on me.

"So, what do you think we should do?" Jake asks.

"How about we give Ellie a taste of her own medicine?" I say. I'm ready to turn the tables for once.

"YEAH!" He raises both eyebrows conspiratorially and gives me a fist bump. "Any ideas?"

"How about we catch her with the most powerful bait out there?"

"Which is …?" He cocks an eyebrow.

"Cécile and Madame Grès."

"Okay. Tell me what to do and I'm there," he announces, standing up from his chair.

"Where are you going? I haven't told you about my idea yet …"

"Ordering a pretzel for you. Before you finish all of mine." He winks.

He comes back with a cheddar-flavoured pretzel and I snap a photo of it for my Instagram page.

"Look at you, back on social media."

"It's about time, don't you think?" I shoot back, referring to my extended silence on Twitter. Although I've been sharing *Bonjour Girl* posts online, I haven't responded to Stella's hurtful comments. This probably makes me look weak.

"Well, you know what they say, sugar plum. Silence is golden and duct tape is silver. You're better off keeping your mouth glued shut. I didn't and look where it got me. Nowhere fast."

He takes a bite of his pretzel, whispers something about revenge under his breath, and smiles, something I haven't seen much of in the last few days. If I can help it, Jake will get his spark and his collection back. May I find the courage and solutions to make it so.

Chapter Thirty-Eight

I SIT IN THE Parsons library across from Jake. We're surrounded by thousands of books about design, art, and fashion. It's heaven, really. I dragged Jake here after class to follow up on our meeting at the pretzel shop.

Why? Last night, as I was looking for a book in Maddie's extensive library to help me with a school project, I came across a quote by French writer Victor Hugo. Its rough translation goes something like this: "To read a book is to see the light. Open it wide, let it shine upon you, let it work its magic." This sparked a flash of inspiration: maybe we can use books to find some creative ideas for responding to Ellie and Stella. Since Cécile's book has been so helpful already, I wonder if some of the answers that elude us can be found in fashion textbooks. Besides, it's fun to look, *n'est-ce pas?*

After I told him about my plan, Jake agreed that the answers to all of life's issues can be found by looking back into fashion history. He thinks we'll find helpful ideas in the Grès archives. I also have Cécile's etiquette book in my bag. Armed with both, I'm confident we will.

This whole ordeal has been a huge burden on my spirit, and I can't wait to get it over with so I can get on with studying, my relationship, and my blog. Thankfully, Jake brought a secret stash of gummy bears; he says it will elevate our mood and help us concentrate. I couldn't agree more.

After asking a charming librarian for help, Jake finds two copies of *Madame Grès: Sphinx of Fashion*. The librarian was curious as to why we needed them, as apparently this particular book has been borrowed a lot lately. Who would have guessed there would be so much renewed interest in this vintage designer?

Jake carries the books over to our table and asks me to speed-read through the first five chapters. He'll focus on the next five.

"I hope we find something …" he says, placing a pencil behind his ear and popping a blue gummy bear into his mouth. "I'm running out of patience."

"These books will help us with Stella and Ellie, I just know it," I say, trying to sound hopeful.

"Really? I think we're on thin ice here. We have no real proof Stella stole my stuff," he whispers. "Maybe we should just call it quits and let the school take care of it."

"Oh, stop it. We both know she's behind this. But why and how — that's what I want find out. Just focus on the book. Look for something out of the ordinary. Something that may lead us to motive." I say, sounding like a private investigator. The truth is, I have my own doubts about this plan. But I'm following my instincts, so we should just go with it.

"Okay, kiddo. If you say so. I'm on it." He pops a red gummy bear into his mouth and cracks open the large hardcover book. I follow his lead and do the same.

I read through a few pages and learn that Madame Grès was considered by fashion historians to be one of "the most important *couturières* of the post-war period." It's amazing to think that my great-grandmother was her muse. Wow. It's worth reading this book just to make this realization.

Apparently, the designer disliked her given name, Germaine Krebs, and replaced it with Barton, the surname of one of her first employers. It was only much later that she took on the surname Grès.

I keep flipping through the pages. They reveal that Madame Grès was a true modernist: she was independent and forward-thinking, and she created an identity shrouded in mystery.

This makes me think of Ellie — mystery and hidden agendas are her thing, too. I still can't believe she managed to fool me, though. What does she have against me? It makes no sense. I recall the look in her eyes when we came face to face in the archive room. I thought I recognized kindness and compassion. Boy, was I completely off base. What a joke and what a shame.

I keep reading and find out that, like today's young entrepreneurs, Grès displayed an early desire to strike out on her own. Yet, while Coco Chanel was a household name and a familiar face, Grès stayed out of the public eye. She wanted to remain enigmatic and do her own thing.

While Jake furiously takes notes for his haute-couture shenanigans, it hits me that even though school has barely begun, just about every student I know has made their pet project known one way or another. Everyone except Ellie.

Could this somehow explain her behaviour? Is she looking for a project of her own? Has she been following me around to copy my ideas? And could this be a motive for her to steal Jake's work?

"I think I'm on to something," I murmur. The words just come out of my mouth.

Jake's head pops up from his book. "Really? So soon? What'd ya find, darlin'?" He puts down his book and pencil, eager to share notes. "Bring it home to daddy."

"Well, um, nothing. That's my clue."

"Excuse me? Are you playing with me?"

"It's about Ellie. She's one of the few people in our class who hasn't declared a major project, right? My gut tells me it's because she doesn't have one. No collection, no creative concept. So she's leeching off others for ideas. Maybe she's pulling another Stella on us."

"Okay …" Jake says, twirling a pencil with his fingers. "So this explains what exactly? That she's in cahoots with Stella to steal my work?"

"I'm not sure but it's a possibility. Maybe Ellie and Stella are both copiers and are using us to get ahead? Ellie's following me around to steal my ideas and Stella is asking Ellie to cover up for her own copying. She knows that we're on to her, right? And maybe the two of them stole your stuff as a way to intimidate us?"

Jake stares at me as though I've just pulled a rabbit out of a hat. Or as though I'm totally losing it. I'm not sure which.

I reach for a gummy bear. The bag is almost empty. I gasp. Jake chuckles.

"You amaze me, Clem. I think this all makes sense. Good going. Now what?"

"It's just a theory," I whisper. I look around the room to make sure no one is eavesdropping.

"You're pretty damn smart, you know that?" He winks. "I'm sure glad I have you on my team."

"Thanks. I like to think I'm streetwise," I shoot back.

"You sure are. New York is working its magic on you, Clem. But answer this question for me: why would Stella or Ellie steal my collection? Wouldn't that be a stupid move on their part? Everyone knows it's mine, even the Parsons faculty."

"Unless they decided to throw it away to get rid of the competition," I blurt out, but I immediately regret it.

Jake's face drops and tears well up in his eyes as though I've just told him his sibling was thrown into the Hudson River. I should have kept my mouth shut with silver duct tape. What a mistake.

He stands up, throws on his jean jacket, and heads toward the exit in a huff.

"Oh yeah? I'm not going to sit around and LET THAT SHIT HAPPEN. We need to act now!" Jake shouts, making every head in the room turn as he walks out of the library. The librarian gives me a puzzled look and I give her a little wave, trying to avoid drawing further attention to myself. I grab my trench coat and follow him out the door under the confused gaze of dozens of Parsons students.

I couldn't care less about the awkward stares. I've gotten used to them. I just hope we're not too late.

Chapter Thirty-Nine

WHEN FORMER STUDENTS said Parsons was competitive, I never thought it could get this bad. I read blog posts written by alumni who complained it was challenging and I even watched their rants on YouTube. But never in my worst nightmares did I imagine I'd be the victim of so much hate. It's painful and makes me feel so vulnerable. I just wish this nightmare would end.

These are the thoughts going through my mind as Jake and I stand outside on Fifth Avenue waiting for Ellie. He's holding a cup of coffee in one hand and chewing on a stir stick. My heart is pounding wildly at the thought of confronting her. I feel betrayed and let down. I hope she doesn't try to pretend everything's fine or deny her role in this ugly mess. That would be insulting, and frankly I can't take any more. But apparently that's what bullies do; one day they're your friend, the next they become your enemy, and vice versa. The cycle is never-ending. But I'm about to put a stop to it.

Ellie's afternoon class ends at five and it's now ten to.

Jake takes a long sip of coffee and throws his cup into the trash. He stands next to me with his arms crossed, leaning against the wall. I know he's beyond pissed. He worked his ass off on his amazing collection and spent a big chunk of his scholarship money on quality fabrics, materials, accessories, and hiring someone to create a website. He put everything into making his dreams come true. Now there's a chance all that effort was for nothing. He looks haggard and even the rhinestones on his jean jacket lack their usual sparkle.

I put my phone away and see Ellie walking toward us. She's dressed in her typical dark attire: black jeans, a T-shirt, a silver jacket, matching earrings, and bulky military boots. She looks lost in her thoughts. Jake zeros in on her like a hawk. She must feel his gaze because she looks up and stops dead in her tracks when she sees us.

"Hey, Ellie, can we have a word?" Jake asks firmly.

"Um, sure. What about?" she responds, her voice cracking.

Jake rolls his eyes and sighs. "Oh please, stop your frickin' nonsense." He points his index finger at her metallic jacket. "I know *you* know what I'm talking about." He moves in closer, inches from her face. She holds steady but I can tell that she's intimidated. I can see that her right hand, the one holding her bag, is trembling. A sign of guilt? We'll find out.

"Okay." She stares down at her biker boots sheepishly. "We shouldn't talk here. Can we go someplace quiet?"

"Well" — Jake looks around before answering — "we sure as hell ain't going to the spa. What do you have in mind? The diner across the street?"

"No! That's way too close to school."

Jake and I exchange glances. The only quiet place we know around here is the Walker Hotel. "Okay, follow me. I know a place," I say, nodding toward 13th Street.

We walk in silence while Jake follows behind, his head hanging low. I just hope this conversation leads somewhere. My friend's morale depends on it. So does mine.

We enter the hotel lobby but this time I don't care about the chic decor; I have other things on my mind. We take a seat and Jake orders some coffees.

"I know what you're thinking," Ellie says quietly. "That I'm a liar and a double crosser. But I didn't sell you out, Clementine. Well, not intentionally, anyway." She fiddles with her napkin.

"What? What do you mean, not intentionally?" I ask. I'm secretly recording this conversation with my iPhone. Who needs Stephanie when you've watched tons of *Scandal* episodes on your laptop?

"Stella's has been on my back since the first day of school," Ellie admits. "It's just been a downward spiral of fucking misery." She lets her head fall into her hands.

Jake nods silently, sipping his second cup of coffee of the afternoon. He sure doesn't need it; he's wound up like a top. I just hope he doesn't get too excited. He tends to get out of control when he does. This could get really ugly.

"When you told me about your great-grandmother and Madame Grès, it gave me an idea for a school project. I starting thinking about creating my own version of those glamorous column dresses. I've been in love with them since I was a kid. I grew up watching old movies with Grace Kelly and Jean Shrimpton. I'm really into retro."

This is a bit surprising. The classic Grès look is so different from Ellie's personal style that I never would have guessed she liked it. This school is full of surprises and oddball characters.

"So, I got this idea — and I admit it was a lousy one — to look in the student archives to see if anyone else had done a modern reinterpretation of those classic dresses. To make a long story short, Stella and I came face to face in the student archive room."

"No way! You caught her in there? That's bonkers," Jake pipes up. I can tell his cappuccino is kicking in now.

I'm not surprised. Stella does what she wants and gets away with everything. Until now, that is. "What was Stella doing there?" I ask, raising my voice slightly so the tiny microphone on my cell can catch it.

Ellie looks around the room before responding. "Trying to destroy the files on the Korean designer whose decal collection she copied. I managed to catch a photo of her doing it, but she bullied me into keeping my mouth shut by threatening to tell the dean I was in there, too. And I feel like such a shit for it. When I took you to the student archives to show you the empty folder, I had no idea Stella was following us. Now she has evidence of both of us being in there."

"So, what the hell does she want from me? Why does she hate me so much?" I ask, totally beside myself. I feel anger boiling up inside but try to keep it together in case I need to share this taped conversation with anybody.

"She's intimidated by you and your blog. I guess something you said or did made her feel insecure."

"Really? I wonder what I said. She's a hot mess. That's all I can say."

"Okay, ladies, and what about me? What happened to *my* collection?!" Jake asks impatiently.

Ellie looks away before responding. I can tell this is painful for her. She's afraid to answer because she's being bullied, too.

"Come on, Ellie, I NEED to know! Did she do it? Did she frickin' steal my stuff?" he asks loudly, his face red and flustered.

She stares at her shoes and nods. "Yes, I heard her joking about it. But I don't know what she did with it. I had nothing to do with it, I swear."

"Ha! And why the hell should I believe YOU?" Jake responds, nearly knocking over our cups of coffee. I hope Ellie gives us what we need; I worry Jake may have a nervous breakdown.

"I know you have no reason to believe me. I was a complete jerk to both of you. I don't deserve your trust but if you let me, I'll show you I'm not lying. And I wasn't involved in taking your collection, Jake, I promise. I know how much work goes into creating your own personal portfolio."

"Oh, do you really? That's rich, coming from someone who hasn't even started working on anything yet," Jake says.

Ellie grasps her cup nervously. "That's not exactly true. If you're willing to follow me, I'd like to show you something …" she says tentatively.

Jake looks at me for a second as if seeking validation. I nod and he asks the waiter to bring our bill. Ellie places a twenty on the table.

"Where are we going?" I ask, confused and a tad exasperated.

"A secret place created in honour of your great-grandmother."

"Really?" Jakes says, looking as bewildered as I am.

This is getting more intriguing by the second. I turn off the recording function on my phone and stand up, feeling re-energized. Against my better judgment, I decide to follow Ellie. *Again.* This time, it had better not be a mistake.

We enter a five-storey walk-up on 12th Street near Avenue A and I get chills, like the ones I got when we were snooping through the school records. A gazillion questions run through my mind: where are we, what will we find, are we safe, and, more importantly, what the hell are we doing here?

Jake is behind me as we follow Ellie up the stairs. The stairs creak under our feet and the sound makes me nervous. We make it to the last floor, and I get knots in the pit of my stomach. What if it's another trap and Stella is waiting for us up there?

Jake watches Ellie unlock the door. He isn't letting her out of his sight, nor will he let her get away with anything, that's for sure. This better be legit for her sake; Jake is under the influence of way too much high-end designer coffee.

It takes a few seconds for Ellie to unlock the door and I hold my breath as she pushes it wide open. My heart in my throat, I tiptoe on the old, creaky wooden floors. The loft space looks like an old garment factory and I imagine the sound of vintage sewing machines whirring in here decades ago, when manufacturing was much bigger in the city.

Ellie opens a second door and Jake and I gasp in unison. This time, I can't believe my eyes. It feels like we just landed on a Paramount Pictures movie set. Layers and layers of dainty pink tulle float from the ceiling, which is covered in tiny silver and pink stars. There are strings of white lights hanging from the wood beams, reminding me of the amazing art installations created by Japanese artist Yayoi Kusama, *Infinity Mirror Rooms*. How did Ellie manage to create this?

Jake's jaw nearly hits the floor when he looks in the centre of the room, where a half-dozen mannequins are dressed in exquisite silk jersey and chiffon dresses.

"What the HELL? THIS IS SICK!" Jake hollers, jumping from mannequin to mannequin like a frantic child let loose in a candy store. "Honey child, YOU made all of this yourself?"

"Yes," Ellie responds shyly. She looks slightly embarrassed to admit it.

"Sweet mother of Jesus!" Jake mumbles under his breath. He's under the same spell I am. Who knew Ellie had so much talent and such a soft, feminine side?

A light-blue pleated dress with tiny pearls at its neckline leaves me breathless. It reminds me of the spectacular couture dresses actresses wear on the red carpet. Next to it, a white column dress holds court, like the dresses Madame Grès created in her time. To my amazement, there are black and white photographs of Cécile's face glued to the top of the mannequins. Where did Ellie find the photo? Then I recall seeing the photograph in that book about Grès at the library. Ellie's idea takes my breath away. The concept is original and it touches me deeply.

On a different mannequin in the far corner is a pink silk chiffon minidress that looks as delicious as a meringue. I could definitely picture myself wearing it to one of Jonathan's upcoming photography exhibits.

"Jeez, Ellie! Why have you been hiding these dresses? They're spectacular! And where are we, anyway?" Jake asks, enthralled.

Ellie shrugs. "A cousin of mine is the building manager. He lets me use this place for free. It's been unoccupied since the last tenant moved out."

"This is the bomb. And so are you." Jake walks over to Ellie and places a hand on her shoulder. "I'm sorry I misjudged you, kiddo. You're a genius and I am humbled." He kneels down on one knee with a flourish. This makes her blush.

I stand in the far corner, staring down at my Adidas sneakers, fighting away tears. I'm not sure if they're tears of joy or sadness. I'm still processing all of this. What I know is this: each in our own way, we've all been victims of Stella's bullying and none of us deserve it. Together, we have far more talent than she'll ever have. I recall Simon Cowell, celebrity judge on the reality show *The X Factor*, responding to a contestant who admitted to having been bullied as a teenager: "Do you know why sometimes people get bullied? Because they're good. Because you're good." His words hit home. I discreetly delete my recording of our conversation at the Walker Hotel. I have all the proof I need that Ellie is one of us. Now, we just need to find a way to stick together and fight back.

"Jake is right, Ellie, you're super talented. These dresses belong on the runway," I say, walking toward them and still trying to wrap my mind around all this beauty. "And I love the old photograph of Cécile you found. That's a very elegant touch. I'm sure she would have loved the way you displayed it." I place my hand on her shoulder as a peace offering.

I can tell Ellie is overwhelmed by the compliments and attention. She stares at the floor and begins to sob quietly. "You're the first people I've shown my work to. I had no idea what I was doing. I was just ... experimenting ..." she says, wiping away some tears.

"Experimenting? Are you kidding? Come on, you're the real deal!" Jake tries to shake her out of it. It hits me that like many artists, including me, Ellie is filled with self-doubt. She clearly has no idea of her worth. That's probably why she was easy prey for Stella. I recall Ellie mentioning something about having mother issues the first time we met. Maybe she never got the encouragement she needed to develop her artistic talents? Whatever it is, she needs to know how amazing she is.

"The designs are locally made. What about the fabrics? Are they imported or locally sourced?" I ask.

"I buy them here in New York. I try to use organic natural fabrics from local textile mills when I can. There are a few exceptions."

"If that's the case, then I'd love to feature you and your work on my blog," I say.

"Really? Even after what I did to you?" She looks surprised.

"It's already forgotten, Ellie," I say. "We need to stick together."

"And YOU, my dear, need enter one of the school competitions," Jake says. "There's no doubt about it. It's time to get out there and show the world what you can do."

She wipes away her tears and stares back at us in confusion.

"Me?"

Jake grabs her by the shoulders and shakes her gently. "Yes, YOU!"

"You deserve to be in the competitions, not me," she counters. "You're doing something that can help people with disabilities. My stuff is just pretty."

"So WHAT?" Jake places his hands on his hips. "First of all, my collection has gone missing, so it's kind of a moot point right now. Second, beauty helps people, Ellie. It helps make life more bearable for people, including me. I'm in awe of your talent. If you don't enter a competition, I'll do it for you!"

"What about Stella? What do we do about her?"

"Pfft, who cares about that snake?" Jake says, his hands flailing in the air dramatically. "You need to STOP giving your power away to her."

As if on cue, the school bully rears her ugly head again. A text from Maddie makes my blood curdle.

Just received anonymous message with picture of YOU looking through student records. Care to explain??? Not happy about this at ALL. Please call ASAP.

Uh-oh. Here we go again. Will this merry-go-round of drama ever stop? Stella must have known that sending the photo to Maddie would hurt me more than anything else she could do with it.

I take a deep breath, look around the room, walk up to a mannequin, and stare into Cécile's eyes. I pray that she'll help me find the stamina, courage, and resilience to fight back.

Chapter Forty

I ENTER MADDIE'S apartment and I can tell she's upset. Usually, she welcomes me with a warm hug. Today, it's with bone-chilling silence.

I walk into the kitchen and see that she's making a jug of iced tea. She barely turns around when I take a seat on one of the stools. She's not just upset; she's really pissed off.

I can't blame her. She took me into her home and under her wing, applied for a scholarship on my behalf, and provided me with love and moral support. What did I do in return? I put all of it in jeopardy because of a silly cat fight with an unstable, angry girl. Maybe I'm the one who needs help.

I'm not sure where to begin or what to say so I lean forward on the counter with my hands pressed together and wait for her to turn around. I'm wearing a sweatshirt that says *BE AWESOME* but I sure don't feel that way. I'm tired and in no mood for a speech but I don't want to lose Maddie's respect, either. It means way too much to me. Although my energy levels are low from trying to deal with all of the drama, I try not to show it. I wish I could make her turn around and face me and say something, just to break this uncomfortable silence.

When Maddie does turn around, her eyes meet mine. She doesn't offer me any iced tea so I know this is about to get rocky.

"Can I at least explain?" I ask meekly.

"Sure, go right ahead. But that photo says a lot, Clementine, especially about your lack of judgment. I mean, what the hell were you doing in student records? Do you understand you could be expelled for this? And do you have any idea what position this puts me in? I know you're under lots of pressure, but this is unacceptable."

I feel terrible and filled with shame. No words come out of my mouth to defend myself. I just want to put all this behind me. I bite my lower lip to keep from crying. I can barely hold back the tears.

"I'm sorry, Maddie. I wasn't thinking clearly. I was just trying to protect myself."

"You know, Clementine, I agreed to have you stay here, even though I had some doubts. Then I helped with the scholarship application so that you could break out on your own, make some money, and eventually become self-sufficient. Just like I did many years ago. And I know it's realistic — I've seen the traffic on your blog. I even gave you Cécile's precious book. And this is how you repay me? By doing something illicit?"

She had doubts about me? Ouch. That hurts. *A lot.* I had no idea she'd thought my staying with her was a bad idea. And now, it's turned into a complete disaster. Tears roll down my cheeks. Her words cut deep but I'm just angry at myself.

I let my pride get in the way of my better judgment over a silly Twitter fight and now there's collateral damage. *Lots of it.* Maybe I should just pack it up and move back to France, even though it's the last thing I want to do.

"It's just that … I've been the victim of bullying … and now Jake's collection has disappeared." I can't help it — the floodgates open wide and I burst into tears.

"What?"

I wipe my tears away with a piece of paper towel. "His fashion collection disappeared. Someone stole it from school."

Maddie looks disgusted. She takes a deep breath and walks over to the cupboard, pulls out two tall glasses, and fills them up in silence while shaking her head. She throws a lemon slice into each glass and hands me one.

"Why didn't you come to me about this?"

"I dunno. We were trying to figure things out on our own."

"Look where that got you. With a compromising photo in my inbox."

"Right. Poor judgment. I get it." I sniffle into my paper towel. She hands me a tissue.

"I can't believe this happened again," she murmurs.

"What do you mean *again*?"

"This isn't the first time this kind of thing has happened. One student had her collection destroyed last year. We never found out who did it. I need to alert faculty about this. It's getting out of hand. Does Jake have any information about who could have done it?"

She's right. Things *are* out of control. I just wish Jake had left his collection pieces under lock and key.

"Clementine, did you hear my question? Do you or Jake have any idea who did it?"

I stare down at my shoes. I know it's Stella but I don't want to say it. I don't want Maddie to do my dirty work for me. I'm sure I can come up with something smart that resolves this once and for all. Enough people have been dragged into the mud and it needs to stop. I just want to move on with my life, my blog, and my relationship with Jonathan.

I take a long, cool sip of iced tea and get a flash. It's a passage I remember from Cécile's book: "A lady is always discreet, and uses her cunning intellect to resolve life's trivial problems."

"No," I finally answer.

Maddie cocks an eyebrow. She knows I have something up my sleeve.

"Whatever you say, Clementine," she says, then pokes my nose. Thankfully, the mood has shifted and she's smiling now. "I'll try to make sure the photo doesn't go around the school, but I don't want any more trouble, understand? I'm so busy with teaching and the TV show, and I think you need to figure this out on your own."

"Mm-hmm."

"You're just like your mother, aren't you?" she says. I react with a frown. I'm not sure what she means by it. In my mind that's either an insult or a reproach.

"You're pig-headed, determined, and despite that girly exterior, you're feisty as hell." She finishes her iced tea in one swoop. "Speaking of your mother, she wants to talk to you." Maddie says, with a strange look on her face.

"Did she contact you?"

Maddie shakes her head and points to the space behind me.

ISABELLE LAFLÈCHE

"Hello, Clementine," my mother says, standing in the middle of the loft in all of her glam glory: a pair of beige suede track pants, a matching cashmere sweater, and designer sneakers. There are several gold necklaces hanging around her neck. They could be medals representing all of her romantic conquests.

I nearly fall off my stool. Maddie grabs my arm to help me maintain my balance.

"What ... when did you get here?"

"This morning. I overheard you crying. Is everything okay, *ma chérie*?"

No, everything is not *okay*, I want to shout, but I keep that to myself for now. I don't want to explode at her in front of Maddie, who shoots me a sideways glance with an *I'll just leave the room now* look.

I think it's best that she go. My mother's visit is totally unexpected, and after what I've been through these last couple of weeks, the last thing I'm in the mood for is a heated discussion. But I realize that she's come at just the right time. We need to clear the air. Otherwise, this ugly situation will remain stuck in my heart forever and prevent me from truly loving myself or anyone else.

I need to get some closure so I can move on. I need that more than anything and I need it now.

After Maddie leaves the room, my mother walks toward the espresso machine in silence. She knows I'm still livid about what she did; I haven't returned any of her calls since I arrived in New York. And there have been many, many calls.

"Would you like a coffee?" she asks, her luxurious brown hair floating just above her shoulders as she pours the dark grounds into the machine. Despite the long flight and probable jet lag, she looks as youthful as ever, probably half her age. And acts like it, too.

"No thanks," I say, following her every move. I'm watching her like a safari explorer watches a lioness waking from her sleep. Or is it a cougar?

She prances elegantly and swiftly around the kitchen, just like she does on stage. She unsurprisingly turns coffee-making into an art form. If only she'd done the same for her personal life and marriage. Ever the soft-spoken gentleman, he manages to tiptoe around her issues. I just can't handle it anymore.

"Clementine, are you ever going to forgive me?" she asks, taking a seat at the kitchen island. I get a whiff of her strong perfume and it turns my stomach. I turn away to breathe some fresh air. I forgot how heavy and musky her expensive eau de toilette can be and right this moment it makes me want to gag.

"No, not really. What you did was unforgivable," I shoot back. I'm not mincing words. It's also had terrible effects on my self-confidence, but I keep that to myself.

"Right. I know." She takes a quick sip of coffee, staring out the window and into the courtyard. "I just want you to know that I talked it over with my therapist and she thinks we need to get this out in the open … to get past it."

"Your therapist? What about me? Did you ever consider how it's affected me?" I shoot back. I'm about to lose it now.

"Yes! That's why I consulted with her and that's why I came here to talk to you."

"So, what's your conclusion?" I ask, although I already know the answer. She's pretty messed up. And thanks to her, so am I.

"My father, Cécile's son, was emotionally distant. I suffered immensely because of it, and now I seek attention from men … much younger men. That's my pattern. It's one that I'm trying to break. I'm not proud of what I've done, you know. I'm terribly ashamed."

"Mm-hmm. So, what now? I'm not sure our relationship will ever be the same. How could it? I was betrayed by my own mother," I say, reeling.

Her face drops and her complexion turns pale. "'I know, Clementine. I haven't been a good mother. And I'm sorry." She puts her elbow on the counter and drops her forehead into her hand. "As a matter of fact, I've been a terrible mother. You deserve so much better." Tears run down her cheeks. This catches me off guard; I haven't seen my mother cry much. She's always been the stoic, over-confident diva, acclaimed artist, and in-demand socialite. Imperturbable, flawless, and at the top of her game. Always. Now, there are cracks in that suit of armour.

I remain silent and I can tell from the look in her eyes that this is causing her more grief. I'm not doing it on purpose to get revenge, though. I'm just thinking things through carefully and weighing my words before I speak.

"Listen, Clementine," she says. "I came to New York to apologize and make amends. What I did was reckless and unforgivable, but I want to change. I can't promise you perfection, I just don't have that in me, but I can promise you this: I'm ready to work hard to become the best version of myself. And that means being a better mother. I'm committed to this journey. I want to heal my past and all the harm I've caused both you and your father. I just hope that I can count on your support." Her mascara runs down her cheeks. I reach for the box of tissues and hand her one.

I think about Jonathan and Jake. What would they do? What would they say? Would they forgive her? I'm not so sure.

Then I think of Cécile. What would she do? Of course, she would forgive her granddaughter. But I try to recall a specific passage of her precious etiquette book, a chapter on indulgence:

> A lady is always indulgent, especially with those who do not act like her. She forgives quickly faux pas and blunders, without making those who perpetrated them feel uncomfortable or embarrassed. She understands if someone else is not yet a lady, thanks to her self-assurance.

What my mother did was worse than a blunder or a faux pas — it was downright disgusting. But she's my mother. Can I move past it? Maybe forgiving her will help me overcome my own self-confidence issues. It may help me get closer to becoming the woman I want to be.

I put my hand on her shoulder and sigh. "Okay, *maman*, I'll do my best. For your sake and Dad's. I can't promise you perfection, because I just don't have it in me, but I'm willing to try."

She cracks a half-smile before jumping into my arms, where she begins to sob. I let her, just like Jonathan let me in the school amphitheatre. It's called coming full circle, and I guess there's something liberating about forgiveness. It takes a heavy load off your back.

"And that boy wasn't for you, anyway. He kept coming on to me when you had your back turned. You deserve better, *ma chérie*."

I know she's right and that's what really hurts. I don't say anything about Jonathan. I'm not ready to share that with her yet so I just remain quiet, trying my best to forgive both her and Charles.

After a few minutes, she breaks the silence.

"*You* were crying earlier. What was that about?"

"Oh, nothing. Just dealing with stuff."

"What kind of stuff?"

"An aggressive classmate."

"Is she hurting you?"

"Not physically, no."

"Want me to get involved? I've been doing Bikram yoga and Pilates. I could kick her *derrière*."

I roll my eyes. I know that she's only half-joking. My mother is addicted to drama, and I don't think that'll ever change. I try to look beyond that and see her genuine concern for me.

"*Non, ça va.* Thanks for the offer though. You always taught me to look out for myself, right?"

She squeezes my shoulder and leans into me.

"Oh, Clementine, you're the mature and reasonable one. I should probably take notes."

"You could start by reading my blog," I say, trying to lighten the mood.

"You have a blog?" She looks surprised and impressed.

"Yes, it's called *Bonjour Girl*."

"What's it about?"

"Eco fashion, ethics, and fashion diversity."

"Oh! I'd love to read it. Why don't you get your computer and I'll make us something to eat. You can show me while I get dinner ready."

"That sounds like a good start."

As I fetch my computer from my room, it hits me that being a lady has some rewards, including having an open and carefree heart, which leads to receiving love and support in return.

While Maddie and my mother chat over dessert, I sneak into my room to text Jonathan and notice that I've got a message from Jake.

Wanna hang out?

Can't right now. Mom is in NY for 48 hours

Oh the famous opera mama!

More like infamous

Ooops. Sounds like there are issues

Yup. Tons. But working through them

If you say so, sweet pea. Wanna share?

Nope

Gotcha

Are you still working on our plan?

Yes. Have some ideas. Will keep you posted

Sounds good. Good night. Hope you dream in technicolor, babe

Right back at ya mon cher ami. Sweet dreams ☺

XXOO

Chapter Forty-One

TODAY IS THE DAY.

After spending yesterday afternoon visiting some museums and enjoying a reconciliatory lunch with my mother, I sit nervously in the dean's office with my laptop on my knees. It holds the interview notes I came up with late last night.

I borrowed one of Maddie's designer pieces for the meeting: a blue and white striped silk dress she bought on a business trip to Milan. I've had my eye on it ever since I moved in with her and I'm grateful she let me wear it today.

I've accessorized it with pretty blue chandelier earrings and navy-blue pumps I picked up on sale when I first got to New York. I knew they'd come in handy. For good luck, I'm wearing a yellow ceramic flower necklace that belonged to Cécile. I feel like Reese Witherspoon at a Hollywood luncheon. Oh, and I finally found the courage to colour a strand of my hair pink. Because that's what badasses do.

My plan will either make or break my future. I've decided that my peace of mind and Jake's sanity are worth the risk. This charade can't go on any longer.

The dean of Parsons School of Design is a tall, elegant, handsome man who spent most of his career working in the fashion industry. Apparently, he was a business consultant for some of the world's top labels and brands before joining Parsons and has successfully co-launched several internet businesses. Despite his impressive resume and stature, he remains very approachable and down-to-earth. He's quite popular with students and faculty members.

I'm here to interview him for *Bonjour Girl*. Since he encourages every student to develop an entrepreneurial spirit, getting him to agree to this meeting didn't take much convincing, but I do have butterflies in my stomach. Who wouldn't, right? I can do this, I tell myself. I just need to execute my plan flawlessly and everyone will be home free.

"Hello, Clementine, nice to have you here. I've heard lots of positive things about you and what you're doing," the dean says, shaking my hand.

"Really?" I respond, dumbfounded. I can't imagine how he would have heard about me. Who told him about my blog?

"Thank you for agreeing to meet with me, Dean Williams. I'm very grateful."

"Please, Clementine, call me James," he says with a friendly glint in his eye. I see why students speak so highly of him.

"Okay, James." I catch myself feeling (and probably looking) insecure and decide to step up my game. If I'm going to make it in the big leagues, I need self-confidence by the bucket load. I clear my throat and imagine that I'm a famous blogger like Garance Doré interviewing Michael Kors. I immediately become more self-assured. I sit up straight in my seat, cross my legs, and let her rip. I just hope this works.

"I'm honoured that you know about my work. I do my best to blog about the industry in a unique way. My goal is to reach the widest audience possible and write about topics that are outside of the fashion mainstream."

"Yes, good for you, Clementine. I read your early posts. I must say that I like your writing style. It's fresh and the topics are super inspiring. Keep it up — it will be a major hit."

Wow, I can't believe this. The dean of Parsons actually reads my blog. This totally cranks up my self-confidence. I smile back gratefully, feeling on top of the world.

"Thank you so much for saying that, it really means a lot. It's competitive out there so I need all the support I can get."

He nods and takes a sip of Perrier. "My pleasure. So what can I do for you?"

I clear my throat. I hope I don't sweat too much in Maddie's dress. This is hard. *Come on, Clementine, you can do this.* "I'd like to ask you about some Parsons student projects that have caught your attention in the past few years; ones that have really stood out."

"Oh boy, that's a tough question. There are so many exciting collections and new projects every year, it's hard to pinpoint only a few. I need to be respectful of the entire student body." He winks.

Rats. He didn't take the bait.

"Right." I think of backing down and changing the subject but this is no time to give up. *Come on, Clementine, you're like your mother: determined and feisty as hell, remember?*

"I understand. I just want to highlight the impressive talent that comes through this school so that it gets the

coverage and reputation it deserves, especially internation-
ally. I know how important it is for the school to attract
foreign students ..."

His eyes light up. "Ah yes, that's true. A large part of
our student body does come from abroad. Just like you.
Well ... let's see, there was a jewellery designer from Kenya
whose collection was so magnificent that several actresses
wore her pieces at last year's Cannes Film Festival."

"Oh! That's exactly what I was looking for! Do you
have any press clippings about that, by any chance?"

"Yes, we keep everything. I'll have my assistant look it
up for you in the student archives."

"And what about Asia? Have you had any superstars
coming from there?" I ask tentatively.

"As you know, some of our top students come from
Asia. There was Wu Fung, who won the womenswear
competition two years ago. Her metallic sweaters were out
of this world. No one had ever seen anything like them
before. She's now working at Chanel in Paris."

"Wow, fantastic!" I say, taking notes. "Any others? Any
men?" Keep it up, Clementine, you're on a roll.

"Ah yes, there's this really talented young man from
South Korea, I forget his name, who made some funky decals to wear on shoes, hats, and cellphones. If I remember
correctly, he had an entire spread in *Vogue Nippon* and won
some prizes for his original accessories."

Bingo. Here we are. I can't believe I did it. I mentally
pat myself on the back.

"Wow, I'd love to feature him on my blog. Is there
any way I could get some more information?" I ask, a little
insistently. But not too much; I don't want this to backfire.

"Um, sure, hold on a sec. I hate forgetting student names … I'll be right back." He stands up and heads off to ask his assistant for help.

I know what he's looking for and what he'll find: an empty student folder, thanks to Stella.

I smile inwardly. My plan is working. *Keep it up, Clementine, and Stella and her bullying will be a thing of the past.* I just hope this long, twisted road helps Jake find his collection. That's all I want. That would make a newsworthy story for *Bonjour Girl.*

I bet it would get tons of shares and retweets, too. But I try not to think that far ahead, because ladies are discreet and know when to put fashionable, sparkly silver duct tape on it.

The dean rushes back into his office looking frazzled. "This is really strange. We can't find it! It's gone!"

"I'm sorry? What do you mean?"

"The contents of that Korean student's file have disappeared."

"Really? That's … surprising." I try to keep a straight face. It's not easy.

"Yes, it is. I asked my assistant to look into the adjacent files, just in case documents were misplaced, and there's nothing in any of them either. I can't believe they've gone missing." He places his Dior reading glasses on the tip of his nose and types up a quick e-mail message. I assume it has something to do with the folder and remain quiet while he sends it off.

I'm proud that my shrewd tactic led to this. I couldn't just come out and tell him about Stella, not when she has those pictures of me.

"I have no idea how this could have happened. We keep such a tight ship around here," James says, looking lost in thought. "It looks as though we may have a record-keeping issue that needs addressing. Anyway, I'll have to get back to you about this, Clementine. I'm really sorry."

"No problem. There's no rush. This can wait."

"I expect that you'll keep this to yourself. The last thing I need is for this to get out."

"Yes, of course. You can count on my discretion."

"Good — I know you're a trustworthy young lady. A lot of weird stuff has happened around here in the last few years. Anyway, take care of yourself, Clementine. Not everyone around here is as nice or loyal as you are." I almost crack up laughing. No kidding. I could write a book about it.

"Did you have any other questions for me?" he asks. I know he's waiting for me to leave his office so he can get back to work.

"Umm … is there anything you'd like to add about the future of the Parsons fashion program?" May as well finish the interview properly. The truth is that I have what I need and would be content leaving his office quickly, but I don't want to be impolite.

"I believe our school is attracting the brightest and most creative minds out there. Students committed to creating the change that the industry so desperately needs. That includes you and your project, Clementine. Thanks for sharing your broad and inclusive vision with the world."

I'm thrilled the dean is taking notice. I try not to blush but it's close to impossible.

"Thank you, James. I really appreciate you taking time out of your busy schedule to meet with me today." I smile gratefully. "I'll send you a draft of our interview before posting it online. Can I assume your assistant will send me details about the Korean designer?"

"Yes, yes of course. Just wait a second while I remind her …" James walks out of his office. Here's the chance I was hoping for — is it really this simple? I get goosebumps and feel a cold drop of sweat trickle down my back.

I need to act fast but for some reason I remain paralyzed. Maybe it's because I'm about to destroy someone's academic future.

Am I game to execute my plan? I have less than five seconds to do it before the dean gets back. In those brief but vivid seconds, I get flashbacks of how horrible I felt after reading Stella's nasty tweets, how devastated Jake was when he found out about his collection, and how Ellie almost gave up showing her spectacular couture because of her low self-esteem. All because of Stella's relentless bullying.

I can't back down. Not now. *Come on Clementine, it's time to do this.*

I pull out the evidence: a photo Ellie took of Stella ripping up the Korean designer's record. I place it in the middle of the dean's desk along with a brochure of Stella's fashion decals.

Just as I'm about to turn around and leave, there's a buzzing from the dean's cell on the desk nearby. I nearly jump out of my skin. I can't help but read the text message.

Hi hon! Made a rezzy at your fave place for dinner in the Village. Can't wait to see you tonight, xoxo

I gasp when I see who it's from: Maddie. And with that, I run out of the office with my heart in my chest, confident that I played my cards right and thrilled for my fairy godmother, too.

Chapter Forty-Two

"YOU'RE NOT GOING to believe what I did." Jake and I are sitting in a small tea joint next to the school. Students come here after class a lot; it's open around the clock. Its hot-pink walls put me in the best mood. I ran here and texted him to meet me as soon as possible. I'm a mess: sweat is pouring down my back (and Maddie's dress) and my hair is all dishevelled. I can tell that Jake ran here, too — he's also sweating bullets.

I decide to shut off my phone, at least for a few minutes, while we talk privately. I know there will be a shitstorm coming my way after James, Maddie, and Stella find out what I've done.

This might get ugly so I need to prepare my squad.

"Sure I will. I know you're capable of anything, sista. You've got that witchy woman vibe going on. You inherited superpowers from Cécile."

Jake takes a large gulp of his bubble tea and stares at me quizzically. He looks much calmer than he has in the last few days. I guess he's come to terms with the situation. Luckily for him, I have not.

"I'm wearing Cécile's necklace for guidance and protection," I say. "I sure needed the extra boost to leave a photo of Stella destroying student records on the dean's desk."

Jake drops his cup of bubble tea to the floor. Its contents splatter everywhere. Thankfully, I jump back in time to avoid getting any on Maddie's dress.

"SAY WHAT? YOU DID NOT!" His eyes grow as wide as saucers.

"I swear. On Cécile's grave, I did!" I'm about to kneel down to wipe up the spilled tea but Jake moves me aside.

"OMG! Let me do that, for god's sake! You're going to ruin your dress!" After cleaning up his own mess, he stands up and gives me a warm, enveloping hug.

"Holy shit, Clem. That was *very* gutsy. I'm so proud of you! How did you manage *that*?"

"It's a long story, but let's just say I caught the dean's attention at the right time and at the right place."

"I bet you did. Well, now we're getting somewhere …" He fist bumps me. "This will get her expelled … and should help me get my collection back pronto."

"Mm-hmm. I hope so."

"You look worried, sugar plum. Why the long face?"

"Stella's the girl who never quits, remember? She's like the evil Energizer bunny."

"Who cares? She's going down. There are no two ways about it. Have you heard anything yet?"

I show him my phone and shake my head. "It's turned off."

"I think you need to turn that baby on. It's party time."

He's right. I go for a last sip of my tea, take a deep breath, and then turn my phone back on. My hands shake as numerous notifications pop up on the screen, including one I've been expecting:

Clementine!! Where are you???? We need to talk in my office NOW!

It's Maddie.

"Hi," I say meekly, walking into Maddie's office.

As expected, James is there, too. Maddie quickly shuts the door. She nods for me to take a seat. I cross my legs and take a deep breath. I try to make myself comfortable as I have a feeling this may take a while.

"Where did you find this?" She points to the incriminating photo of Stella.

I look up at them. I'm shaking, I'm sweating. I don't want Ellie to get in trouble.

"Do I really have to say? The photo speaks for itself, doesn't it?"

Both James and Maddie exchange glances. I smile inwardly. I must admit that they do make a really cute couple.

"Yes, it does," James responds calmly. He's sitting on the corner of Maddie's desk, with his shirt sleeves rolled up and his designer reading glasses perched on top of his head. "But we need more details, Clementine. And why go through the trouble of interviewing me for your blog if all you wanted was to show me this photo?"

I clear my throat. That's a very good question and there's no way around it: I need to tell the truth. Nothing else will fly.

"I did it," I say, staring down at my shoes, "because I'm guilty of breaking into the student archives, too. I was afraid to come out and say it directly. I wanted you to see this photo first." I'm embarrassed to admit this in front of the dean. I just hope this won't be used against me and that I won't be expelled.

Maddie looks at me and smiles. "Clementine's mother is an opera singer. Theatre runs in the family."

I grin back. She's probably right. Drama and theatrics run deep in my blood. "I was only trying to find out why Stella was bullying me and my friend Jake, not to destroy or steal anything, I swear."

They look at each other and then back at me.

"I know I shouldn't have done it. Now I'm trying to do what's right."

James uncrosses his arms, leans forward, and pats me on the shoulder gently, as if to reassure me. "Good going, Clementine. Doing the right thing is always the best course of action."

What a relief — it's as if a huge weight has been lifted from my shoulders.

"I see that guts, intelligence, and determination run in your family. I'm impressed and I commend you for bringing this to our attention. You can breathe now. I'll take over from here." He stands, putting on his jacket and winking at Maddie on his way out.

Phew. This was a major gamble, but it worked out. I should know something about taking risks: it runs in my family. My dad took risks by launching a business in a new country and by marrying my dramatic and unpredictable mother. She took some professional risks (and personal ones, too — but I'm trying to move past that) to become the renowned singer she is. In my heart, I know they would be proud, and so would Cécile.

"Well done," Maddie says with a grin.

"Does that mean I still have a place to live?"

She smirks. I try to guess what she's thinking. Is she proud, embarrassed, or ashamed?

"Of course you do. But you're sailing close to the wind, my dear; tone it down a notch, okay? I want no more drama in my life or in my home." This lightens the mood — I can breathe easy. I'm not going to end up on the street after all. I'm relieved Maddie trusts my better judgment. I just need to make sure it lasts.

Chapter Forty-Three

I SIT ACROSS from Jonathan at Brigitte, an art-filled restaurant in Chinatown renowned for its cool design. It's a favourite hangout among fashionistas and bloggers and appears regularly on Instagram. I feel right at home in this modern and colourful decor. It's the perfect place to meet on a Friday morning.

After the whole Stella ordeal, I'm thrilled to be spending time with Jonathan. We're enjoying some café au lait and a delicious breakfast.

Maddie and James asked that I stay away from Parsons today while they meet with Stella to tell her that she's being expelled. Deep down, I'm feeling really anxious about it, but I try not to show it. Instead, I stuff my face with avocado toast.

I hardly slept last night after I found out about the meeting. I played out all kinds of scary scenarios in my mind, including one where Stella hires a hit man to finish me off. Her empire is about to crumble and I know she won't go down without a good fight. I need to remind myself that Stella is the master of her own destiny. I had nothing to do with her unethical behaviour.

I take a sip of my coffee and try to forget about it. I need to concentrate on the beautiful man sitting in front of me.

"Finally, some well-deserved time alone."

"Yes. Finally indeed." Jonathan sighs and kisses my hand.

I know Jonathan's been stressed out about work in addition to his own legal issues. I haven't asked him about his claim yet. I don't want to kill the moment.

"I still can't believe what you pulled off, Clementine. You're like the heroine in a detective novel."

I nod. "I'm just relieved it's over. I wasn't trying to prove anything, I just wanted to protect my own reputation and my blog."

"And you managed all that without anyone's help," he says. "You're much stronger and braver than I am. I've been leaning on Stephanie to fight my battles, but you did it on your own. You're a champ." He runs his finger over mine.

"I can't afford her services anyway." I shrug. "Maybe one day, though."

"One day? With your blog taking off, it'll come sooner than you think. I just hope you won't forget me when you get famous."

"How could I? I'm hopelessly infatuated with the hottest photographer in New York. Who also happens to be the object of lots of female attention," I say in jest.

"I'm happy to report my skeletons have officially been pulled out of the closet. Julia finally dropped her claim against me. I just found out this morning. I wanted to tell you in person."

"Hooray!" I lift my cup and we clink our coffees. "Here's to getting rid of energy vampires. We should go to a Fashion Week event to celebrate! Is there some fabulous party or runway show we could attend?" I ask.

"A party? A runway show? What's the matter? Breakfast doesn't cut it, Miss International Fashion Blogger Extraordinaire?" Jonathan says, laughing. "Besides, Fashion Week pretty much ended yesterday." I'm about to say that this place suits me just fine and I'm happy just chilling with him when a young girl approaches our table. She's in her early teens and is wearing bright-red eyeglasses, a black and white polka-dot vintage dress, a topknot in her hair, and ballerina flats. She approaches our table shyly and Jonathan addresses her first.

"Hello there. Can we help you?"

She turns to me. "Um, I wanted to talk to you, Clementine. I'm a major fan of *Bonjour Girl* … so I just, um, wanted to say *bonjour* and ask if we could take a selfie." She holds out her cellphone and I blush with pride. I have a fan! A real fan! Jonathan grins and gives me the thumbs-up.

"What's your name, sweetie?"

"Alicia."

"You're in luck, Alicia. We have a professional photographer right here."

She sits beside me at the pink table and we make goofy faces while Jonathan takes pictures of us with different Instagram filters. I can tell this has made her day, but the truth is she's made mine.

"I'm really happy you came over to introduce yourself, Alicia. You just made my day. Stay in touch, okay? And thanks for reading *Bonjour Girl*."

After she walks away, it occurs to me that being in the public eye comes with certain responsibilities, including being true to your own values. If I'm going to inspire a generation of young women, I need to act like a role model. This confirms I did the right thing about Stella.

Jonathan leans in to kiss me. "Here's to dating the most inspirational woman in New York," he says. "How lucky am I?"

I kiss him back softly and it hits me that I don't need to be seen at trendy places or fashion shows to boost my self-worth. I have all the loving attention I need right here. And, most importantly, inside myself.

"If I'm inspirational, what are you, then?" I respond, reaching for that hair.

Unfortunately, the buzzing of my phone interrupts us.

It's a text from Jake. I take a deep breath before reading it. I just pray he's finally got good news. That would be another breath of fresh air. And I can't get enough of that.

Chapter Forty-Four

OMG. Just got call from dean's office. CALL ME!

I feel a tight knot in the pit of my stomach. I move my coffee and toast out of the way, put my elbows on the table, and dial Jake's number.

"Hi, what's up?" I ask, sitting on the edge of my seat. I tremble slightly. Jonathan watches me silently.

"You're not going to believe this, Clem, but she confessed! Stella confessed to everything! Including stealing my collection. Apparently she read about Brian Kim in a fashion magazine when she was thinking of transferring out of law school. She broke into the records the first week of class in her first year at Parsons to get all the details of his collection and how he produced it. Crazy!"

Phew. I let out a loud sigh of relief. It worked. Jake sounds elated.

"I'm so happy it wasn't destroyed. Where it is?"

"It's in some dingy warehouse near Canal Street where Stella stores some of her fancy schmancy patches. I'm in a cab with Ellie and we're on our way there now."

I whisper the news to Jonathan and he looks relieved, too.

His shoulders soften and he smiles. His warm chestnut eyes look into mine, making me melt. I wish we could stay here alone a bit longer but I need to be there for Jake. I just do.

"I'm in Chinatown with Jonathan. How about I meet you there? What's the address?"

"5900 Canal. Eighth floor. I just asked our cab driver to step on it — my future awaits!"

"Okay, I'll be there in fifteen." I just hope there won't be any unpleasant surprises when we get there.

I put down my phone and ask Jonathan whether he wants to join me. It's for a good cause. We can always celebrate, just the two of us, later. Right now, I want to be there for my friend the way he's been there for me.

"Of course I'll join you. You know you can count on me for stuff like this." He stands up first and throws on his jean jacket.

That's music to my ears. I extend my hand as we walk out of the café and onto the busy sidewalk, on our way to my BFF's moment of glory.

Jonathan and I get there before Jake and Ellie. Thankfully, the security guard downstairs knows to let us in. We walk up the eight floors in silence. Once we've made it to the designated room number, Jonathan pushes the metal door open with his foot.

We enter the huge space and the floors creak under our feet, reminding me of the storage space Ellie uses for her collection, minus the attractive details, feminine charm, and sophistication. It doesn't matter; we're here to rescue Jake's stuff, not to showcase it.

I walk around and take in the contents of this rundown storage space: there are racks and racks of garment bags, plastic containers, and lots and lots of dust. I sneeze as we walk by a large wooden table covered with a huge white plastic cover.

I stare at it for a few seconds before Jonathan pulls the cover off the table. Underneath, we find piles of colourful fashion decals. Not the original versions made by the Korean designer, of course; these are Stella's copies. I see now that they're far from being the real deal. These decals look sad to me, pathetic even.

The floor creaks behind us and I shriek.

"*BONJOUR, Bonjour Girl! C'est moi!*" Jake moves in for a hug. Ellie remains two steps behind. I walk over to Ellie and give her a peck on the cheek. She nods and smiles. All is forgotten and forgiven. We're all on the same team now.

I can tell by the grateful look in her eyes that my friendly gesture brings comfort. Just like the rest of us, she's been carrying a heavy burden.

"Okay, friends, I wanna find my stuff. LET'S DO THIS!" Jake says, rubbing his hands together. He walks past Stella's patch collection with a look of disgust. "Ew, gross. I hope my clothes were stored with better care than those revolting things."

Jonathan walks into an adjacent room and Jake is quick to follow him. I stand in the doorway, watching them inspect every nook and cranny. Finally, Jake opens a nondescript closet door at the far end.

"HALLELUJAH!" he shouts. All of his precious garments, fabrics, and supplies come falling out on his head. "It's a frickin' miracle!"

Ellie and I gleefully watch Jake and Jonathan pick up his pieces and put them in protective plastic bags. We hug, because we know that in the end, hard work, talent, and honesty prevailed.

I'm about to kneel down and help them when my phone makes a pinging sound.

There it is. The text comes as no big surprise. I've been expecting it all day. I already know who it is. I try to remain calm and stoic and strong as titanium. To mentally prepare, I play Destiny's Child's hit song "Survivor" in the back of my mind, with Beyoncé belting out the chorus.

Bien joué Clementine. You found a way to bring me down. I guess you're not just a pretty face. You better watch your back though, I'll find a way to get back at ya Bonjour Girl.

Why can't Stella just drop it? This woman's audacity and spite are beyond belief. Should I make a big deal out of this and ruin Jake's special moment? Stella would like that, I'm sure. But I decide not to let Stella's message get under my skin. I try to see it for what it is: a pathetic attempt to get attention by someone who's clearly hurting inside. *A lot.* She's already cut me to the bone. I'm not letting her go any further. I've had more than enough.

I delete the message. Jonathan comes over and kisses me tenderly on the side of the head.

"We need to protect these fine things if they're going to win the big Parsons competition at the end of the year, right?" I say, and Jake turns around and grins. My heart nearly bursts at seeing my friend so happy.

I must admit that I'm pretty happy, too.

"Who says we have to wait that long?" Ellie blurts out, putting her hands on her hips defiantly. She seems to be back to her sassy, bold, confident self.

We all give her a puzzled look.

"Whaddya mean, sugar?" asks Jake.

Ellie blushes. "I may have entered your collection in another competition."

"You did *what*?"

"I won't say which one. Not until we hear back."

"We?" Jake asks, raising an eyebrow. "I guess we're on the same team now, are we?"

"You bet. And I couldn't have dreamed of better team-mates," Ellie says. And this time, I know she really means it.

Chapter Forty-Five

TONIGHT IS TURNING OUT to be perfect in more ways than one. James and Jonathan are over at Maddie's. We're having a casual dinner, just the four of us. I must admit that it feels weird to have the Parsons dean over for dinner, but I like it since Maddie hasn't stopping smiling since he showed up with a bottle of champagne and a bouquet of pink roses. I'm just thrilled to see her so happy.

We're celebrating Maddie and James coming out of the closet with their relationship. They told the school faculty they were dating and, other than a few raised eyebrows, all went well.

Maddie made her delicious vegan pad thai and I helped her make dessert. I'm half French so pastry runs in my blood.

"More wine?" James asks Jonathan.

"Absolutely, it's a great pick. Where's it from?" Jonathan asks.

"Italy," James says. "I visited the vineyard while travelling for work last year. I was there to develop a liaison with the Istituto Marangoni in Milan. We'll be launching an exchange program with them as well as with several schools around the globe, including one in Shanghai." He takes a long, deliberate sip of wine. He and Maddie exchange furtive glances.

I wonder what that's about? I hope Maddie isn't going to tell us that she's moving to Milan or Shanghai. My head begins to spin at the thought of it. Although I've made friends in New York and have a boyfriend I adore, Maddie is my rock. I can't lose her right now, especially after what I've been through with Stella and my mom.

I stare at her quizzically and gently kick her foot under the table. She sees the look on my face and pokes James's shoulder.

I worry it might bad news.

"What's going on? Don't tell me it's about Stella?" I say, my heart rate going up. I don't think I can handle any more surprises or heartache.

"No. She's gone," James says quietly.

"That's a relief," Jonathan says. "Did you find out what was up with her? Why she was such bully and a thief?"

James twirls his glass of wine pensively. I can tell he's hesitant to tell us about it. "Normally I wouldn't reveal personal student information but given Stella is no longer with us, I can tell you this: she flunked all her first-year law school exams because of family problems. Her parents were having financial difficulties. So she decided to switch to fashion school after receiving a grant from a local non-profit that supported her work."

"I guess she was desperate to make money quickly," Maddie chimes in, "so she launched her decal business and, as they say, the rest is history. I think she turned on you because she found out about your scholarship. She was jealous of your ideas and became envious and bitter because of her circumstances."

Despite everything Stella put me through, I can't help but feel sad for her. I guess we don't choose our family dramas — they somehow choose us. It's too bad Stella channelled her pain by hurting others rather than focusing on her own creative projects. I would gladly have interviewed her on my blog had she chosen to focus on an original concept instead of stealing one.

"Thanks for telling me. You can count on my discretion. It really helps to understand what happened. I'm ready to move on."

"Yes, it's time to move on, indeed." Jonathan lifts his glass.

"So, what are you two hiding from us?" I ask. I'm dying to know.

"We thought we'd bring it up over dessert but I guess now is probably just as good a time," Maddie says, beaming. Are these two getting married? So soon?

James clears his throat. "Clementine, given your talent and the popularity of your website, Maddie and I thought you'd be a great fit for the new exchange program in Shanghai. We're sending a dozen of our students there to spend a semester developing their skills. In your case, it would be journalism and technology. You could even cover fashion events and make that one of your key projects for next year."

"Shanghai?" This is a major surprise. But I can't help but wonder if my father has anything to do with this. He's been trying to get me to go back to China to study for years.

Although my father is from Beijing, I haven't spent much time in China. But I know the fashion industry is buzzing with tons of new players and retailers. I've been keeping an eye on the Chinese fashion scene through blogs and Chinese web platforms.

My dad has been feeding me articles about Angelica Cheung, the founding editor-in-chief of *Vogue China*, who managed to convince Condé Nast to launch the magazine years ago. She's considered a publishing powerhouse and commands respect and authority for sending the magazine's readership numbers into the stratosphere. Millions of Chinese women slavishly read the magazine. Cheung has said that her goal is to inspire Chinese women and make them independent, strong, courageous, positive, and loving. I also adhere to these values. It's too bad one of my classmates did not.

"Yes, there's so much happening there right now. Parsons is partnering with Condé Nast as it expands into the world of education. Together, we plan to offer courses on a range of topics that play a crucial role in China's fashion industry. In addition to classes about photography, styling, marketing, and fashion design, there will be courses about China's digital fashion world."

It does sound pretty awesome. I can't believe my ears.

"It would be perfect for you," Maddie chimes in.

"You'd be right at the forefront of emerging fashion on the local and international scene. There's tons of talent over there; it's just a question of continuous support and time. And you'd be part of it all," James continues.

Wow. I sit back in my chair and try to take it all in. I wasn't expecting this, especially not now, when I'm finally settling in at Parsons and in New York. And what about Jonathan? A semester abroad would mean a long-distance relationship, which I know can be challenging. I turn to him. He smiles back and grabs hold of my hand.

"This sounds like a terrific opportunity, Clementine. Don't worry, I'll come and visit. I have clients in Asia. And it's only for a semester."

I close my eyes and imagine what Jake would say if he were here at the table. *GIRL, ARE YOU FOR REAL? Are you hesitating to take up this amazing opportunity because of some dude? You know you want it. SO JUST DO IT!*

I burst out laughing while everyone at the table just stares.

"I was just thinking how ridiculous it would be to turn down such an amazing offer."

Jonathan nods approvingly and kisses my hand.

"Count me in," I say, clapping my hands. "And thank you, James, for thinking of me. I promise to make you and Parsons proud." Jonathan puts his hand on my knee and kisses me softly.

Despite some setbacks, now more than ever, I'm convinced that coming to New York and attending Parsons was the best decision I ever made.

"So, I guess you no longer have any doubts about me," I say to Maddie.

"None whatsoever. The only doubt I really had was whether you had the maturity to survive in the crazy New York jungle, and you've proven that you've got it, hands down."

I smile gratefully in response.

Here's my two cents' worth: when you step into who you truly are and pursue your life purpose with passion, it's amazing how the universe opens its doors and sends you gifts. I'm overwhelmed with gratitude for the gift that I've just been offered. I vow not to disappoint those who are offering it to me.

Chapter Forty-Six

"NOW THIS IS WHAT I call class," Jake says, lifting his glass of champagne and looking terribly chic in his nifty tuxedo. We're at the Parsons Fashion School semi-annual gala, where students are rewarded for their exceptional work and contribution to the school's visibility and reputation this semester. It's also the last school event before the holidays.

Jake sits next to Ellie, who, for a change, is not dressed in dark colours, but a dazzling white column dress. Her hair is swept up on the non-shaved side with a crystal-encrusted hair clip and her eyes are made up with a smoky grey and silver palette. She's dropped the goth look in favour of grace and elegance, and she looks like a Hollywood starlet from the 1940s. Jake also invited his blogger friend Adelina, who showed up wearing one of Jake's blue and white creations and a navy-blue fedora. Not only is she stunning, she's hilarious, too. She's been cracking jokes non-stop since she showed up at the cocktail party earlier. I have a feeling we're in for some major laughs tonight.

The three of them are seated across from Jonathan and me. I'm wearing a cream-coloured chiffon dress made by

Ellie and accessorized with a clementine-coloured shawl that Jake made me for the occasion. I also had my nails done with tiny pearls and a light-pink polish that matches my look perfectly. I decided to go for minimal makeup and hair, preferring to let Ellie's dress shine.

Jonathan looks amazing in his sharp black suit, the one he wears for important client meetings. He's also wearing a crisp white shirt and this delicious cologne he brought back from France. I smile inwardly. He looks so handsome — I'm really lucky to have met him. I'm just happy to be with a man who supports my work *and* smells this good.

Maddie and James are here, too, sitting at the head table with tonight's guest of honour, *Vogue* magazine's Anna Windsome. That's one of the reasons I love studying at Parsons: the glam factor can't be beat.

In her book, *Why Fashion Matters*, London College of Fashion professor Frances Corner asks the question: When the online world offers so much in terms of visibility and information, why are students leaving their homes in increasing numbers to study at institutions such as Parsons? Her answer: to develop skills and foster a sense of community.

A sense of community is what I've found by coming to New York and that's what we're celebrating here tonight.

"Cheers to you, my friend, and congrats on your nomination. It's well deserved!" Jonathan says, clinking his glass against Jake's.

Jake is beaming. Not only did he receive a grant to create his own collection, but thanks to Ellie he was nominated for an award tonight in a special category for those who advance social issues in fashion. Although he's not ready to branch out on his own, this nomination will help him get the coveted internship with a fashion label that he so dearly wants. More importantly, he followed his intuition and it's proving to be a winning strategy.

Thanks to Jake, Ellie was also nominated for her breathtaking work. Jake shared photos of her showroom and her collection on his Instagram profile and the reaction was quick and astounding — the photos went viral in a matter of hours. Parsons quickly contacted Jake to find out who made the dresses. Ellie also received an invitation from a small museum in Normandy to partake in an exhibit about Madame Grès. They asked to borrow her pieces this summer. She literally jumped up and down and rolled around on the floor when she found out. Talk about nailing it.

I'm so happy my own great-grandmother was the inspiration behind Ellie's jewel of a collection. I'm sure Cécile is staring down at us, beaming.

Jake interrupts my musings by suggesting I lift my dinner plate. Underneath, I find a handwritten note from Brian Kim, the Korean designer who won awards for his decal collection. In his letter, he personally thanks me for protecting his designs. I know Jake has something to do with this and I give him a thumbs-up. I'm glad Jake reached out to Brian; after all, he's a former Parsons student and has a right to know. In helping myself, I also did some good for somebody else. It was all worth it.

After our entree is served, silence fills the room as Anna Windsome walks on stage in her signature tweed shift dress to address the audience. She begins by welcoming the students and congratulating the nominees on the important work being done at Parsons. "You're all paving the way to the future," she says, and I get a frisson down my spine. This was the main reason I decided to come to New York and launch my blog. She continues by thanking James for his impressive contribution to the fashion industry. I crane my neck to look over at his table and see Maddie looking at him admiringly; this makes my heart sing. Tonight, cheesy as it sounds, love is the air.

A video of the nominees' work is played on a large screen above the stage and our table goes wild when images of Jake's work appear. Even Anna looks impressed by his collection — that's no small feat. He's asked to stand before the cheering crowd.

Tears well up in his eyes as he takes a bow, and this makes me teary, too. I know how hard Jake fought to get here; that makes tonight even more special.

"My only worry," Windsome continues, "is for any of you going straight from school to starting your own business. Just remember one thing: it's tough out there. Take your time, get some valuable experience, and watch your backs."

Jake gives me a conspiratorial nod. He mouths the words "No kidding!" This makes me giggle.

"I personally would advise you to think carefully before you start your own business, and consider working for a designer or a company whose work you admire before you do. You'll be in a better place strategically, financially, and emotionally. And then when you're ready, you can count on me for support," she finishes, and the crowd begins to laugh. Jake lifts his hands in the air, whistles, and claps. I know this comment did not fall on deaf ears. He'll be calling her sooner than she expects.

I wink at Jake after Anna Windsome finishes her speech. It's my friend's strategy to find an internship and I know it's Ellie's strategy, too. She told me during the cocktail reception earlier that she's looking to intern for one of the major labels in Paris. Given her amazing talent, I have no doubt she will. From her chaise longue in her boudoir in the sky, Cécile will see to it that she does.

As for me, I hope to continue writing and posting on my blog to grow my readership. After I get back from China, I'm also looking to intern for a newspaper or magazine, to develop my writing skills. We'll see what the future brings.

I'm pulled out of my thoughts when I suddenly hear my name being called out by the editor-in-chief of *Vogue* magazine. I nearly spit out my wine.

I turn and see my blog header displayed on the large screen above the stage. "What's happening? What did she say?" I whisper to Jonathan, half in awe, half in shock.

"Oh, Anna Windsome just said your blog gets a special mention tonight in the social issues category for broadening the scope of how beauty and fashion are portrayed in the media. That's all."

I turn beet red as the clapping roars around me. I have no idea who proposed my blog. Was it Jake, Ellie, Maddie, or James?

I stand up, holding on to Jonathan's hand to steady myself. I take a bow while mentally thanking my parents for sending me here and Cécile for her inspiration. It's all her doing. And I am one grateful great-granddaughter.

"What is this?" I ask Jonathan, stars in my eyes. We're sitting on a bench overlooking Central Park. After the Parsons event at Lincoln Center, we decided to take a long, leisurely stroll. We even stopped in a local diner on the Upper West Side for some burgers and fries.

I was feeling so giddy about Anna Windsome mentioning my blog that I hardly touched my food during dinner. Because of all I've been through, her mentioning *Bonjour Girl* is all the more special.

"It's a gift. Something I thought you'd like. Open it," he says, kissing me softly on the cheek. "It's your big night. It's something to mark the occasion." He wraps his wool scarf around my neck to keep me warm.

I unwrap the present and my heart swells when I find a vintage book inside the silver wrapping paper. It's entitled *Classic French Fashions* and the cover shows gorgeous illustrations of women wearing delicate flapper dresses.

"I know how much you love vintage fashion and books."

I'm touched by his thoughtful gesture and feel tears well up in my eyes. I can't believe I ever thought this man could betray me. That was so ridiculous. I couldn't have been more wrong. "This is terrific! I love it. Thank you."

"That's not all …" He takes the book and opens the front cover. The pages have all been glued together and a hole has been cut out of the centre to turn the book into a gift box. Inside, there's a tiny red velvet pouch.

"What? What is this? There's more?" I protest but deep down I'm squealing with happiness.

He grins mischievously. "Wait. You haven't seen what's in it yet." He nods for me to continue unwrapping.

I untie the pouch's strings and a delicate silver ring with a small ruby falls into the palm of my hand.

"It's beautiful."

"It belonged to another famous woman."

"Oh?"

"My grandmother. She wasn't as famous as Cécile but she had a big heart, just like you. It represents my love." He slips it onto my index finger.

"I want you to wear it and think of me while you're in Shanghai."

I look down at my hand and it begins to tremble. I wasn't expecting this supremely romantic gesture tonight, on top of everything else. Can a person be too happy? I think not.

"I promise to wear it every day. I love you, Jonathan," I say, tears running down my cheeks.

"Since your parents are in Europe, I was hoping you'd join my family for Christmas this year. My mother is dying to meet you, especially after I asked her for that ring."

"I can't imagine spending the holidays in better company. It'll be the best Christmas ever. And I can't wait to meet your parents."

Despite recent challenges, life has turned out so much better than I could have imagined. I kiss Jonathan back, this time with all the passion of four generations of fiery French women.

What surprises await me in Shanghai? I'm not sure, but I'm hoping for the good kind. Right now, I'm just happy I followed my instincts.

Because that's what a lady does best.

Acknowledgements

Whether putting together fashion collections or writing novels, designers and writers cannot create their respective works of art without the precious help of a select few.

In that regard, I'd like to thank Daniaile Jarry, my manager extraordinaire, who in addition to having great panache also recognized the potential of this story and provided unrelenting encouragement and support.

Thank you to my editor, Jess Shulman, for her terrific work and upbeat personality, and for making *Bonjour Girl* the best it can possibly be.

I'd like to thank Isabelle Rayle-Doiron, Camille Auger, Tina Avon, and Gina Roitman from the bottom of my heart for their precious feedback and collaboration. This book wouldn't have seen the light of day without you. A special thanks to Debbie Stasson for being a cheerleader from a distance.

Thank you to Scott Fraser and the rest of the terrific Dundurn team for your immense enthusiasm. It's a real pleasure to work with you all.

Thanks to Marie Geneviève Cyr, Stéphane Jean, and Marie-Ève Faust for bringing a touch of elegance and inspiration to my life. Thank you to my friend Sophie Lymburner for offering me the most magical place to write; I am immensely grateful. And thank you to my family and dear friends for your unwavering support.

And thank you to all the smart, stylish, and sassy women out there, young and not so young, who kick ass every day. You are my true inspiration, and my admiration for you is boundless.